ABOUT THE BOOK

There was only one thing to do—escape. At least that's what the four Linnet children thought when they found themselves in the care of a grandmother who on the one hand despised dogs and on the other hand believed in boarding schools and instant obedience.

And escape they did—into a beautiful world knee deep in bluebells, presided over by an admirable uncle, peopled by such romantic characters as Ezra, a one-legged gardener who talked to bees, Lady Alicia who refused to go outdoors except in the moonlight, and Emma Cobley, a witch who was at the heart of whatever unhappiness there was in the village of High Barton. Allied with Emma Cobley, there were giants and magic cats but in the end, although they created some hair-raising episodes, they were no match for the Linnets.

This is Elizabeth Goudge at her magical best, creating a story that is bound to live happily ever after in the hearts of its readers.

ABOUT THE AUTHOR

ELIZABETH GOUDGE was born in 1900 at Wells, in Somerset, England, where her father was the principal of the Theological College. She has lived in Ely, Oxford and Devonshire. She now has a seventeenth-century cottage in Oxfordshire.

Her fame as a novelist is worldwide. Not only are her novels best sellers throughout the English-speaking world, they are equally well known in translation in Europe.

LINNETS

AND

VALERIANS

by Elizabeth Goudge

Illustrated by Ian Ribbons

COWARD-McCANN, INC., NEW YORK

© 1964 BY ELIZABETH GOUDGE
FIRST AMERICAN EDITION 1964

SECOND IMPRESSION

Library of Congress Catalog Card Number: 64-17997

Manufactured in the United States of America

082012

CONTENTS

1

The Escape

Robert gave the storeroom door a resounding kick, merely for his own satisfaction for he knew that only the kick of a giant would have made any impression on its strong oak panels, and sat down cross-legged on the floor to consider the situation. Betsy was roaring in the bathroom, Timothy was yelling in the broom cupboard, Nan was sobbing in the linen room and Absolom was barking his head off in the small cupboard where the boots were kept. None of them could get out for everything in this house locked firmly on insubordinate children. Grandmother said they were insubordinate; Father only thought them high-spirited. But it was what Grandmama thought that counted now for Father had gone to Egypt, on his way back to India and his regiment, and they had to stay behind and live with Grandmama.

They had no wish to live with her for she was a very autocratic old lady, a grandmother of a type that was to be met with in 1912, the date of this story, but is now extinct. She believed that children should be instantly obedient and she did not like dogs. She said that Absolom had fleas and must be given away, and as if that was not enough she had arranged for Robert and Nan to go to boarding school while her companion Miss Bolt taught Timothy and Betsy at home. The children were in despair. They did not want to be educated and they did not want to be separated, either from each other or Absolom.

Robert listened. He was not disturbed by Betsy's roars for she liked roaring and there was a window in the bathroom, but Timothy's yells had a hysterical note. It was dark in the broom cupboard and he didn't like the dark. Nan's sobs he could not actually hear for she was a quiet person, but he guessed she was sobbing. Absolom was now not only barking but hurling his body against the door of the boot cupboard with resounding thuds. It's like the Bastille, thought Robert.

And then suddenly he knew what they would do and it was so simple that he wondered he had not thought of it before. Escape. People always escaped from prison if they could. The question was, could they? Robert was ten years old, stocky and strong, and he had a penknife, green eyes and red hair, and when a question like this presented itself to his mind he did not ask it twice. He had heaved a small tin trunk on top of a larger one, poised a hatbox on top and mounted to the summit while the question was still passing through his mind. The high window had not been opened for a long time and it was covered with ivy outside, but the penknife and obstinacy got it open and clear. To get himself off the hatbox and through it called for both agility and courage, and he was pleased with himself when after a considerable struggle he landed outside on the flat bit of roof that made a platform for the rainwater tank. He decided he would be a burglar of international reputation when he grew up. Until this morning he had been going to be an engine driver but he realized now that he could do better than that. Any man of normal intelligence can drive an engine but only a superman can be a master burglar, and there was probably more money in it.

But great gifts take their toll and after the struggle through the window and the ivy Robert found he was hot, dirty and breathless, and he sat down to cool off. It was comfortable with his back against the rainwater tank and the spring sunshine was warm on his face. And from up here on the roof of the old house there was a grand view. He had not known it was like this beyond Grandmama's house. Four years ago Father had brought them all home from India to visit her, but he had only been six years old then and in the strangeness and confusion of being in a new country he had not noticed his surroundings very much, and this time they had been kept within the large enclosed garden, except when they had gone for short walks through the town with the Thunderbolt. There had been the train journeys from the boat to London and from London to Grandmama, but the knowledge that Father would go back to India without them, cutting short his time in England because of a selfish desire to go exploring in Egypt, was so dreadful that again he had not noticed much. He had had no idea that England was like this.

The town was an old one, with attractive crooked houses and winding narrow streets, and beyond it was a green land of meadows and woods, and streams that glinted in the westering sun. And beyond the greenness and the glinting rose the ramparts of the mountains. They were really no more than high hills, misty and blue, but they seemed to Robert higher than they were because they rose so abruptly from the green plain, and because their blueness was almost lost in the blue of the sky. They were mysterious and exciting and their silence called louder than any trumpet. The weathercock on the church tower told Robert that they lay due west.

He stood up and looked around him to get his bearings. He remembered that Elsie the housemaid's bedroom was beside the storeroom. Behind him and the tank was the storeroom window, to right and left sloping roof, in front of him the sheer drop down to the garden. It made him feel dizzy to stand above that drop and look sideways, but he saw the dormer window only a few feet away from him and the gutter below it looked strong. All the same he never knew how he did it. And yet there was not much to it really and if it hadn't been for that drop it would have seemed a mere nothing, for it only meant stepping onto the gutter and then, facing inward with his body leaning against the sloping roof and his fingers gripping the irregular tiles, edging along step by step until he came to the window, whose casements opened inward and were mercifully wide at the time. After that it was just a question of taking a leap onto Elsie's dressing table. It was that stepping onto the gutter that was the worst part.

Nevertheless, lying on Elsie's bedroom floor all mixed up in her brush and comb and a crochet mat that had been on the dressing table, and damp because a bottle of violet scent had smashed all over him, Robert found he was sweating profusely and trembling like an aspen leaf. He did not know what an aspen leaf was but he knew it was what you trembled like when a moment of supreme crisis was safely passed. At first there was only one thought in his mind; was there more money in burglary or acrobatics? How much did those fellows get who walked on tightropes in circuses?

Robert's thoughts ran on money so constantly because he wanted a pony and though he had been saving for it for a long time he still only had sixpence. That was because he kept seeing other things he wanted, like the penknife, and Absolom whom he had bought in London, when Father's back was turned, from a waiter in a hotel where they had stayed, only half a quid because he was a mongrel.

Robert staggered to his feet and went out into the passage, where he found to his satisfaction that all the keys had been left in the doors; which just showed that the Thunderbolt had not yet realized that Robert was a force to be reckoned with. Betsy and Absolom were still roaring and barking but Timothy wasn't yelling anymore and Robert let him out first because he didn't like the dark. He was eight years old and supposed by Father to be delicate. "Come on out, you little devil," said Robert kindly. "Keep your mouth shut and run straight downstairs and out to the rubbish heap."

Timothy picked himself up from among the brooms and sped down the stairs as though airborne, for he was very lightly made with smooth gold hair and very blue eyes. But these effeminate embellishments were not his fault and were no indication of weakness of character. He could yell, kick and bite with the best and it was only the dark that frightened him.

"Stop that row, Betsy," said Robert as he cautiously unlocked and opened the bathroom door. Caution was necessary with Betsy for she always emerged from anywhere as though shot from a catapult and her small round body was very hard. Robert sidestepped skillfully and she landed out in the passage on her nose, her roars soaring to a fine crescendo. Robert lifted her up by the gathers of her smock with one hand and clamped the other over her mouth. Her face was crimson and her green eyes shot sparks. Her rough red curls were as angry as they could be all over her little bullet head and she kicked out at Robert's shins with all her strength. Robert kicked back, but gently, for she was only six and he was fond of her because she reminded him of himself when young. "Another screech out of you, Betsy, and I'll skin you alive," he said. "Go straight down to the rubbish heap and wait there till I come."

She made for the stairs, thumping down from step to step as though she weighed a ton. She was always very heavy on her feet when she was in a passion, for anger does weigh heavy. But she did not roar anymore for where she trusted she was obedient and she trusted Robert. All the children trusted each other and their father, and he them. To be separated from him was the most awful thing that had ever happened to them, for Mother dying five years ago was now a little dim to everyone except Father, and Betsy did not remember it at all. But they understood that they had to be parted from Father, for he had explained about the new place where his regiment was going being too hot for children, and they knew it was not for always. Nevertheless Betsy, as she thumped downstairs, was calling over and over inside herself, Father, Father. But it didn't do any good. He was in Egypt by this time and he didn't hear.

Robert let Nan out next. She had stopped sobbing and was counting the linen to see how many pillowslips Grandmama had. She was twelve years old and, as the eldest of the family, of a domesticated turn of mind.

"Come to the rubbish heap, Nan," he said. "I've an idea."

Nan nodded and followed him, waiting while he let out Absolom and stowed him under his arm. "You smell dreadful," she said.

"Elsie's violet scent. I smashed it all over myself."

She nodded again and ran with him down the stairs. She did not ask him why he was drenched in Elsie's scent, for after long experience she had found it best not to know what Robert had been doing, so that when questioned by authority she need not lie. Nan was truthful, loving and serene and it was hard that her hair was sandy and straight and her nose too large for she was such a dear person that she deserved to be beautiful, but people do not always get their deserts in this world. She and Robert ran down the stairs shoulder to shoulder, very companionably, for they got on well together. Though he was two years younger, the number of ideas that he had made him seem older than his age. Nan did not have many ideas of her own because it was she who had to deal with what happened after Robert had had his.

To reach the garden door they had to pass the drawing room where Grandmama was entertaining a tea party with the Thunderbolt to help her, but there was such a clatter of cups and saucers and voices that there was no danger of their footsteps being heard. It was this tea party that had been the cause of their all being put into the Bastille. Grandmama had arranged it to show off her grandchildren of whom, had they but known it, she was extremely proud, but they were not socially minded children and they disliked parties. It had been Robert's idea that they should barricade themselves in one of the hen houses at the bottom of the orchard, with rhubarb stalks for weapons. The Thunderbolt's idea, after she and the gardener had found them and overcome the defense, too late for them to be cleaned up for the tea party, had been to lock them up until they should apologize; which they would not have done had she left them there all night for they were not apologizing children.

And here it should be said that neither the Thunderbolt nor Grandmama was really as bad as the the children thought they were. Grandmama could be charming to those who obeyed her and three of her four sons, the children's father among them, were devoted to her. Only her eldest son Ambrose had not inherited from his father that yielding gentleness which Grandmama found so pleasing in her younger sons. The children had not seen Uncle Ambrose for he lived some distance away and did not like either visiting or being visited. Also he had been a schoolmaster and upon retirement had been heard to remark that he hoped never to set eyes on a child again. But even he could appreciate Grandmama from a distance and the children would perhaps have done so close to had they given themselves time. The Thunderbolt too had a bark worse than her bite and was only engaged just now in trying to get the children sufficiently under control for it to be possible to live with them. But it takes a long time to learn to appreciate the excellent motives of those who are trying to control you and patient waiting was not the strong point of the Linnet children. They had the charming surname of Linnet and it was a pity it did not suit them.

The rubbish heap was at the bottom of the kitchen garden, hidden from the world by a tall yew hedge that bordered the garden on the west. It was private, and a good place for counsels of war. Usually they sat cross-legged on the rough grass for the discussion of their affairs but today Robert did not stop to sit down before announcing, "We're escaping. We will walk to the mountains and earn our living there."

"Are there mountains?" asked Nan cautiously. Robert had such a fine imagination that it was necessary to distinguish between what was there and what he thought was there. They were sometimes the same but not always.

"I've seen them," said Robert. "Westward where the sun sets." And he swung around dramatically with one arm outflung toward the yew hedge. Should he be the greatest actor of the age? he suddenly wondered. Would there be more money in being a great actor than in burglary or acrobatics? He was so busy wondering that he did not actually look at the yew hedge and it was Timothy who yelled, "Look!"

Behind the hedge the sky was a bright gold. It dazzled the eyes and got inside the head and exploded there as a wild desire for wings so that one could take off and soar up into it. There was a bird up there who had done just that, and his song came down to the earth he had left in a clear fall of music that was lovelier than anything the children had ever heard. Leaning against the yew hedge was a ladder that the gardener had forgotten to take away. Timothy was up it in a flash. His smooth fair head showed for a moment gold against the gold of the sky and then he was gone. Robert gave a gasp of astonishment and then he leapt after Timothy, Absolom still under his arm. Betsy scrambled after him clutching at Absolom's plume of a tail to help herself up, and Nan came last rather more soberly. She was not expecting to take off into the golden sky as the lark had and it did just cross her mind that it might not be as easy on the other side of the hedge as Robert seemed to think. But she climbed steadily to the top of the hedge, for Father had told her to look after the others, and resignedly she fell off it onto the struggling mass of the other four down below.

At first there was a good deal of noise, for though they had fallen onto the grass along the edge of a narrow lane it had been a considerable fall. Betsy was roaring because she had bumped herself, Absolom was yelping because she still had hold of his tail, and the boys were shouting at them both to stop their din.

"Do you want to bring the Thunderbolt out on us?" asked Nan as soon as she could make herself heard. "Because if you don't, keep quiet."

They disentangled themselves in a sudden silence, got up and looked about them. The lane ran between gardens and backs of houses and only a short distance to their right turned left toward the sunset. "That's the way," said Robert, and ran down it, the others after him, Absolom bringing up the rear with his tongue out and his ears flopping. He was a medium-sized mongrel, dirty white, very hairy, and apt to get caught in bushes because he was so hairy. His great dark eyes were his only beauty but it was difficult to see them through the thicket of hair that fell over them. But he could run fast. He had to.

The lane brought them to the back streets of the little town and they followed these toward the sunset. Beyond the town the road began to climb steeply between woods and fields. Streams ran through the fields, quick-running streams that had come down from the hills, and butter-cups lay in pools of gold beside them. Birds were sing-ing everywhere, in the woods and beside the streams. The air, coming down from the hills as the streams had, was cool and yet the golden sun gave a warm edge to it. It made them want to sing and so they sang, not with any particular words but just humming and whistling, laughing and calling out to each other as the birds were doing. They felt happy and it was a long time since they had. It was wonderful to be happy again.

And then gradually one by one they began to leave the birds to sing alone. Betsy stopped first and complained that her legs were aching and Nan said, "You'd better carry her, Robert." He took her on his back willingly, being fond of her, but that silenced him too for she was heavy. Then Timothy stopped whistling because actually Father had been quite correct in considering him not as strong as the others. Then Nan stopped singing because she was beginning to feel worried. It was getting dusky under the trees and when she looked up at the bits of sky that showed through the pattern of branches they were no longer gold but rose-colored. The cool air no longer had an edge of warmth but was downright chilly and they had not brought their coats with them. She and Betsy were only wearing their linen smocks, Betsy's green to match her wicked eyes and hers blue to tone with hers, that were gray-blue, quiet and gentle. The boys wore linen sailor suits, which were the fashion for the male young in those days, very dirty after the hen-house fight, but there's no warmth in dirt. And still they were not up in Robert's mountains but only climbing the lower slopes and the slopes of mountains can last a long time, Nan knew. It would be dark when they got there and how did they know if they would find anywhere to sleep or anything to eat when they arrived? She began to think that Robert's latest idea had not been one of his best, but she did not say so because when an idea has hardened into consequences it is too late to change it for another. That is why ideas should never be put into practice the moment you have them. They should be chewed like cud for twenty-four hours.

But the children tonight were to have a luck greater than they deserved, for rounding a corner they saw a thatched inn beside the road, with light shining from a curtained window. They knew it was an inn because the painted sign of a wheatsheaf hung over the door. A pony and cart stood outside. The cart was the type known in

those days as a governess cart and there was plenty of
room in it for four children and a dog. The pony was
looking at them over his shoulder and he seemed to like
them for he whinnied softly. He was piebald, chestnut
and white, fat but not too fat. There was no one with him
and the reins were loosely knotted around an old thorn
tree. He was the pony of Robert's dreams and before he
knew what he was doing he had spilled Betsy off his back
onto the seat of the cart and untied the reins from the
tree. Then he picked up Absolom and dropped him on
top of Betsy. "Get in," he said to the other two. Timothy
scrambled in at once but Nan hesitated. "It's stealing,"
she said.

"Borrowing," said Robert. "There's a difference."

Nan thought to herself that it was hard to tell the
difference sometimes, but she got in because just at that
moment her loving anxiety to get Timothy and Betsy and
Absolom wherever it was they were going rather got the
better of her honesty.

They drove off at a good pace, Robert holding the
reins. There was no whip but they did not need it, so
eager was the strong brisk little pony to take them
wherever it was they were going. He seemed to know
exactly where that was for whenever they came to a turn
in the road he did not hesitate. Robert was in an ecstasy.
His red hair lifted on his head with the wind of their
going and his green eyes shone like lamps. He had never
driven a pony and cart before but he did it as though to
the manner born. He felt as though he and the pony were

one person. "He's called Roy," he shouted to the others. "Rob-Roy. Rob's Roy. I'm Rob and he's Roy." And throwing back his head he began to sing again. Over their heads the sky was a mysterious green and a few stars were showing.

The others were glad to be off their feet but less ecstatic because they were cold and hungry. However Timothy, flung off the seat to the floor as Rob-Roy whirled them around a corner, made in his prostrate position a most timely discovery. Under one seat was an old rug full of holes and a bag of apples and under the other a basket of groceries: crackers and cheese, slices of cold ham, a jar of pickles, lump sugar, a pot of marmalade, eight cans of sardines and a bar of Sunlight soap. "Stop!" yelled Timothy and they stopped by a gorse bush and had a gorgeous meal. They did not forget the pony and Absolom. Rob-Roy crunched up four apples and a quarter of a pound of lump sugar in his strong white teeth and Absolom had eight crackers and a quarter of a pound of cheese. When they had finished eating, there was nothing left except half a pot of marmalade, the soap and sardines, and they all felt completely different.

From then on it was a wonderful drive, and when the road was so steep that Rob-Roy could only go at a walking pace they looked about them in wonder, for they seemed to be climbing to the top of the world. Great hills shouldered up into that strange green sky, and below they fell steeply away into deep valleys filled with mist. The shadows on the hills were the color of grapes. Then gradually the color drained away. The sky changed from green to deep blue, the stars grew brighter, and a hidden moon shone behind a hill that had an outcrop of rock like a castle or a city on its crest, and another rock like a lion's head beneath it. It grew steadily colder and even with the rug and after all they had eaten they began to shiver. They were a bit scared, too, for it was strange and lonely and they didn't seem to be coming to wherever it was they were going. But no one cried or complained for though insubordinate they were courageous. Nan did say just once, "Robert, are you quite sure Rob-Roy knows where we're going?" but after Robert had answered very snappily, "Can't you see he knows?" she did not say anything more. But she could tell by his snappishness that Robert was a bit worried too.

And then the moon sailed up from behind the hill and the whole world was washed in silver. They could see more now: low stone walls, clumps of thorn trees blown all one way by the prevailing wind, and ahead of them a cluster of cottages on a small hill with lights showing in their windows and a tall church tower rising behind them. Rob-Roy quickened his pace. He rattled them down a slope and over an old stone bridge that crossed a little river, and then uphill again toward the village. Just at the foot of the village street he turned left through an open gate in a stone wall, jolted them over the cobbles of a yard and stopped dead in front of a stable door. They had arrived.

2

Where They Went

They jumped eagerly out of the cart and looked
about them. The yard was enclosed by the stable and
three high stone walls and had a pump in the middle of it.
One wall was built against the hillside and a flight of
stone steps led up beside it to a door at the top. Beyond
the door there seemed to be a garden on the slope of the
hill and above it a house. They could not see any lighted
windows but there was a glimmer through the trees that
made them think there must be a light in one of the
downstairs rooms.

"But we must stable Rob-Roy first," said Robert.
None of them had unharnessed a pony before but by dint

of unfastening every buckle they could find they got Rob-Roy free and led him into the stable. In the moonlight flooding through the open door they could see a rough towel hanging from a nail on the wall and with this Robert rubbed him down and they put the rug from the cart over him. There was hay in the manger and water in the bucket and he immediately made himself at home. They kissed him and patted him and said, "Good night Rob-Roy," and they felt he liked them.

They came out and shut the stable door and climbed up the stone steps beside the wall. It seemed to be an old wall, built of rough gray stone, with small ferns and plants growing in the crannies. The door at the top of the steps had a stone arch over it and seemed old too but the latch lifted easily and they went through into the garden. It was queer and creepy in the garden because there were so many tall bushes and odd steps here and there. Then the bushes vanished and they came out on a sloping lawn and there was the house up above them, its granite walls covered with creepers and a terrace running along in front of the French windows of the ground floor.

It was the center one that was lighted, and framed in the shadows of the creepers it was like a picture hung on a dark wall. There was a table in the window and in front of it an elderly gentleman dressed in black sat writing with a large quill pen, an oil lamp beside him on the table and piles of books all around him on the floor. He had a big domed forehead with white hair sprouting up on either side of it, and white whiskers, but the rest of his face was clean-shaven. His eyes beneath bushy white eyebrows were looking down at the paper but Nan was quite sure they were bright and fierce. He was writing with great concentration, his pen spluttering and his grim mouth working. He was a most alarming figure altogether for his broad strong shoulders suggested he would be at least six feet tall when he stood up. The children and Absolom drew nearer, both terrified and attracted, for behind him they could see in the glimmer of firelight a great globe of the world shining like a second moon, and perched on the high carved back of the chair was a little owl. As the children watched, it spread its wings and flapped them twice and hooted. They had now come so close that they were standing at the bottom of a flight of four narrow steps that led up from the lawn to the terrace exactly in front of the window. The owl hooted again in warning and the elderly gentleman looked up.

It was no good running away for, caught in the beam of lamplight, he could see them as clearly as though it were broad daylight. Nor could they have run if they had tried, for his terrible gaze transfixed them. At first he was as still as they were, his face a mask of incredulous anger, and then he rose slowly to his feet, so slowly that it seemed his great height would never cease rising toward the ceiling. His big strong chin was propped up on a stiff white high collar that seemed to make him stiffer and taller than ever. He unfastened the French window, flung it wide and came out onto the terrace.

"What on earth?" he inquired in a terrible deep voice,

gazing down at them huddled together at the foot of the steps.

Robert was usually the family spokesman but his tongue was sticking to the roof of his mouth and it was Nan who replied. "Please, sir, four children and a dog."

"I have my eyesight," said the elderly gentleman, "and have already observed that there are four children and a dog, but may I be permitted to inquire what four children and a dog are doing on my lawn at this time of night?"

"It's where we've come to," said Nan.

"That also I observe. But how did you come?"

Robert's tongue came unstuck and he said, "Rob-Roy brought us, sir. Rob-Roy, my pony. He brought us in the cart."

"And where have you left this pony and cart?"

"Rob-Roy is in the stable," said Robert, "and the cart in the yard."

"My yard?"

"Yes, sir."

"I also possess a pony and cart," said the elderly gentleman. "My gardener drove to the town this afternoon to fetch my groceries and I am momentarily expecting his return. What do you suppose my own pony, Jason by name, will make of an intruder in his stable?"

Nan suddenly turned very white and then all by herself she mounted the steps and came to the elderly gentleman. They were all brave children but she was the bravest. She looked up at him where he stood with his hands behind his back and his legs wide apart, glaring down at her, and she said, "Rob-Roy isn't really Robert's pony. He only calls him that because he loves him so. Rob's Roy. We'd walked a long way uphill and we were dreadfully tired, especially Betsy because she's only six, and we saw the pony and cart outside an inn with a wheatsheaf painted on the sign, and we got in and Rob-Roy, I mean Jason, brought us here." Then she turned as red as she had been white, swallowed hard and whispered, "I'm afraid we've eaten all the groceries except half a pot of marmalade, the soap and eight cans of sardines."

Her voice died away and she began to tremble and to her horror she could feel a few hot tears trickling over her cheekbones and down in front of her ears, but she did not take her eyes from the elderly gentleman's face or flinch when he shot out a large brown wrinkled hand, gripped her shoulder and swung her around so that the lamplight fell on her face. It fell on his face too and she ceased to be afraid. He was not exactly smiling but there was a slight twitching at the corners of his grim mouth and the grip on her shoulder, though it hurt her, was reassuring. And then a very odd thing happened to her. From one moment to another she loved him.

"Stealing, eh?" he said. "Were you running away by any chance?"

Nan nodded.

"From whom?"

"Grandmama and Miss Bolt."

"Merciful heavens!" he ejaculated. "What's your name?"

"Anna Linnet," said Nan.

The elderly gentleman gave a deep groan and looked down at the others. "You three down there. Come up. Come in. Bring the dog. Might as well go the whole way. If there is anything I dislike more than a child it's a dog. Merciful heavens! And I trusted never to set eyes on a child again."

He made a despairing gesture and led the way into his library. The children followed in single file, Absolom bringing up the rear with his tail between his legs. Then he caught sight of the owl, barked joyously and leapt up into the elderly gentleman's chair. The owl took off and floated to the top of a large oil painting of some ruins and a thunderstorm that hung over the fireplace. Then he opened his beak, said, "Hick," and a pellet shaped like a plum stone shot out of it and hit Absolom on the nose. Glancing off onto the carpet the pellet broke open and disintegrated into a collection of small beaks and claws and a penny. "Do not do that again," said the elderly gentleman to Absolom. "If Hector is annoyed he shoots out undigested matter in this unpleasant fashion. You, boy, what's your name? Speak up. What? Timothy? Shovel up the beaks and claws and put them in the fire. You may keep the penny. Sit down. Do not touch my books or my papers. In twenty minutes I shall for my sins be with you again. Merciful heavens, here's a kettle of fish!"

He left the room, banging the door behind him. They heard his footsteps in the hall and another door banged.

"Is he quite right in his head?" asked Robert hoarsely.

"Quite right," said Nan. "Let's sit down, like he told us, and get warm."

They sat in front of the fire and looked about them. It was a big room but the bookcases that lined the walls could not hold the number of books the elderly gentleman possessed and they had overflowed onto the chairs and the floor. Where the carpet could be seen it was deep crimson, and so were the velvet curtains at the three long windows, but they were faded and torn and the deep leather armchairs had the stuffing bursting out of them. The mantelpiece was comfortably littered with pipes and tobacco jars, and the grandfather clock and the wonderful globe of the world were as kindly presences in the room as the glowing fire. Suddenly they felt befriended, in spite of Hector's outraged gaze. It was a friendly room, smelling of leather and tobacco and burning logs and home. Absolom expressed the feelings of them all when he flopped down on the woolly hearthrug in front of the fire, laid his chin on his extended paws, sighed twice and fell asleep. Betsy fell asleep too, in Nan's arms in the deepest armchair, and the boys sat on the rug by Absolom and contentedly fed the fire with fir cones from a basket that stood on the hearth. The grandfather clock ticked gently and Hector's expression slowly changed from outrage to resignation.

And then suddenly their drowsy peace was shattered

by the sound of a quickly trotting horse coming from the direction of the village. The rider came past the house, slowing down where the hill was steep, crossed the bridge at the bottom and then urged his horse to a canter up the long slope beyond. The sound of the hoofs died away in the distance and the children looked at each other in dismay. There were no telephones in those days, and only rich people had cars, so urgent messages were often carried on horseback.

"Has he sent a message to Grandmama?" gasped Timothy.

"How could he?" asked Nan. "He doesn't know where she lives."

"Don't be such a fool, Tim," said Robert.

Yet in spite of the impossibility of a message being sent to Grandmama they all felt a little uneasy, and still more so when the elderly gentleman returned looking grimmer than ever and capable of anything. "I see nothing to be done but for you to stay the night," he growled. "Dog and all. Merciful heavens, what an infliction! Since nothing is left of my groceries except marmalade and soap and Hector's sardines I presume you are not hungry. You are however extremely dirty and one of you is smelling abominably of violet scent. I dislike scent. That is why I am a bachelor. You must wash and get to bed. I know nothing of the routine of getting children to bed but you, I presume"—and he pointed a long forefinger at Nan—"can superintend the horrid business. I'll show you where the bed is and provide you with hot water and then I do not wish to hear a chirp out of any of you until the morning."

He led the way out of the room and they followed him exactly as the children had followed the Pied Piper. He was even more severe with them than Grandmama and the Thunderbolt yet they would have done anything he told them and followed him anywhere. And so would Absolom, who flopped along keeping as near him as he possibly could. Out in the hall the elderly gentleman lit the two brass candlesticks that stood on the table, took one himself and gave the other to the children. "That's Ezra Oake's candle," he said. "He is my gardener and general factotum and sleeps in the house. When you appropriated Jason and the cart he was in the Wheatsheaf and I must warn you that when he returns, having no doubt strengthened himself with strong drink for the walk home, it is possible that he may create a considerable disturbance. If so, do not be alarmed."

"How will he go to bed if we have his candle?" asked Nan.

"In the dark," said the elderly gentleman. "Give me the child. She is too heavy for your strength. This way to the kitchen." He took Betsy from Nan, settling her in the curve of his free arm in a way that seemed to Nan very handy for a man who did not like children, and led the way down the passage. It was a glorious house. It had not been spring-cleaned for years. Delicate festoons of spiders' webs swayed beautifully in the draft all the way down the passage and when they reached the big stone-floored kitchen it was the most wonderful place they had ever seen. Apart from the settle by the hearth and the black kettle murmuring gently on top of the range, everything was in the wrong place. A basket full of a cat and six kittens was on the drain board, the dishes and plates and two pairs of boots were stacked on the table, the cuckoo clock was in the sink, the saucepans were on the floor, and the mantelpiece, windowsills and cupboard were crowded with plants in pots, sacking and string and seedboxes. Some women, but no men or children, might have considered this a dirty kitchen but they would have been wrong. It was not dirty because it smelled right. It smelled of onions, herbs, geraniums and good earth, but not dirt. Cobwebs were spun between the rafters but the washing-up had been done before the cat and the cuckoo clock had been put on the drainboard and into the sink, and the copper saucepans on the floor were so bright that you could see your face in them. Nan, Robert and Timothy sighed with delight and wanted to look at the kittens but the elderly gentleman would not let them linger. Handing his candle to Robert he picked up the steaming kettle and led them all out again. "I'll not have Andromache disturbed," he said. "Her kittens were born only last Wednesday."

He led them up a staircase, down a passage and into a room full of moonlight so bright that its reflection in the polished oak of the old wavy floor was almost dazzling. There was a four-poster bed with maroon curtains and a flight of steps leading up to it, a bow-fronted chest of drawers and a vast washstand with two sets of willow-patterned jugs and basins.

"My spare room," said the elderly gentleman. "It has never been slept in, for if there is one thing I dislike more than paying visits it is receiving them. As to the condition of the bedding, if any, I am unable to inform you." He set down the steaming kettle on the washstand and lifted the patchwork quilt which lay on the bed. Under it was a pile of feather pillows and blankets but no sheets. "Are they damp?" he asked a little anxiously. "I should not like the child to catch cold."

He did not so much as glance at Betsy as he spoke but yet Nan knew he liked Betsy, and liked her. What he felt about the boys she was not so sure.

"Betsy never catches cold," she reassured him. "Timothy does but I'll make him keep his combinations on."

"Combinations of what?" asked the elderly gentleman.

"Just combinations," said Nan. "What we wear next to our skins."

"Ah," said the elderly gentleman. "Combinations. I must behold them at some future and more suitable occasion, for the extension of knowledge has always been of prime importance to me. Good night."

Laying Betsy down on the bed, he took his candle from Robert and walked out of the room without a backward glance. Yet they looked at each other with dancing eyes, for if he had really intended to turn them adrift tomorrow he would not have expressed a wish to see their combinations.

"We'll do everything he tells us," said Robert. "We'll wash. Come on."

Robert hated washing, and he hated doing what he was told, so it was all the more extraordinary that it was he who poured hot water into one of the big basins, rummaged out a bath towel from under the bedding, a piece of hard yellow soap from a cupboard under the washstand, and fell upon Timothy. There was no washcloth but he soaped Timothy's face and neck good and hard with the soap in direct contact with the skin, ducked his head in the basin and then rubbed him dry. Timothy yelled once, kicked twice and then submitted. Nan woke up Betsy, washed her face, took off her smock and petticoat and tucked her back into bed again. Then she washed her own face and hands, took off her smock and helped the boys with their sailor suits. Followed by Absolom they climbed up the little flight of steps and settled themselves joyously in the big bed. With the girls at the top, the boys at the bottom and Absolom in the middle there was plenty of room for all of them. It was cozy and soft with all the feather pillows and a featherbed, and about eight blankets. Their combinations, excellent garments but as out of fashion now as the kind of grandmother Grandmama was, clung warmly. The moonlight lay in benediction upon the bed and they were immensely happy and presently immensely sleepy.

Yet suddenly Nan raised her head from the deep hollow in her feather pillow and asked, "Robert, did *you* wash?"

There was no answer. He was asleep and so were Timothy, Betsy and Absolom. For a moment Nan felt annoyed, then she dropped her head back onto the hollowed pillow again. What did it matter? She was too warm and happy to mind. It was nice sleeping in blankets, with no chilly sheets. She gave a sigh of contentment and closed her eyes.

A few hours later she suddenly woke up again, and in a moment she was sitting bolt upright with trickles of fear running down her spine. She had been awakened by a tremendous crash, followed by a piercing yell and then yowling and hooting. She was so terrified that for a moment or two she forgot about Ezra Oake, and then she heard a tenor voice caroling out a rollicking song that was like a spring wind, and the sea on a fine day and suet pudding with treacle. It was punctuated by the sound of castanets, and an extraordinary thumping sound, and was so exciting that her fear vanished and she woke the others so that they could hear it too. "It's Ezra Oake," she said. "He's come home and fallen into the saucepans. But now he's singing and I think Hector and Andromache are singing too. And he's dancing. Come on."

All four children had the gift of waking instantly from the deepest of sleeps if there was anything exciting going on. They rolled out of bed onto the floor without bothering to go down the steps, picked themselves up and made for the door. Nothing except being picked up and dropped woke Absolom and so he remained in bed and asleep. They raced down the passage and down the stairs to the kitchen, where a glorious sight met their eyes. A man with a wooden leg was dancing in the bright moonlight, two saucepan lids held in his hands as castanets, singing as he danced. Hector was perched on a flowerpot on the mantlepiece hooting like mad and Andromache was yowling melodiously on top of a pile of dishes on the kitchen table. To complete the perfection it only needed the cuckoo clock to join in, which it immediately did, cuckooing twelve times down inside the sink, and after the cuckooing came the sound of a great bell tolling far up in the sky. The children only paused for a moment at the door and then they leapt in and began to dance too, stamping their feet and clapping their hands and trying to join in the song that was like a spring wind and the sea on a fine day and suet pudding with treacle. They did not get the words properly that night but they caught the tune. They could have sung and danced forever only suddenly the man tripped over a saucepan, fell on his back on the settle, stretched out his legs and was instantly asleep.

Andromache returned to her box, where she could be heard purring contentedly to her kittens, Hector flitted away into the passage and back to the library and the children gazed in adoration at the man.

He was a little man, not much bigger than Robert, and he lay with his brown gardener's hands placidly folded on his chest. His rosy wrinkled face was even in sleep extraordinarily kind. He had a short gray beard but there was not a single hair on his acorn-colored head. His brown corduroy trousers were fastened below the knee with string on his real leg but on the wooden leg they were folded back to show the fascinating bee that was carved and painted upon its round polished surface. He had a mustard-colored waistcoat, a full-skirted beech-brown coat and a scarlet handkerchief knotted around his throat. In the moonlight all these wonderful colors were muted and the moon lent them mystery. With a sigh of satisfaction the children tiptoed out of the kitchen and up the stairs and back to their room. One by one they climbed the flight of steps that led up into the big bed, fell among the blankets and pillows and Absolom and snuggled down. They were asleep at once and did not see the fading of the moonlight and the growing of the dawn, or hear the morning chorus of the birds and the sound of the sheep bleating on the hills.

They woke up to a smell of fried sausages and were quickly dressed and pursuing it. Just at first, after they had caught up with it in the kitchen, they wondered if that wonderful interval of song and dance in the middle of the night had been a dream, because the man who was frying the sausages, turning them over and over in the huge iron pan with a long two-pronged fork, was wearing a shepherd's smock tied around the waist with string. But when he turned his head it was Ezra Oake all right, and when he saw them he smiled. He had the most wonderful smile, which seemed to run up into all the wrinkles on his face. His eyes were bright blue.

"Lucky us weren't out of sausages," he said. "Nor bread. If it had been pickles and cheese you was wanting for your breakfast you'd have had none." And he winked one eye and chuckled. He had a deep rumbling chuckle and a husky voice. The children gathered around him fascinated by the interior of the frying pan which contained not only sausages but bread, eggs and kidneys, all sizzling gloriously.

"Nothing like a good fry for breakfast," said Ezra. "And a nice strong cup of tea. Settles the stomach."

The cuckoo clock in the sink struck ten.

"Ten?" gasped the children.

"Aye," said Ezra. "Ten. The Master he had his breakfast and he was off in the cart two hours ago."

"Where to?" said Robert, and fear clutched at their hearts.

"Down to town," said Ezra.

"Why?" whispered Nan.

"Us be short of cheese, pickles, biscuits, ham, sugar and marmalade," said Ezra, and again he winked. "But I reckon us should be thankful Hector has his sardines. He takes the huff if he don't get his breakfast."

The children now saw that Hector was sitting at the open window above the sink with an open can in front of him. As they watched he stretched out a claw and delicately removed a sardine. It went down at one

swallow and he removed another. Andromache was looking at them over the top of her basket, a tortoiseshell cat with apprehensive green eyes.

"Better put the dog out," said Ezra.

Nan grasped Absolom's collar and pulled him past Andromache's basket and out into the garden. The back door opened right into the little yard behind the house, where there was a well and a clothesline. Opposite the back door four steps led up to a small walled kitchen garden on the slope of the hill. At the top of the garden under the wall were four beehives, and beyond the wall was an old gray church with a tower that soared so far into the sky that it took Nan's breath away. A door in the wall beside the beehives led from the garden to the churchyard. There was a jumble of whitewashed thatched cottages grouped around the church, and on the other side of the lane, and smoke was curling lazily up from their crooked chimneys. She shut her eyes and smelled flowers, woodsmoke and sausages and heard a real cuckoo calling and the sheep bleating, and what she heard and smelled matched what she had seen. Yet it seemed too good to be true.

"Be you hungry, maid?"

She opened her eyes and it was true and Ezra was beside her. She looked up at him and smiled and he smiled back and again she felt that the midnight dancing had been a dream, for this Ezra did not seem quite the same as the other. That had been a many-colored, gay, fantastic creature; this was a kindly, earthy, sober man who moved slowly on his wooden leg, and this morning his corduroy trouser leg was pulled down to hide the bee that was carved and painted on it. But perhaps the bee was no longer there. Perhaps there were two Ezras, a midnight one and a daytime one, for anything was possible in a place like this. The daytime Ezra was looking tired and old and she was filled with remorse.

"Because we took Rob-Roy, I mean Jason, and the cart, you had to walk all the way home from the Wheatsheaf on your wooden leg," she said.

He laughed and lowered his voice to a husky whisper. "As I be now, maid, I couldn't have done it," he said. "But as I were then I done it easy."

And with this cryptic remark he led her back to the kitchen where the other three had already started their breakfast. Ezra had put everything that was on the kitchen table on the floor and pushed the settle up to it, with four piles of sacks of varying heights on it so that each child would be at exactly the right height for comfortable eating. He himself sat opposite them behind a large black teapot and presided with a wonderful benignity. When breakfast was over they helped him to wash up, a process which involved the removal of the cuckoo clock and Andromache and her kittens to the floor, the placing of the frying pan and crockery and knives and forks in the sink, the turning of the cold water on full blast, the emptying of the kettle of boiling water on top of the resultant whirlpool, the stirring of the mixture as though it were a Christmas pudding and then its removal to the drainboard where it was left to dry by itself, because Andromache had all the drying-up cloths to make the basket soft for her kittens.

When they had finished, Ezra asked, "Will you be staying for dinner?"

"What's for dinner?" asked Timothy.

"Fried steak and onions and rhubarb pie," said Ezra.

"Yes," they said in chorus.

"Then be off with you and let me get to me pastry," said Ezra. "And don't speak to them bees. Not yet." They obeyed him instantly because obedience, which had seemed so difficult at Grandmama's, came easily here, and they were out in the yard before they realized they had got there. But Nan came back to ask, "Will the elderly gentleman be back to dinner?"

"Couldn't say," said Ezra. "Over and above that little matter of the groceries the Master had a call to make in town."

Nan ran back to the others feeling uneasy and found them grouped about the well looking uneasy too. Though they had brazened it out about dinner the mere suggestion that they might not be staying for it had upset them terribly. "I shall stay here until Father comes home," said Betsy suddenly. "And then I shall go on staying here, with Father."

"Sh!" the others hissed at her. It seemed to them dreadfully dangerous to put it into words like that, for lately the things they didn't want to happen were the things that happened and the logic of this was that if you pretended not to want what you really wanted dreadfully you would be more likely to get it.

"But I think it would be all right to explore the garden," said Nan. "Only not to want too much to play in it every day."

"Come on," said Robert.

It was a wonderful garden, quite different from Grandmama's. Hers had been a sort of continuation of the house, dreadfully tidy and a place where you had to step carefully and not touch things. This garden was also a continuation of the house but untidy, unexpected, comfortable and homey. They explored the kitchen garden first and it seemed made for them. The grass paths between the miniature box hedges were just the right width for children running in single file, and the tangle of apple trees, currant and gooseberry bushes, flowers, weeds, vegetables and herbs that the paths intersected was so wild that leaping through it couldn't make it much wilder than it was. Betsy, who loved picking flowers, picked a bunch of periwinkles and primroses but there were so many that no holes were left. When the children reached the top of the garden they stood at a little distance from the beehives and surveyed them with awe but they did not speak. Even if Ezra had not forbidden them to do so they would not have presumed, for there was a strangeness there. It was like standing on the frontier of a foreign country. You would have to know something of the customs and a few words of the language before you dared to go over.

An exciting tunnel of yew trees beside the house led to the front garden. At the lower end of the sloping lawn was a mulberry tree, its lower limbs held up by stakes of crotched wood. Its branches grew out from the main trunk in such a way that to climb the tree would be as easy as running upstairs. Timothy, who loved climbing trees, dared not look too long and they all ran determinedly past it to the part of the garden down below that they had not seen properly last night. They found it now to be a rough grassy slope planted with rhododendrons and azaleas and flaming with glorious colors. The path, with steps here and there, descended steeply among them and as they came down they could look right over the wall of the stableyard and see the river and the bridge and the stretch of the moor beyond. The road down which they had driven last night was looped like a ribbon around the shoulder of a hill that was blue and green with bluebells and ferns. Stone walls divided the wilderness into fields in which sheep were feeding, and cows and a few ponies.

They sat down under a flame-colored rhododendron and gazed, with the sun on their faces, and then they shut their eyes and listened. They could hear the voice of the little river as it tumbled over the stones in its shallow bed, the sheep bleating, the humming of the bees, but at first nothing else, and then suddenly there was the sound of a pony's trotting feet and their eyes flew open. The little cart was coming down the hill at a brisk pace, Rob-Roy in fine fettle and the elderly gentleman apparently in fine fettle too for he was sitting very upright with a tall hat set jauntily on his head, his whip held upright like a king's scepter. As he rattled over the bridge they saw that he was swaying a little as though in time to music. Could he be singing? It didn't seem possible that so terrible and statuesque a person could be doing such an unsuitable thing, yet as the cart disappeared from sight and slowed up on the hill they distinctly heard the strains of "The British Grenadiers" floating up to them. They jumped up and raced down to the arched door in the wall, pulled it open and ran down the steps to the stableyard as he drove in, Absolom at their heels. The moment the elderly gentleman had pulled Rob-Roy to a standstill they had surrounded him.

"Ah," he said, grimly surveying their eager anxious faces. "You slept well, I see. Breakfasted well also, I trust. I see no signs of fatigue or starvation on your grubby faces. Robert, look after your pony. You three, carry up the groceries. The luggage follows in the delivery cart."

He stalked up the steps to the garden door with his hands folded in the small of his back and the three followed. His back looked very grim, yet he had returned with a great many groceries, far more than he and Ezra would need, and peeping into one bag Nan saw that it was full of dog biscuits. And what did he mean by the luggage following in the delivery cart? As they went up through the garden the church clock struck one, a gong boomed inside the house and he said, "Ah! Luncheon! I breakfasted early. What's for luncheon?"

"Fried steak and onions and rhubarb pie," said Nan.

"Ah," said the elderly gentleman. "There is in my pocket a package of peppermint lozenges for indigestion if the need for them should subsequently arise."

Ten minutes later they were all sitting around the table in the cool paneled dining room with steaming plates of steak and onions before them. Ezra, with a large apron tied over his shepherd's smock, was serving spring greens and baked potatoes. Absolom was under the table with a dog biscuit. Hector was on top of the marble clock on the mantelpiece with a dead mouse. The dining room window looked out on the village street and the scent of the flowers that were growing in the garden of the cottage opposite came in warm gusts through the window. At first there was no conversation because everyone was too hungry, but presently Ezra asked, "Will the young ladies an' gentlemen be stayin' for tea?"

"Use your intelligence, Ezra," said the elderly gentleman severely. "Did you not take note of the muffins and strawberry jam I brought back from town? You know my personal abhorrence of muffins and strawberry jam."

"Very good, sir," said Ezra and left the room with a broad grin on his face.

"Ezra's mental processes are always somewhat slow on the morning after an evening's visit to the Wheatsheaf," explained the elderly gentleman. "I trust you were not disturbed in the night? He has, I fear, this one regrettable failing. In all else he is the soul of rectitude."

The children laid down their knives and forks and gazed at the elderly gentleman in astonishment. A failing? Did he consider it a failing to sing and dance in the moonlight? "It was grand in the night," said Timothy. "We sang and danced too. It was grand."

It was the elderly gentleman's turn to be astonished. "You danced in the night?" he ejaculated. "What am I clasping to my bosom? Four young bacchanalians? It will be but a short period now before my gray hairs are brought with sorrow to the grave. It surprises me that your grandmother and the excellent Miss Bolt have survived so long. It does not surprise me that my suggestion of shouldering the burden in their place should have been received with such profound and touching gratitude. Never in my sixty-five years of mortal life have I seen my poor old mother so favorably impressed by a humble suggestion of my own. Ah, here comes Ezra with the rhubarb tart. Place it in front of Miss Nan, Ezra. If we are to have a mistress of this house, an infliction which by the mercy of God we have hitherto escaped, at least let her relieve us of some labor. What are you gaping at, Ezra? I should have thought the strong family likeness between Miss Betsy and myself would have informed you that these young people are my relatives. They are my nephews and nieces, the children of my youngest brother. They are to live with us for the present. I feel for you, Ezra. I feel for myself. This has come upon us for our sins. Nan, my dear, why are you crying? If there is one thing I dislike more than a child it's a crying child, and let me tell you, my dear . . ."

He got no further for, sobbing with joy, Nan had flung herself into his arms. Betsy followed, scrambling up onto his left knee, Nan being now settled on his right, held within the curve of his right arm. For a few moments there was pandemonium, the boys cheering, Ezra laughing and stamping his wooden leg on the floor, Absolom barking and Hector hooting and flapping his wings.

"That will do," said the elderly gentleman sternly. "The rhubarb tart grows cold. I am partial to rhubarb tart. Nan, return to your duties. Betsy, get down. Boys, hold your tongues. Hector, hold your beak. Ezra, you may go. Down, Absolom."

In a moment order was restored and they were all eating rhubarb tart in a wonderful golden silence, one of those musical silences rich with the chiming of unheard bells and the ring of silent laughter. When the tart was finished the elderly gentleman, now so marvelously transformed into Uncle Ambrose, got up and said, "Your joy, children, had been premature. I intend to impose conditions upon your sojourn with me. You will keep them or go to your Uncle Edgar, who lives in Birmingham and will dislike you even more than I do myself. Come into my study."

He left the room with Hector on his shoulder and they followed him gravely but with their joy no whit diminished. They were prepared to fulfill any conditions and they knew very well that Uncle Ambrose did not dislike them. Does a man buy muffins and strawberry jam for those whom he dislikes? In the study Uncle Ambrose stood with his back to the fire and motioned the children to sit down. He looked very awe-inspiring, he was so tall, and Hector on his shoulder made him look taller than ever for Hector had a way of elongating himself when he wanted to look alarming. By stretching he could add five inches to his height and when he did this on Uncle Ambrose's shoulder the feathers on the top of his head nearly touched the ceiling.

"It appears," said Uncle Ambrose, "that you children wish to live with me. Why, I cannot imagine. It also appears that I am willing that you should do so, and that not only to relieve my poor old mother of the exhaustion of your society. I must tell you that I have a devouring passion, not for children themselves, for I abominate children, but for educating them. For thirty years I educated boys. When I retired from my labors I had caned more boys into bishoprics and the Cabinet, and into the law, than any headmaster living. My boys lived to bless me for their sore backsides and I've lived to miss them. Yes, I've missed my boys these last five years. You live with your Uncle Ambrose only on condition that he educates you. Is that understood?"

Nan replied steadily, "You can do what you like with us so long as you let us stay with you and each other and Absolom. Grandmama was going to send me and Robert to boarding school, and give Absolom away because of fleas, and that's partly why we ran away. We have to stay with each other."

"Nan to boarding school?" ejaculated Uncle Ambrose. "By Hector, no! I don't hold with boarding schools for girls. Home's the place for girls, though they should have a classical education there. I have always maintained that women would not be the feather-headed fools they are were they given a classical education from earliest infancy." He shot out a finger at Betsy. "Can she read?"

"No," said Nan.

"What's her age?"

"Six," said Nan.

"Six and not read? I could read Homer at four. She'll read him by eight. As for you, Robert, the excellent Miss Bolt tells me that you can read and write but no more. Do you suppose I will send you to boarding school to bring shame upon the name of Linnet until I have given you a thorough grounding in at least the rudiments of a gentlemanly education? I shall not. Now, children, which is it to be? Education or your Uncle Edgar at Birmingham?"

They replied in unison, "Education," but they all looked a little pale and Timothy inquired in a brave but slightly wavering voice, "For how long every day are we to be educated?"

"Nine till one," said Uncle Ambrose promptly.

"Not nine till one for Betsy?" asked Nan.

"Certainly. Why not? She shall have milk and a ginger cookie at eleven."

"Will there be homework?" asked Robert, and he looked a bit miserable for he hated learning anything.

"For yourself and Nan, yes. It will be of an hour's duration, six P.M. until seven P.M., and will take place under my personal supervision, and if you do not come home in time for it you will go supperless to bed. For the rest of each day you will be free to go where you like and do what you like. Only don't disturb me for in the intervals between my parish duties I am writing a book, a study of the Dialogues of Plato, and if you don't know who he is you soon will. Your education will start tomorrow at nine sharp. Now we will each have a peppermint lozenge."

Inserting finger and thumb into a waistcoat pocket he produced a white package and handed it around. The peppermints were good but a bit on the strong side and Absolom's eyes watered before he could get his down. Hector did not try to swallow his. He said "Hick," and sent it to the top of the grandfather clock.

"I shall now take a short nap," said Uncle Ambrose. "Tea is at five with muffins and strawberry jam. You may come to meals or not, just as you please, but if you do not come to meals you will go without them. Be off with you."

They made off immediately. Nan, the last out, looked back as she closed the door. Uncle Ambrose had already made himself comfortable in the biggest armchair and spread his large white silk handkerchief over his head. Hector had perched on the back of the chair and as Nan watched he slowly sank down and down into himself, his head sinking into his shoulders until he was nothing but a large round ball of feathers with two great eyes glaring out of it. Then one eye closed but the other stayed open and winked at her. Then that closed too and Nan went out and shut the door softly behind her.

3

Emma Cobley's Shop

"Today we will be back for tea," said Robert as he opened the front door. "Do you suppose there'll be muffins every day?"

No one answered him for the front door had opened on a new marvel, the porch with four stone steps leading down from it to the village street. It was a stone porch, deep and cool with seats on either side. They sat down instantly, two a side with Absolom between them, looked at each other happily and swung their legs. "Free to go where you like and do what you like." Such a thing had never been said to them before. If a slight chill had touched their hearts as the thought of being classically educated it had been dispersed by that superb sentence. Wonderful adventures shone ahead.

"Not far today," said Timothy, "because of the muffins."

"A reconnaissance today," said Robert. "Exploration of the terrain." He was rather fond of using long words picked up from his soldier father. He always hoped the younger children would ask him what he meant but they never did. They were not interested in self-improvement nor for that matter was Robert. It was just that he liked to feel grand. "Come on."

They got up and climbed down the steps to the road. The door of the cottage opposite was open and just within it a very old man sat on a Windsor chair smoking a pipe. They smiled at him and he smiled at them and then they went on up the hill to the village green at the top. It was pocket-handkerchief size and had cottages grouped about it. One was an inn, the Bulldog, with a swinging sign of a fierce brindled creature, another had a mailbox outside it and a window filled with bootlaces, bottles of boiled sweets, cakes of soap, birdseed, picture postcards, hairpins, onions and a black cat asleep. Over the low green door beside the window was a sign on which was painted EMMA COBLEY, POST OFFICE AND GENERAL STORES. Also opening onto the village green was the lych-gate of the church and beyond it the churchyard.

From the green a lane led away uphill under arching trees and disappeared into a wood that looked vast as a forest in a picture. Rising high into the sky above the wood was the great hill with the outcrop of rock on top, like a castle, and below it the rock like a lion keeping guard, that they had seen last night. The Bulldog was on one side of this lane and the angle of the other was formed by stone walls with tall iron gates facing toward the green. Within the gates a moss-grown drive disappeared into a dark mass of evergreens. There were pillars on each side of the gates with stone lions on top of the pillars and sitting on top of one of the lions was a monkey, who chattered at them angrily. Apart from the monkey there was no one about.

Robert summed it up. "There's the shop, the Bulldog, that wood, the hill with the rocks on top and whatever is inside those gates. Where shall we go first?"

"I want some sweets," said Betsy.

"The shop, then," said Robert. "Has anyone any money? You have, Timothy. You have the penny Hector hicked out."

"And you have sixpence," said Timothy. "The sixpence you were saving up to get a pony. You don't want it now you've got Rob-Roy."

"I might want it for something else," said Robert.

"Don't be horrid, Robert," said Nan. "You're the elder. You pay this time and Tim next time. We shall need all you have for we must get a stamp and a postcard as well as sweets. I think it would be nice to send a postcard to Grandmama. I think perhaps we behaved badly when we were with her. We didn't see it at the time but I think perhaps we did. I'd like to send her a post-card."

Robert capitulated willingly for he didn't want to be horrid. "All right," he said. "The shop. But it won't be much of an adventure."

He was wrong. Little did they know as they approached Emma Cobley's low green door what her acquaintance was eventually to lead to. They got inside the shop with difficulty for when they knocked nothing happened, and when they turned the handle and pushed the door nothing happened either. Then suddenly it gave way and to the furious jangling of a little bell fastened to it inside they fell into a warm stuffy darkness strongly scented with soap and onions, and a great many other smells that could not be identified in the confusion of the moment. Then came a most dreadful sound, a noise of snarling hate that froze their blood in horror, and something leapt at them out of the darkness. It was as big as a calf and Absolom barked madly and Betsy screamed.

"I've got it," panted Robert, on the floor with his hands gripping a furry throat that seemed to sink in and in under his fingers.

"So have I," gasped Timothy, gripping a long ropelike tail. And then he yelled, for the creature had suddenly got free and was on his chest, thrusting sharp talons right through his sailor suit into his skin and gazing down into his face out of terrible blazing yellow eyes.

"It's the cat," said Nan suddenly. "Don't yell, Timothy, it's only the cat." Bending over Timothy, she picked the cat up in her arms and suddenly he went

all soft and purry and everyone's curdled blood began to run freely in their veins again. "He was asleep and we frightened him. Poor cat. Don't growl, Absolom."

"He may be a cat now," said Timothy morosely, for he had a lump coming up on the back of his head where it had hit the floor when the cat attacked him, "but he wasn't when he jumped at me. He was as big as a tiger."

"Don't be a fool, Tim," said Robert, and he said it all the more crossly because he was inclined to think that Timothy was right. He felt quite sure that his hands had not met around that great throat.

"Well, he's a cat now," said Nan, as she put him back in the window. "And this is a shop and we've come to buy sweets, a stamp and a postcard for Grandmama."

"There's no one to buy them from," said Robert.

"Yes there is," said Timothy suddenly. "Look."

They all swung around and their hearts were beating almost as hard as when the cat had jumped at them. When they had first fallen into the shop the darkness, after the sunlight outside, had seemed complete, but now that their eyes were growing accustomed to the dim light they could see that the small low-ceilinged room had a counter piled high with boxes and bags full of every conceivable thing, and shelves all around the walls crowded with rows of bottles, and more boxes. Bunches of herbs hung from the ceiling and in the far corner behind the counter, perched on a high stool, was a little old woman knitting a red woolen muffler. Absolom, who was thoroughly upset, growled at her but she took no notice.

"Good day, my maids, good day, young masters," she said in a birdlike chirping voice, nodding at them as pleasantly as though their entry into her shop had been a perfectly normal one. "And what would you be wanting?"

"A picture postcard for our grandmother, please," said Nan. "And a stamp. And some sweets. We've sixpence. Where is it, Robert?"

There were a few anxious moments while they all stood in a row in front of the counter and Robert searched the pockets of his sailor suit and found nothing, and then the old lady pointed with a knitting needle to a corner of the room. It had fallen out of his pocket during the scrimmage with the cat and rolled away behind a box of potatoes. Robert, as he retrieved it, wondered how she had known it was there. How, amidst all the noise and confusion, could she have seen such a small thing as a sixpence fall out of his pocket and roll away? He felt a bit uncomfortable but he brought it to her and she took it from him, put it into a tin box beside her and smiled at him. She had a small brown wrinkled nutcracker face and beady black eyes like a robin's. Their bright glance seemed to Robert to pierce right through his eyes and come out at the back of his head. Though she looked old her voice was remarkably clear and she seemed as full of vigor as Betsy. She wore an old-fashioned snow-white mobcap, such as the children had seen in pictures, a voluminous black dress and a little red shawl crossed over her chest.

"Sixpence is a lot of money, dearie," she said. "You must spend it to the best advantage."

She rolled up her knitting and got down from her stool and she was taller than she had looked sitting down but small-boned, neat and dainty. With quick darting movements she took a cardboard box from under the counter and laid out five postcards for the children's inspection. They were of the church, the inn, the shop, the dark wood with the great hill behind it, and the gateway with the pillars. Then she took a sheet of green stamps out of a teapot with roses on it and tore one off.

"Can't you make your minds up, my dears?" she asked them as they argued over the postcards. "Send your grannie the church."

"The one of the inn is nice," said Nan.

"Look!" said Robert. "It's a different sign. Not the horrid bulldog. What is it?"

"A bird," said Timothy. "A wonderful bird!"

He bent to look closer but Emma Cobley quickly took the postcard away and put it back in the cardboard box. "That's a very old postcard," she said. "I'd forgotten I had it. Send your grannie the church. That'll please her, your Uncle Ambrose being Vicar." Then as she saw their astonished faces she said, "Emma Cobley knows all about you. It was a boy from across the green who took the message to your grannie last night to say you were safe. My door was open and I heard the Vicar give the message. And old Tom Biddle who was a-setting in his doorway opposite the Vicarage dining room window while you were having dinner tells me you're to stay. Well, my dears, welcome to High Barton, but don't you never climb to the top of Lion Tor."

"Why not?" asked Robert.

"It's a dangerous place for children," said Emma, her bright glance piercing him again. "Something nasty might happen to you there. Now you've fourpence-ha'penny to lay out in sweets. There's a lot of sweets can be bought for fourpence-ha'penny." Turning

around, she took from the shelves behind her one glass
jar after another filled with sweets of every color of the
rainbow. They looked wonderful standing in a row on
the counter with the light from the window just touching them, far more magical than sweets usually look.

It was true that in those days a great many sweets
could be bought for fourpence-ha'penny. After a heated
discussion which lasted a full ten minutes they chose a
pennyworth of peppermint lumps that looked like
striped brown bees, a pennyworth of boiled lemon
sweets the color of pale honey, a penny-ha'pennyworth
of satin pralines in colors of pink and mauve, and a
pennyworth of licorice. And out of pure goodness of
heart Emma Cobley added for nothing a package of
sherbet. They did not know what that was and she
had to show them how to put a pinch of the powder
on their tongues and then stand with their tongues
out enjoying the glorious refreshing fizz. If they had
felt any fear of her it vanished with the fizz, and when
they looked at the black cat peacefully asleep in the
window he looked so very ordinary that they no longer
believed he had been as big as a tiger. They had just
imagined it.

"Frederick," said Emma, following the direction of
their eyes. "A sweet cat. A dear, pretty, loving, gentle
cat."

Though the scratches on his chest were still smarting,
Timothy kept silent during this eulogy, but something
made him glance at Absolom and he was standing by

the door with his tail between his legs, tucked down and in so very firmly it could scarcely be seen, and when Robert opened the door he vanished like a streak of lightning.

They said good-bye to Emma and went out into the sunshine sucking pralines. They were crisp and crackling on the outside and soft and gooey inside. The moment when the teeth crashed through from the outside was sheer heaven.

"Not too many," said Nan. "Remember the muffins and strawberry jam. We must leave room."

"The food's good here," said Robert.

"Everything's good here," said Nan.

Timothy forbore to mention the cat Frederick. Instead he said, "Fancy Uncle Ambrose being Vicar. He's not dressed right. Grandmama's vicar had a stiff white piece of cardboard around his neck. Uncle Ambrose has that folded white thing."

"Uncle Ambrose would never dress like all the other vicars," said Nan with a touch of pride. "Uncle Ambrose would always be different."

"He said he'd been a schoolmaster," said Timothy. "How can he be a parson too?"

"Very clever men can be both," said Nan. "Uncle Ambrose is both. Look. There's the delivery cart."

From where they stood munching they could look down the hill toward the Vicarage, and drawn up outside the porch was a covered wagon drawn by a big gray horse. The delivery man and Ezra were lifting out their trunks. Betsy's doll Gertrude and Nan's sewing basket, Timothy's box of soldiers and Robert's water pistol, all they possessed was in those boxes. Now they knew they had really arrived. Now they knew without any doubt that they were here for good. They stuffed their sweets into their pockets, Robert took Betsy on his back, and yelling hurrah they raced down the hill.

The rest of that day passed like a happy dream. Tea came up to their fullest expectations, with no scrimping of butter on the muffins and the strawberries in the jam large and juicy. It was great fun unpacking their belongings and putting them away in their rooms. For they had two rooms now. Ezra had put sheets on the four-poster in the spare room for Nan and Betsy and the boys were to sleep in the dressing room opening out of it. At present they had only blankets and pillows on the floor but they did not mind this because Uncle Ambrose said that presently they would borrow a couple of beds from Lady Alicia, and her name had such a soft silky sound that they were sure they would be comfortable.

After the unpacking, Betsy suddenly said she felt sick, so she was given a cup of warm milk to settle her and put to bed and very soon she was comfortable and asleep. Her digestion was really very good for her age but it had been a bit strained that day. The others did not feel sick but they did feel disinclined for anything solid for supper, so they had milk and biscuits in the kitchen with Ezra, and Absolom had boiled cabbage and some scraps left over from dinner.

"Since you've come to stay," said Ezra when they had finished, "we must tell the bees."

"Tell the bees?" ejaculated Robert. "But bees don't understand when you talk to them."

"Never let me hear you say that again," said Ezra sternly. "Bees understand every word you say. They be the most wonderful creatures God ever made. If men were to have one-quarter of the wisdom of the bees this wicked world would be a better place, and so I be telling you."

"We did see the hives this morning," said Nan, "but we didn't dare go near."

"That's right," said Ezra. "They don't like you near till they've been told about you. Now come along with me. Step quiet and keep civil tongues in your heads and behave yourselves seemly."

He led the way up the garden, and Robert, Nan, Timothy and Absolom followed him in single file. The sun had set and the sky was a deep blue with one star shining above the tall dark church tower. The wallflowers by the beehives smelled wonderful but in the dim light their deep red had turned to a mysterious velvety darkness. It was very quiet, for the birds and the lambs had gone to bed. The hives were quiet too with only a few late bees coming home with the last load of honey. When they were all in, Ezra brought the children quite close to the hives and touched his forehead in salutation, and Nan curtsied and Robert and Timothy bowed. Absolom lowered his tail and touched the ground with his nose. It came quite naturally to do this. It is what they would have done if they had found themselves suddenly in the presence of royalty.

"Madam queens and noble bees," said Ezra, "there be four children come to bide in this house, nephews and nieces of the Master. Their names be Robert, Nan, Timothy and Betsy. The three eldest, they are here with old Ezra and they've made their reverence to thee. The little 'un, she be poorly, but in the morning I'll bring her to make her curtsy. There be a dog, Absolom, a good dog. They be good children. Have a care of 'em and let no harm come to 'em. Have a care of 'em in the wood and on the hill. Good night to you, madam queens and noble bees, good night to you from the Master, from Hector and Andromache and her four kittens, from Jason now called Rob-Roy, from Nan, Robert, Timothy and the little un that's poorly. From Absolom and from Ezra. Good night from all that lives and breathes in house and garden, the mice in the wainscot and the spiders round about and all that wears fur or feather in your dominion. Good night from all your subjects, madam queens and noble bees."

He touched his forehead again and the children bowed and curtsied and said good night, and then they went solemnly back to the house again in single file.

"Can bees take care of you?" asked Timothy wonderingly, when they were back in the kitchen and Ezra had lit the oil lamp that hung from the central beam and they were sitting around the fire.

"The Vicarage bees, I reckon they saved my life," said Ezra. "There's always been bees at the Vicarage and from a boy I've loved 'em, and so they saved my life. I were a shepherd once and one spring I was up on the moor with my sheep and a lamb strayed. It was evening when I found it, caught in a thorn tree and bleating something pitiful. I ran towards it and sudden I felt the ground give way beneath I and I fell. It was one of the workings of an old tin mine, all overgrown with brambles so that running quick I didn't see it. I fell a long ways down and I knew when I got to the bottom as I'd hurt meself real bad for I couldn't get up, not nohow. I was scared as I'd never be found, and I never would have been but for the Vicarage bees. They swarmed that morning and your uncle he ran after with a spare skep in his hand, and they led him on till they brought him where the lamb and I was, and then they settled theirselves hanging from the bough of a tree just on the near side of the pit, bringing the Vicar up sharp. I was near a goner but I hollered and he heard me. He fetched help from the village and I was took to horspital. They took me leg off but they saved me life and when I come back to the village again the Vicar he took me to be his man for I be too lame now to be a shepherd. I was that grateful to the bees that I carved a bee on me wooden leg and painted it ever so pretty. Do you say now, young uns, as bees don't take care of you? If you're good to the bees the bees they'll be good to you. But you must mind your manners with 'em. They like a bit of courtesy."

"Is it dangerous in the wood and on the hill that you asked the bees to take care of us there?" asked Nan.

"There's dangers if you don't keep your wits about you," said Ezra. "But if you want to go there you won't come to no real harm now I've told the bees to look after you."

Timothy's head was already nodding, and the others were feeling sleepy too, but Robert had enough wits left to put his hand in his pocket and bring out one of the bags of sweets that they had bought from Emma Cobley. He peeped inside. It was what was left of the pennyworth of bee-striped round peppermints and feeling them to be appropriate to the occasion, he offered them to Ezra. He did not want to, for he liked them himself, but courtesy had been stressed and he felt he should. The effect on Ezra was alarming. He shot up out of his chair like a Jack-in-the-box and roared out, "Where did you get them sweets?"

"From the shop on the green," said Robert.

"Emma Cobley's?"

"Yes," said Robert.

"Then don't you never go there no more," thundered Ezra. "I don't buy nothing at Emma Cobley's. The Vicar, he buys his stamps from Emma, that being his duty being Vicar, but I wouldn't get so much as a bootlace there not to save me life. I gets our groceries in the town. When you want sweets you tell me and I'll buy 'em in town for yee. But don't yee get 'em from Emma."

He was so angry that for a few moments no one dared speak and then Nan said gently, "But she seems a very nice old lady."

"Handsome is as handsome does," said Ezra.

"But what *does* she do?" asked Timothy.

"Never you mind," said Ezra. "And as for that cat of hers, that Frederick, you can ask Hector and Andromache about Frederick. They'll tell ye."

His mouth set like a trap and it was obvious that he was not going to tell them any more, and since they did not know how to converse intelligibly with Hector or Andromache there seemed no way of acquiring further information. Discouraged, they went to bed. But they did not stay discouraged for when they slept they dreamed of bees, thousands of bees rustling all about them in a murmurous, musical, protecting cloud.

4

Lady Alicia

Breakfast was at eight o'clock in the kitchen, and Ezra told them that at nine o'clock punctually they were to go to the library to be educated. Nan had feared as much and had put them into clean clothes and seen to it that their hands were clean and their hair well brushed.

"Come in," said Uncle Ambrose in a terrible voice when they knocked at the library door. They entered timidly and found him standing with his back to the fireplace, that was without a fire this morning because it was so warm. His hands were clasped under his coattails and his eyebrows beetled. Hector was perched on the clock behind him. The writing table had been cleared and was out in the middle of the room, with the big high-backed chair at one end and four smaller chairs, two on each side of the table. There was one cushion on Timothy's and two on Betsy's.

"Girls to the right, boys to the left," thundered Uncle Ambrose and when they had taken their places he stalked forward and seated himself in his chair. Hector spread his wings and glided from the clock to its high back where he drew himself up to his fullest height and winked at the children over Uncle Ambrose's head. His wink was wonderfully reassuring. Evidently he liked them now and in this business of education was on their side.

"I observe that you are slightly more prepossessing in appearance than I had previously supposed," said Uncle Ambrose, his glance resting with stern pleasure on their clean clothes and sleek heads. "You are not bad-looking children. If I can succeed in inserting a little knowledge into your vacant heads you may yet bring honor to the name of Linnet. An old and honored name and a charming bird. Linnets and nightingales sang in the enchanted groves that clothed the lower slopes of Mount Hymettus, that sacred mountain above Athens that in the summer season is as purple with heather and as musical with bees as our own Lion Tor above Linden Wood. Where's Athens?"

The question shot out at Robert as though from a pistol and Uncle Ambrose's terrible bright glance seemed to reach right down into his head like a hook. It groped about there and came up with something.

"In Greece, sir," gasped Robert.

"Where's Greece?" Uncle Ambrose shot at Timothy.

"In the Mediterranean," was hooked out of Timothy. He stumbled over the long word but he remembered Father using it on the ship that brought them home.

"Do you, child, know anything whatever about Greece?" Uncle Ambrose asked Nan.

"It has a wine-dark sea," said Nan. It was a phrase she had heard once and forgotten. It had needed Uncle Ambrose's brilliant hooking glance to make her remember it again.

"Good," said Uncle Ambrose and passed on to Betsy. "You, child? What do you know of Greece?"

Betsy had not understood much of what had passed but she remembered her nursery nightlight burning in a little pan of grease and she said, "It is a bright light."

Uncle Ambrose leaned back in his chair and stared at her and his jaw dropped. Then an expression of great tenderness came over his face and he said, "Child, you are right. A bright light. One of the brightest the world has known. But that you should know that, a child of your age. I am astonished. Out of the mouths of babes and sucklings."

He smiled at Betsy as though he loved her very dearly and she smiled back at him. The other three, though well aware of the nightlight in Betsy's mind, did not give her away. They never gave each other away. Also it would be useful if Uncle Ambrose should become taken with Betsy. She would be able to wheedle things out of him.

"Sir," said Robert suddenly, "what about pocket money?"

"Pocket money?" ejaculated Uncle Ambrose.

"Yes, sir. I had sixpence but it's spent now. Do you give us pocket money?"

"I do not," said Uncle Ambrose sternly.

"Betsy likes sweets," said Robert. "They're good for her. I mean the plain hard kind. Grandmama said so."

"I do not *give* pocket money," said Uncle Ambrose more gently, his eyes on Betsy's shock of red curls in the sunshine, "but it can be earned."

"How, sir?" asked Timothy.

"Threepence for a bucket of snails collected in the garden," said Uncle Ambrose. "Sixpence for a barrow-ful of weeds similarly come by. Sixpence a week for grooming Jason-Rob-Roy and polishing his harness. Six-pence a week for darning the socks of the male members of the family. A penny for any child who helps Ezra with the washing-up. Sixpence a week for cleaning the shoes of the entire household. These tasks may be di-vided among yourselves as you wish excepting only that Robert, single-handed, tackles the snails." His terrible eyes searched out the thoughts Robert thought he had hidden so carefully. "No, Robert, not the pony only, leaving the less congenial tasks to the weaker sex. Pony and snails or no pony. You are likely to earn a considerable income. Let that console you."

He opened a drawer, took something out and laid it in the center of the table. It was a slender little switch.

"I do not like caning boys," said Uncle Ambrose, "though I have of course caned hundreds in the course of my professional duties. Upon a girl I would never practice corporal punishment. Nevertheless, Robert and Timothy, any serious wrongdoing, and under that heading I include deliberate disobedience, lying, stealing, and any form of unkindness, will be punished with this switch. There is one more thing that will cause you to be laid over a chair with your posteriors uppermost, and that is interrupting the process of education with conversation upon irrelevant matters. For this once, Robert, we will pass it over but if it occurs again you will know what to expect. We will now return to that bright light, the land of Greece. Before you learn her language, her history and her literature I will tell you of the land itself. I have traveled there, and shall endeavor to travel there again in your company. Attention, please."

Uncle Ambrose did not have to call for attention twice for in a few moments he had them spellbound. He was, they discovered, the most wonderful storyteller in the world. Who would have thought that education was like this? He told them first about the land itself, and he took down books from his shelves and showed them pictures of the glories he had seen, mountains crowned with ruined palaces, statues and temples and shrines beside the sea. And all he described they saw with their inside eyes, so that the pictures in the books were scarcely necessary, and the words that he used fell chiming so that they remembered the sequence of them as one remembers the sequence of the notes in a tune. Milk and crackers were brought by Ezra at eleven o'clock and devoured and then they were sent into the garden for ten minutes. When they came back again it was even better, for Uncle Ambrose told them a story about one of the Grecian heroes. He told them about Jason and the Golden Fleece. He had in front of him a box filled with the letters of the alphabet cut out in cardboard and painted in different colors (had he been up half the night making them? Nan wondered) and with these he set out Jason's name for Betsy on the table top, and made her do it. And she learned to make "bright light" too, and her own name. She learned quickly and easily, and the other three learned to repeat after Uncle Ambrose lines of poetry that he spoke for them, first in Greek and then in English. There was a bit about the evening star that made them think of Ezra and stuck in their minds. "Star of evening, bringing all things that bright dawn has scattered, you bring the sheep, you bring the goat, you bring the child back to its mother." It was wonderful how Uncle Ambrose seemed to keep the three things going at once, telling stories, speaking poetry and helping Betsy with her colored letters, as though he were a conjurer tossing three balls in the air. When one o'clock struck from the church tower and Ezra sounded the gong they could not, apart from their hunger, realize it was dinnertime already.

"Enjoyed yourselves?" said Uncle Ambrose.

"Yes!" they chorused.

"Enjoyed yourselves enough to want to learn the history of this country, its language and poetry? And in due course the history, language and poetry of other countries, including your own?"

"Yes!" they said.

"Together with the knowledge of such kindred subjects as mathematics, geography, and grammar? Education is a mosaic of beauty. The various colored fragments are interrelated."

Understanding failed them but they still said yes.

"Very well then," said Uncle Ambrose. "Tomorrow we start work."

They gazed at him openmouthed and Betsy said in a small voice, "Haven't we been working this morning?"

"Working? By Hector, no!" said Uncle Ambrose. "That was mere titillation of the appetite. Tomorrow I shall teach you how to lay the foundation stone of all education: hard work. Robert, do not look so downcast. Believe me, I will teach even you to find sweated labor entirely admirable. Go and wash your hands. I smell liver and bacon."

At dinner Uncle Ambrose was quite gay and chatty. "The education of the very young is something at which I have not hitherto tried my hand," he said to the world at large. "I taught the sixth form in my teaching days. But I have had my theories and I am not displeased at being compelled to put them into practice. Ezra, what's to follow? Apple dumplings, I trust."

"No, sir. Junket, sir. Miss Betsy was poorly yesterday."

"Ah yes," said Uncle Ambrose resignedly. "You delivered my note to Lady Alicia?"

"Yes, sir. And waited for the reply. Her ladyship will be pleased to lend yee two cots, two goose feather mattresses and two patchwork counterpanes. I be to take the cart to the Manor this afternoon and Moses Glory Glory Alleluja will give 'em to me."

Four pairs of pleading eyes fixed themselves on Uncle Ambrose's face. "Certainly," he said. "Did I not say you could go where you liked and do what you liked in hours not devoted to education? It is most unlikely that you will see Lady Alicia, who has lived in strict seclusion for thirty years, but if you do, present my compliments. Ezra, these children will accompany you on your errand in order, I gather, to set eyes upon a man whose name it appears intrigues them. Ezra, if I am to eat junket it must be to the accompaniment of nutmeg, sugar and cream."

"Very good, sir," said Ezra.

An hour later Ezra and the children, Betsy's doll Gertrude, with whom she had been reunited yesterday, Absolom, Rob-Roy and the pony cart were driving up the hill to the village. Old Tom Biddle, who seemed to sit permanently just inside his front door, nodded and smiled as they went by and called out to Ezra, "See the little maid don't get her eyes scratched out."

Ezra, who did not seem to like Tom Biddle, growled and muttered to the children, "The old varmint! Today's the second day I be forgetting to shut the dining room window."

"Who could scratch out Betsy's eyes?" asked Nan anxiously. "Not Moses Glory Glory Alleluja?"

"Lor' no! Moses wouldn't hurt a fly. He means Abednego. But if you don't worrit Abednego he won't do you no harm. Likes to keep himself to himself, Abednego does. But worrit Abednego and I won't be answerable for no consequences."

"We won't worrit Abednego," they promised. They had reached the green and Ezra drove around it and stopped in front of the iron gates between the stone pillars with lions on top. The monkey was not there today. So this was the home of Lady Alicia. The children looked at each other with sparkling eyes and then the boys and Nan scrambled out of the cart to help Ezra get the gates open. Betsy stayed where she was for she had Gertrude in her arms, and looking around she saw the cat Frederick come out of the shop. He sat down on the doorstep and became absorbed in washing behind his ears but she knew very well that he was keeping his eye on them.

The gates opened reluctantly, as though they seldom did, and did not want to now, and Ezra led Rob-Roy and the cart through. Nan and the boys did not get in again for the drive beyond the gates led into such a thicket of evergreens that they had to go ahead, pushing the branches back to make a way through for the cart. But though they made a way through they didn't seem to come through. The shrubbery appeared endless, a tangled dark forest of yews, laurels and rhododendrons, and the moss under their feet was so thick and soft that the wheels, and Rob-Roy's hoofs, made no sound. Absolom did not like it very much and kept his tail tucked down.

"Lady Alicia, she don't like visitors," explained Ezra. "Moses and Abednego, they comes and goes over the wall."

After that he did not say any more, for the strange twilit place imposed its own silence. It was a relief when they saw light breaking through the thinning evergreens and knew they were coming out into the open again. Presently the moss under their feet turned golden-green and an archway cut in the yews straight ahead was ablaze with sun. The children began to run, full of joy, and then suddenly there stepped into the archway, blocking out almost all of the sunshine, the most alarming figure.

He was a coal-black giant with a big head and long loose arms. He had a curved knife in one hand and stood a little crouched, as though ready to spring at them. Absolom growled and the children stopped dead so suddenly that Ezra, leading Rob-Roy, bumped into Timothy.

"Get on then," said Ezra, annoyed. "What's come to yee? That's only Moses Glory Glory Alleluja. Don't hurt the poor chap's feelings now. Gentle as a dove he be."

Nan walked bravely forward, for she was a child who would not have liked to hurt the feelings of the devil himself. The others followed, and the nearer they came to Moses Glory Glory Alleluja the less terrible he appeared, and when they were actually through the arch of yew and close to him, he was suddenly changed by some miracle of the sunlight from a figure of fear into one of the most attractive men they had ever seen. He was a Negro with white hair, tall but stooped about the shoulders, his face folded into deep lines of age and kindness. His eyes were sad but his smile, as he looked at the children, was as wide with pleasure as Ezra's. He wore the tattered remnants of a coat of a dark green uniform, from which one brass button still hung by a thread, as though he had once been a coachman or footman, a gardener's corduroy trousers and a sack apron tied around his waist. The knife in his hand was a scythe with which he was trying to clear a path through

the mass of grass and docks and nettles in which he stood knee-deep. Nan held out her hand to him.

"The children," he said with delight and took Nan's hand in his. He had a fascinating hand, large as a ham, coal-black but with a pink palm. All the children shook hands and Absolom removed his tail from between his legs and wagged it. How, they all wondered, could they have felt afraid of this glorious man? After their father, Uncle Ambrose and Ezra, he was without doubt God's masterpiece.

"They're good children as children go," Ezra informed him. "And Absolom's a good dog. Have yee got these here beds up at the house?"

"Got 'em at the back door," said Moses. "Put the children in the cart or their legs will be stung."

They piled into the cart again and followed in the wake of Moses and Ezra, swaying through the green sea of grass and docks and nettles. Presently they realized to their astonishment that once it had been an orchard or a garden, for apple trees in full bloom and tall black cypresses grew up out of it, and ahead of them were two great trees of japonica covered with flaming blossom. The sun was bright and hot and there was the hum of bees.

"Our bees?" Robert asked.

"Aye," said Ezra. "Very fond of Linden Manor, our bees be."

They walked between the japonica trees, where the mossy drive appeared again from beneath the weeds and grasses, and there before them was the Manor. It was an old house built of weathered gray granite with a stone-tiled roof. It was surrounded by unpruned rose-bushes, and its dormer windows peered like eyes through the hairy creepers that had climbed right up to the roof and even in places to the tall chimneys. From the front there seemed no entrance; briars grew over the pillared porch of the front door and all the downstairs windows had blind eyes, for their curtains were drawn. There was a stone terrace in front of the house but the weeds had pushed up the paving stones. Directly behind it Lion Tor towered to the sky, and Linden Wood surrounded the house and its ruined garden as a moat surrounds a castle, completely cutting it off from the world beyond. Hot, murmurous with bees, the place cast a spell.

Turning right, Moses led them to the back of the house where the wood came pressing almost up to the walls. It was full of great linden trees, oaks and beeches all dressed in their bright spring green. There was a cob-bled yard behind the house with a tumbledown stable to one side. The back door was open and the monkey was sitting on the doorstep playing cat's-cradle. He was a sad-eyed gray monkey with an irritable expres-sion, wearing a tattered green coat like the one that Moses wore, and when he saw the children he chattered with annoyance and leapt back into the house.

"Children, do not worrit Abednego," cautioned Mo-ses.

"We won't," they said.

"Where be beds?" asked Ezra.

"In the kitchen," said Moses.

The back door opened straight into the big kitchen. It was a dark dreary place, not at all like the bright happy kitchen at the Vicarage. It had a well in the middle of the floor and a big oak cupboard stretched from floor to ceiling. On the top of the cupboard was Abednego, still chattering with annoyance. By the well there were two cots, two feather mattresses and two little folded quilts. Moses, Ezra and the boys carried the beds and mattresses out to the cart, and Nan followed with the quilts in her arms. They smelled faintly of cedarwood and they were made of hundreds of diamond-shaped patches of silk, satin, velvet and brocade of all the colors of the rainbow. She was so absorbed in them that she did not notice, as she stepped into the sunlight, that Betsy had stayed in the kitchen.

Betsy was gazing at Abednego. He was about her size but he had the face of a very old man and he was hairy like Absolom. The queer mixture of man, child and creature fascinated her. And so did his long tail which hung down over the willow-patterned china on the cupboard like a velvet bell-rope. Mechanically rocking Gertrude in her arms she stared and stared, and Abednego stopped chattering and stared at Gertrude, who was a very beautiful doll with red cheeks, golden hair, a blue silk dress, a lace petticoat and red shoes.

Betsy said afterward that she did not mean to worrit Abednego and had no intention of pulling his tail. She merely wanted to stroke it to see if it was as velvety as it looked. Standing on tiptoe and stretching up her left hand she did so, and like a snake striking down came Abednego's long hairy arm and skinny hand and snatched Gertrude from the crook of her right arm. Before she had time even to get her breath he had leapt from the top of the cupboard, wrenched open the door beside it and vanished, carrying Gertrude with him. At once Betsy dashed in pursuit for she was a brave child and though she was no more than mildly fond of Gertrude she had a very strong sense of personal property.

The door closed behind her and she was in darkness. She ran and ran, and felt as she ran that the strange dark tunnel was taking her right into the heart of a mountain. She forgot this was a house. Now and then a faint glimmer of light suggested that other tunnels led off to right and left but she kept straight on because she very soon became so frightened that she could not stop. She was brave but she thought she heard long swift loping footsteps padding up behind her and she pictured some creature rather like Abednego but more horrible reaching out for her with furry paws. She very soon forgot about Gertrude and even about the others and home; she forgot about everything except the hairy creature coming behind her. Then she tripped over something and fell headlong. She did not hurt herself, partly because she was so well cushioned with fat and partly because she fell on something soft, but she was startled and for a few moments she could only lie still with her face pressed against the softness.

Then she heard not the footsteps of the hairy creature but a soft humming. It was so familiar and reassuring that immediately all the fear went out of her and she sat up and opened her eyes. The first thing she saw was a slanting sunbeam, and slowly and happily revolving in it, as though bathing their wings in the gold, were three bees. It was not total darkness about her now but a dim green underwater light with the sunbeam slanting through it. She thought at first that she was sitting on thick green moss in a cavern in the mountain. Then she realized that this must be a house after all because she was sitting on a green carpet. The long dark passage had led her into the hall of the house and she had tripped on the carpet because it was ragged at the edges. Under the carpet the hall was paved with stone, like the passage, and it smelled cold and dark because the windows were all closed and covered with green velvet curtains. They were old and shabby and there was a big hole in one of them. It was through this hole that the sunbeam slanted. Betsy didn't know how the bees had got in. If they had followed her up the passage then they had been with her all the time and she needn't have been so frightened. Uncarpeted stairs led up from the hall into darkness and their curved balustrade was festooned with cobwebs. Betsy had thought the cobwebs at the Vicarage were glorious but they were nothing to these, which looked as though they had been here for a hundred years, growing more intricate and marvelous all the time.

She got up and smoothed her frock and the bees stopped revolving in the sunbeam and led the way to the stairs. She followed them, going slowly step by step up through the thick curtains of shadows that dropped from some high unseen roof. But there must have been light coming from somewhere for there seemed always a gleam of gold on the bees' wings. She reached the top of the stairs and the bees led her along a dark landing, then up two steps and along a corridor with rows of doors, and up more steps and along another corridor, and then they stopped before a door that was not quite dark because through a large empty keyhole another sunbeam had thrust as much of itself as it was able to do. In this small beam the bees once more revolved, bathing themselves in the gold, and Betsy lifted the latch of the door and walked in. They followed her and she closed the door behind the four of them.

"What are you doing here?"

The voice was sharply imperious but Betsy was so pleased to hear a human voice again that she did not mind, and it was wonderful to come out into the sunlight of an uncurtained room. Though it was a very strange room. The first thing Betsy noticed was a needlework picture hanging on the wall close to her. It showed men on horseback, with falcons on their wrists, riding through a forest glade toward a town built high up on a mountain that rose above the tops of the tallest trees. The town had steep roofs and towers and pinnacles like a cathedral, but was so far away in the sky that it might have been fashioned out of clouds and rainbows. The furniture in the room was old and dark and the dark wavy floor reflected the light like water. The curtains were dim gold and the small shoes of the lady were gold too, and set side by side on a purple velvet footstool.

She was strange as her room, very small and upright in her big carved chair. Her black silk dress was shiny, long and full, and when she moved it rustled and reflected the light just as the floor did. In some places there were slits in the silk as though it were very old and she herself looked old, with a lot of white hair piled up untidily on top of her small head and a nose so thin as to be almost transparent. Her face was bleached as though she was never in the sunshine and her tiny hands looked like claws holding the carved birds on her chair, and so weighed down by their load of rings that Betsy was quite sure she would not be able to lift them however hard she tried. And then suddenly one hand flew up with a flash of diamonds and the fingers gripped Betsy's shoulder like pincers, the wrinkled eyelids lifted and blue fire shone out from eyes that were as young as Betsy's. And at that moment the three bees flew out of the open window. For a moment Betsy felt abandoned and then she thought that the bees wouldn't have left her if it hadn't been all right.

"I asked you, child, what are you doing here? Have you no tongue in your head?"

"I am looking for my doll Gertrude," said Betsy.

"And why should you expect to find your doll Gertrude in my private boudoir?"

"Abednego might have brought her here. Abednego has stolen her."

"In what circumstances?" asked the lady.

"We came to fetch the beds," said Betsy. "And I went into the kitchen with Gertrude, and Abednego was sitting on the cupboard and he took her out of my arms and ran away with her and I ran after."

"I see," said the lady. "And who are the *we* who came to fetch the beds?"

"Nan my sister, Robert and Timothy my brothers, Absolom our dog, Ezra, Rob-Roy the pony and the cart. Uncle Ambrose stayed at home but if you are Lady Alicia he presents his compliments."

"I beg that you will thank him," said Lady Alicia, "and present mine. I do not know your uncle personally, for I dislike being visited, but I correspond with him on occasions. You may sit down, child, on that chair and describe your Uncle Ambrose to me."

Betsy hoisted herself onto a chair in front of Lady Alicia and sat with her legs dangling. The sun shone on her rough red curls, and her cotton frock was the color of the new green beech leaves. In the old room she looked very fresh and new and a great deal more beautiful than in actual fact she was. "My Uncle Ambrose," she said, "is the very nicest kind of man. He loves me."

A ripple of something that might have been amusement, or perhaps memory, passed over Lady Alicia's face and she asked, "He has informed you of the fact?"

Betsy shook her flaming head. "But I know," she said.

"One does," agreed Lady Alicia. "But if you return his affection you should inform him of the fact. Not necessarily in words."

"I've told him," said Betsy, "like this." And she slipped off her chair, went to Lady Alicia and leaned close to her, fluttering her long eyelashes against the old lady's cheek. "That's a butterfly kiss," she said. "I do it to Uncle Ambrose, Nan and Father. And you. Nobody else. Where's my doll Gertrude?"

Lady Alicia's voice was no longer imperious but soft and slightly shaky as she said, "We must summon Abednego. But I have lost my silver bell."

"It's on top of the bookcase," said Betsy.

Lady Alicia gave an exclamation of annoyance. "He puts it beyond my reach," she said querulously. "He does it on purpose."

"I'll get it," said Betsy and climbing up on one of the chairs she brought it down.

"Ring it outside the door," said Lady Alicia. "Ring it for a long time."

Betsy did so. It was a small silver bell but it rang out in a marvelous manner, clear and sweet and loud as though it were ten times its size, and echoes woke up in the house and answered it, ringing and ringing away and away like birdsong in the wood. "That should fetch him," said Betsy and came back to Lady Alicia. "Have you any little girls?" she asked, climbing back on her chair.

"No," said Lady Alicia.

"Little boys?" asked Betsy.

"A long time ago I had one little boy, called Francis," said Lady Alicia, and her blue eyes were hooded again and once more her hands looked as though she would never be able to lift them from the carved birds.

"Did you lose him?" inquired Betsy with interest.

"Yes," said Lady Alicia.

"Where did you lose him?"

"On Lion Tor," said Lady Alicia in a voice dry as dust. "Thirty years ago. He was eight years old."

"Timothy is eight," said Betsy.

She was sorry Lady Alicia had this habit of losing things because she could see it made her unhappy, but she did not know how to say so. It was a relief when padding footsteps were heard in the passage and Abednego knocked at the door.

"Come in," said Lady Alicia, unhooding her eyes, and he entered, put his feet together and bowed.

"What have you done with this little girl's doll?" He straightened, chattering with vexation, but his eyes were piteous. "Abednego, you know quite well that you cannot keep this doll. Go and fetch it."

He went out, muttering monkey curses under his breath, and from behind he looked about a hundred years old. Lady Alicia apologized to Betsy. "You must forgive him, child. This is not so much a case of stealing as of thwarted paternity."

"What's that?" asked Betsy.

"When my late husband brought him from Africa to be my page he was a very young monkey and so, you see, parted from his own people he has never had the pleasure of bringing up a family."

"Did you lose your husband too?" asked Betsy.

"No, he lost himself. He was an explorer. He used to travel all over the world digging up vanished cities. And then he also vanished."

"Perhaps he'll turn up," said Betsy hopefully.

"Not, I think, after twenty-seven years," said Lady Alicia. She sounded sad but Betsy thought she had got over her husband losing himself in foreign parts a good deal better than she had got over herself mislaying her little boy on Lion Tor.

Abednego returned with Gertrude in the crook of his left arm and advanced toward Betsy with dragging footsteps. He stood in front of her, his eyes hot and angry as well as miserable, but he did not say any more rude things. He took Gertrude out of his cradling left arm with his right hand and held her rosy face briefly against his cheek, and then gave her back to Betsy. She looked up at him and saw that there were two wet tear-tracks smudged down his furry face from his eyes to the corners of his large ugly mouth. He was not weeping now, not in front of her, but he had wept.

Now Betsy was not an unselfish or even an outstand-
ingly loving child, but she suddenly remembered her
father saying good-bye to her before he went away. He
had picked her up, holding her with her cheek against
his face, and then had put her on Grandmama's lap and
gone out of the room without saying a single word. And
then there was the old lady, so heavy and dusty because
she had lost her little boy. And now there was Abednego. Three times now this strange adult thing had
touched her. She was well aware that her feeling for
Gertrude was not this thing but something far less
admirable, and looking up into Abednego's face she
fought a battle inside herself with the thing that it was,
a sort of grabbing thing, and then she held Gertrude
out to him. "You have her," she said.

Abednego stared at her, stupefied.

"My dear, are you giving your doll to Abednego as a
permanent gift?" asked Lady Alicia.

"Yes," said Betsy. "I want him to have Gertrude for
his."

"Abednego, you may take the doll," said Lady Alicia.
"She is now your doll."

Abednego snatched Gertrude out of Betsy's hand
and clutched her to the breast of his shabby green velvet
coat. His eyes blazing like lamps, and chattering madly,
he leapt around the room, to the top of the bookcase
and then to the back of Lady Alicia's chair, from there
to the mantelpiece and then to the windowsill. Then
he came back to Betsy and stretching out his right hand

he touched her cheek and her hair, and then gently laid the hand on her chest. His eyes were soft and mild and the excited chattering had changed to crooning. Betsy smiled at him, aware that he loved her now and would always love her.

"Child, you have made a friend," said Lady Alicia, "and a more valuable one than you realize. Abednego, fetch the tea. We will partake of it the three of us together and then we will play at jackstraws."

5

The Cave in the Rock

Packing the beds, mattresses and quilts into the little cart and tying them firmly into place with pieces of string, so they would not fall out on the homeward journey, took quite a long time, and they were all so absorbed by it that it was not until the job was finished that Nan said suddenly, "Where's Betsy?"

There was a moment of consternation and then Nan said, "She'll be in the wood picking bluebells," and began to run across the yard. But Ezra ran after her and caught her wrist. "You don't go into that there wood alone, maid," he said firmly. "I be coming with you."

"Come back, both of you," called Robert. He had jumped up onto the parapet of the well and was looking very Napoleonic and important, and he spoke so loudly that they obeyed him. "Campaigns must be planned," he informed them, "and troops deployed in coordinated action. But first of all, where was this child last seen?"

To their shame no one knew but Nan ran back into the kitchen and looked under the table and behind the roller towel that was hanging beside the sink. She never even saw the door in the dark corner that had so mysteriously closed itself behind Betsy, and perhaps would have taken no notice of it if she had, so sure was she that Betsy was in the wood. She ran back to the others and heard Robert asking, "What does this child like doing best?"

"Don't be so silly, Robert!" she said angrily, for there was no doubt Robert was showing off. "You know perfectly well what she likes doing best. Picking flowers. She's in the wood."

"There are flowers in what used to be the garden," said Robert. "Now then. Ezra, Nan and Absolom will go to the wood, Timothy and I to the garden with Moses Glory Glory Alleluja to show us where to look, and we'll unharness Rob-Roy and put him in the stable till we come back."

People who are quite sure what one ought to do are always obeyed, even if what they think one ought to do isn't what one ought to do, and everyone immediately did what Robert said without further discussion. Robert himself, jumping off the well to unharness Rob-Roy, decided he would be a great general. There was probably less money in it than in burglary or the stage but it would please Father.

Nan, Ezra and Absolom set off for the wood, making for the part of it that was directly opposite them across the yard, for that was the way they thought Betsy would have gone. "You see she loves picking flowers," said Nan again, "and look at those bluebells. They're like the sky fallen down."

She was close to tears and Ezra said soothingly, "Now don't yee take on, maid. Remember our bees be about."

There was no visible path through the wood but they made their way upward, wading in and out of pools of bluebells. There were other flowers too, white ones with veined petals like the wings of moths that Ezra said were anemones, sorrel smelling sweetly of hay, and late wood violets. Nan would have felt herself in heaven had it not been that Betsy was lost. The way grew steeper and she asked anxiously, "Aren't we climbing toward Lion Tor?"

"Aye," said Ezra. "But don't yee fret. The little maid could never have climbed that far. Absolom, where be off to?"

There was a whirring of wings and a great clattering cry, for Absolom had started a cock pheasant. There was a gleam of purple and crimson and green and then the great bird flew off with Absolom in pursuit, and Ezra stumping after shouting at Absolom to come back, for pheasants are valuable birds and must not be pursued by dogs. Nan stayed where she was, knee-deep in bluebells, for she knew that Ezra on his wooden leg had as much chance of catching up with Absolom as he had of catching the pheasant. They would both soon be back.

Yet they were out of sight and she felt lonely. Far up above her head, in the galleries of the trees, among the interlacing sunbeams, the birds were singing, but they seemed far removed from her and only a few of the sunbeams pierced down to where she was. Yet a few did and turning to one of them for company she saw four bees revolving in it, turning slowly around and around as though bathing their wings in the gold, and now that she saw them she could hear their low humming. They came from the sunbeam, flew around her head and then moved slowly away to the left. She followed them because she found she had to.

They led her uphill among rocks and brambles but they found the way through for her so that she did not fall or hurt herself. They led her to where a wall of rock had forced itself through the hillside. She realized she had come a long way up the hill, that the trees were thinning and that up above her she could hear the baaing of sheep out on the hillside. A narrow path led steeply upward along the face of the wall of rock and Nan climbed it, following the bees. She had no doubt that Betsy had been this way because here and there she found flowers lying on the path, anemones and sorrel and a few violets, and she picked them up because she did not want them to die. Yet it was not like Betsy to drop the flowers she had picked and Nan was surprised she had managed to climb so far by herself.

The path grew steeper and Nan found she had climbed above the tops of the trees. She turned around with her back to the rock and she almost forgot her anxiety for Betsy in wonder and awe. For here was another country. The rustling green that had made the ceiling of the country below was the floor of this one, and it rippled to her feet like the sea. She climbed up farther and saw high white clouds sailing over her head and she knew that if she were to go up above them the marvel would be repeated. Over her head there was world upon world, and below her feet too, going down and down forever. It was her first experience of the heights and the abyss and she felt a little dizzy and very small and alone on the rock-face.

She climbed on farther and then stopped, finding her way barred by a boulder of rock thrust out across the path like the paw of some great beast. The bees had vanished and she began to feel frightened. She wanted to go back, down to the safe floor of the wood where Ezra and Absolom were, for these other dizzy worlds were not where she belonged. And surely Betsy could not have come this way. She could not have climbed over the boulder. Yet somebody had climbed over it because halfway up lay a white anemone like a dying moth, and because the somebody might possibly have been a scared Betsy, who had gone on because she was too frightened to go back, Nan went on too. She reached the dropped anemone, rescued it, scrambled to the top of the boulder and began to climb down the other side, and now it was suddenly easy because below her she was aware of refuge. It seemed no time at all before her feet sank into soft grass and she knew she was safe.

She stood and looked about her and she wondered if there was any place anywhere more lovely and strange than this, poised here halfway between the world of the trees and of the clouds. It was a miniature green valley, almost like a garden, held in a cleft of the rock. The two spurs of rock that contained it on each side were both the same shape, like the paws and forearms of a huge beast, and viewed from this side they were not menacing but protective, as though the beast held the garden in his arms. A small stream ran down the center of it and fell over the edge of the cliff down to the trees below, and the banks of the stream were thick with water forget-me-nots and green ferns. There were flowers everywhere in the grass and more ferns and little rowan trees grew up the sides of the valley. Nan put her flowers into a pool between two stones at the edge of the stream, to get a good drink, and she had a drink herself, lifting the water in her cupped hands. Then she sat down to rest and for the first time looked up at the rock at the head of the valley and saw it shaped like the chest of the beast, and up above it, against the sky, was the huge shaggy lion's head. Now she knew where she was, between the paws of the Lion who kept guard beneath the tor.

She knew where she was but she still did not know where Betsy was. She called her but there was no answer and taking her flowers out of the water, she began to search the little valley, following a path beside the stream. It took her only a few minutes to reach its source, bubbling out of the rock near the head of the valley. She walked a little farther and the path brought her out into an open space in front of the lion's chest. Only now the mass of rock became less like a lion than a house. What from a distance had looked like the lion's mouth was the mouth of a door-shaped cave up above her in the rock-face. Rough steps had been cut diagonally in the rock, leading up to the door, and at the bottom of them was a wooden workbench, a saw and ax, a pile of logs and a waterpot. Evidently the Lion was inhabited. He was alive.

Still carefully carrying the flowers Nan climbed the steps with a beating heart. She was not afraid, for she knew there was nothing to be afraid of in this place, but life for the last few days had been not quite what she was accustomed to and she did wonder what was going to happen next. She reached the top of the steps, came to the mouth of the cave and looked in. There seemed no one about and she very timidly went inside. At once she felt as though she had gone back thousands of years, right back to the time when people had no homes except the caves, when they dressed in skins,

hunted the wild beasts and drew wonderful pictures on
the cave walls. There was a picture in this cave, on the
wall opposite her, but she could see it only dimly because smoke drifted between her and it, smoke going
up in a waving blue column from the fireplace of stones
in the center of the cave to a hole far up above in the
roof. The floor of the cave was spread with dried ferns
and there was a table of rough planks laid on logs of
wood, a few pots and pans beside the fire, and bunches
of dried herbs hanging on the walls. Light came into the
cave from its opening and from the hole in the roof
above and Nan found she could see quite well. She
crept cautiously around the fire because she very much
wanted to see the picture on the wall.

It wasn't one of the long-ago cavemen's pictures because it wasn't of wild animals. It was of men in tall
hats with falcons on their wrists riding through a forest,
and up above them was a town with towers and pinnacles perched on a mountaintop. Nan was reminded
at once of Linden Wood and Lion Tor. The outlines of
the picture had been incised in the rock with a sharp
tool and the colors carefully applied within the outlines. It was not an oil painting and it looked as though
the artist had got the colors from roots and flowers. The
picture was not very clear yet Nan could feel the mystery of the wood, and the airy-lightness of the towers
in the sky.

She moved on around the cave and there were other
pictures on the walls, more like the cavemen's pictures

because they portrayed hares, foxes, squirrels, striped badgers and all sorts of birds. She did not yet know the names of the birds and beasts but the little pictures made her love them. In one corner she found a bed of dried heather spread with old sacks and near it some roughly made wooden dishes, a clay pot full of wild flowers, and a basket of woven reeds containing dry wrinkled apples, nuts and queer-looking roots. But no Betsy. She was on the point of going out again when she noticed a curtain of hide hanging on the wall, lifted it and saw a narrow fissure in the wall of the cave, just wide enough for a man to squeeze through, and beyond it a roughly made wooden ladder ascending a sloping chimney in the rock. Pale green light filtered down the chimney, so she supposed it led up to the hillside above. She dropped the curtain and drew back, for the ladder was so steep and the rungs so far apart that she did not think Betsy could possibly have gone up it.

But after a moment or two she realized that someone was coming down it for she heard heavy footsteps slowly descending. Had it not been for Betsy she would have run away, but she had to ask whoever it was whether he, or it, had seen Betsy. So, trembling, she stood her ground.

He came out backward from behind the curtain and with deep relief she saw he was a man, not a thing, a tall man with bent shoulders and tawny hair and beard. He turned around, straightened up and saw her. His jaw dropped in consternation and a look of alarm came

into his golden-brown eyes. He was dressed in the odd-
est assortment of ragged garments and seemed to be
what Grandmama called a tramp. She did not like them
and had a notice on her gate which said NO TRAMPS. NO
VENDORS. BEWARE OF THE DOG. But Nan liked this man
on sight just as she had liked Ezra and Moses Glory
Glory Alleluja. He was big and strong, and golden like
a lion, yet at sight of her he had begun to tremble too,
and because he was frightened she ceased to be afraid.
To reassure him she held out to him the flowers she
was still carrying. He took them with joy, his whole face
lighting up, counted them carefully and added them to
the other flowers in the clay pot.

"You dropped them?" asked Nan.

He nodded and smiled at her and taking a wrinkled
apple from a basket he held it out to her. To please him
she took it and ate it but it was dry as a piece of leather.
He opened his mouth and made a strange sound, an
expression of deep sorrow came over his face, and Nan
knew that he was dumb. She knew because they had
had a dumb servant in India, and he had made those
same strange noises and his face had worn that same
look of bewildered sorrow. Nan had grown very clever
at saying for him what he wanted to say and she found
she could do the same for this man. "You were picking
flowers in the wood down below," she said, "and you
heard voices and a dog barking and you ran away and
climbed up above the treetops home again, but in your
hurry you dropped some of the flowers. One must not

drop flowers for then they die. It was only my voice you heard, and Ezra's, and our dog barking at a pheasant, and we wouldn't do anything to hurt you."

An expression of relief came over the tramp's face and taking her hand he bent down and kissed it. His gesture was gentle and courteous and she thought that after all he couldn't be quite an ordinary tramp, not the sort you warn off by notices on the gate about savage dogs that aren't there, and he would understand how anxious she was about Betsy. Leaving her hand in his she told him about Betsy being lost. He looked sad and shook his head to show her that Betsy was not here, and he pointed up the ladder down which he had come and shook his head again to tell her that Betsy was not up there with the sheep on the hillside. Then, taking Nan with him, he went to the mouth of the cave and stood looking out, his hand over his eyes. They saw no one at first and then the tramp gave a croak of pleasure, for down below them in the small valley was a little white figure scurrying along by the stream. But it wasn't Betsy, it was Absolom. "It's Absolom, our dog," said Nan, and she and the man climbed down the steps to the valley.

Absolom came bounding to meet them, his tongue out and his ears flapping, very proud of himself that he had found Nan. He had a bit of paper fastened to his collar with a piece of gardener's string and Nan took it and read it. On one side of it, in Uncle Ambrose's beautiful handwriting, was a list of the groceries that Ezra had bought and the children had found in the cart and eaten, and on the other side crookedly printed words had been inscribed so painfully and laboriously that in places the pencil point had dug right through the paper.

Dear maid come back I cant get up them rocks on wooden leg nor couldnt the little un get up em no harm in Daft Davie but your uncle wouldnt like it dear maid come back now respectfully Ezra Oake.

Nan was glad she had not read the message aloud because of the word daft. If this man was Daft Davie he was not daft and she felt hot with indignation that anyone should call him so.

"It is Ezra," she said, "and he's down below in the wood and he is anxious about me but he can't come up because of his wooden leg. So as Betsy isn't here I must go back."

Daft Davie looked very bewildered and so Nan told him how they had come to live with Uncle Ambrose for always, and she would see him again. Then she said good-bye and ran off down the valley with Absolom. Just before she climbed up over the Lion's paw she turned and looked back and there was Daft Davie at the top of the steps just outside the entrance to his cave. He was watching her go away and he looked very sad. She waved to him, and she felt sad too, but she knew she would see him again, and his wonderful home inside the Lion's head.

Ezra was waiting for her and Absolom at the foot of

the cliff and he was pleased to see them again for he had been anxious. He was also annoyed. "Give I the slip like that again, maid," he said, "and I'll tell on you to your uncle."

"But I had to go," said Nan. "The bees said so. There were four of them turning around and around in the sunbeam and they led me on."

"Well now," said Ezra, astonished, "what were they thinking on? The little 'un wasn't up there."

"I must have had to go there," said Nan, "or the bees wouldn't have said so."

"That they wouldn't," agreed Ezra. "Don't know, I'm sure. Well, us better be getting back to Manor. You've been gone nigh an hour and we 'aven't found the little 'un."

As they went Nan said, "I like Daft Davie and I like his house. Who is he?"

"Used to live over to Pizzleton, village down on the other side of Lion Tor. Worked for the blacksmith there. But the village boys laughed at him, being dumb and peculiar as you might say, and threw stones and that, and he ran away and he's lived on Lion Tor ever since. He earns a bit now and again, helping with the lambing and the harvesting, selling baskets and such like. Clever with his hands. But he's daft, poor chap. No harm in 'im."

They were back again in the yard by the well but there were no signs of the others and no signs of Betsy.

6

The Garden of
the Fountain

The second search party, Timothy, Robert and
Moses, put Rob-Roy in the stable and set out for the
gardens.

"Where do the best flowers grow?" asked Robert.

"In the garden of the fountain to the west of the
house," said Moses. "There's wallflower and sweetbrier
there, and come the summer there'll be night-scented
stock and mignonette. I plant there all things that be
sweet to smell beneath the moon."

"Don't they smell sweet beneath the sun too?" asked Timothy.

"They do, young master, but it be beneath the moon that milady paces the garden of the fountain upon my arm."

"Does Lady Alicia only go out at night?" asked the astonished Robert.

"Only at night, young master."

"Why does she only go out at night?"

Moses smiled and shook his head and gave no answer. Timothy thought that he was not a very communicative person. He spoke slowly, as though he were not used to talking, and his deep soft voice would begin a sentence with power and then die sadly away to a mere breath of sound. Yet he did not seem a dying sort of person for somewhere at the back of his dark eyes there was fire. Robert did not notice these things about Moses because he was a practical person, always much occupied in telling people what they ought to do, but Timothy was not practical and following where Robert led he was able to notice things. As Moses led them silently through the tall grass that bordered the terrace in front of the house he noticed three things. There was an uncurtained window upstairs and it was a little open, and three bees flew out of it as he watched. Those were two things. The third was the great wisteria vine that grew up the side of the house and had such thick branches that it would be possible to climb it.

They came around to the west side of the house and

through an archway into a small garden entirely enclosed by yew hedges. In the middle of it was a fountain
with a statue in the center, and there were winding grass
paths and flower beds full of dark red wallflowers, south-
ernwood, lemon verbena and thyme. And there were
hedges of lavender and sweetbrier, rosemary bushes
grown almost as large as trees, and an arbor grown over
with honeysuckle. There was nothing growing here that
was not sweet smelling and the little place was most
lovingly taken care of.

"Do you take care of it?" Timothy asked Moses.

Moses smiled and nodded. "Moses is gardener to
milady," he said. "And chef to milady. And butler to
milady and once he was coachman. But the horses are
dead now and the rats have eaten holes in the seats of
the carriage. No more horses." He had begun to speak
with a sort of forlorn pride but now his deep voice sank
away into inaudible sorrow and Timothy wanted to cry.

Robert didn't because he was not listening. Being
practical he was looking for Betsy. "She's not in the
arbor," he called out. "Let's look behind all the bushes."

Moses joined him in the search but Timothy felt
quite sure that Betsy was not here. If she had been she
would have heard their voices and called out to them.
He wandered off by himself to the center of the garden
where the fountain was. There was no longer any water
in the marble basin and the man sitting on the rock in
the center of it had moss growing on him and he looked
heavy and weary. Yet he wasn't old, because the beard

that flowed over his chest was crisply curly, and his hair, bound with a garland, was curly too. And the muscles of his back and bare arms were so strong that one expected him to be holding a sword or spear. But he wasn't; he was holding in his left hand some queer sort of musical instrument made of reeds, the hand raised as though he had only just taken it from his lips, and his right hand was lifted too as though he was calling to someone to listen to the echo of his vanished music. His face was strong and sad and two strange little horns grew out of his head. Timothy had not noticed the horns at first because they were almost hidden in the curly hair, and when he did notice them he began to feel a little scared. Then he looked down at the rock on which the man was sitting and had the shock of his life, because he saw suddenly that the man was only a man as far as the waist. Below the waist he was an animal with hairy goat-shaped legs and hoofs instead of feet. Panic seized Timothy and with one part of himself he wanted to scream and run away, yet with the other part of himself he wanted to look again at the listening face and because he was a plucky child he stayed where he was and lifted his eyes. Looking up he was not aware now of heaviness or weariness but of power and loneliness. He was still afraid, but differently afraid. He no longer wanted to scream but he did want to be clear outside this garden, and suddenly he ran through the archway in the yew hedge and back to the place where he had seen the three bees.

He looked up at the window and they were no longer there but he could hear a faint reassuring humming in the pale wisteria flowers over his head, and partly because he loved climbing trees and partly because he wanted to be up there with the bees, he began to climb up the wisteria. It was quite an easy climb for an agile small boy and so enjoyable that he forgot his panic in the garden, and in a few minutes he was on the flat top of the porch and not far below the open window. He climbed up a little farther, the porch below giving him a sense of not having to fall far if he were to lose his footing, and presently he was right under it and heard a murmur of voices mingling with the murmur of the bees. There were three voices, an old lady's voice, a chattering monkey voice, and the other was Betsy's. Timothy climbed down to the top of the porch again, slowly so as not to make a noise, and standing there he noticed a small uncurtained window almost hidden behind the wisteria to his left, a window that was neither upstairs nor downstairs but somewhere between the two. He walked cautiously to the edge of the porch and peeped through it, and he had another shock, for sitting on the floor of the little room inside, a room no bigger than a cupboard, was Frederick the cat washing behind his ears. Feeling eyes on him, Frederick turned his head and saw Timothy. They looked at each other and Timothy was so fascinated by Frederick's unblinking stare that he could not look away.

Then Frederick began to swell. He swelled and

swelled and his blazing eyes grew larger. One great paw struck the glass of the window and it cracked. Timothy did not wait any longer. He had no recollection of climbing down the wisteria. The next thing he knew he was running under the arch of yew into the garden of the fountain as though he were running home, and the great stone man in the center was no longer a frightening thing but a rock of defense.

Moses and Robert came from behind a tree. "She's not here," said Robert. "We've looked everywhere."

"Of course she isn't here," said Timothy. "She's upstairs with Lady Alicia. I climbed up into the wisteria and heard them talking."

"With milady?" ejaculated Moses. "But milady does not see visitors."

"If Betsy just walked in how could she help seeing her?" said Robert. "What do we do now? Wait till Betsy comes out?"

"No," said Timothy. "We must go and fetch her because the cat is in the house. I saw him through that little window by the porch and if Betsy runs through the house by herself he might catch her."

Moses growled and he suddenly looked so alarming that Robert and Timothy gazed at him in astonishment. "That cat!" he muttered. "Let Moses leave one door open and that cat creeps in. That cat's a bad cat. What he come here for? Let Moses get his hands on that cat and he'll strangle him!" This was a new Moses, big and angry, with his sad eyes burning in his face, his teeth showing and his hands clasping and unclasping themselves against his sides as though they itched for the feel of Frederick's throat between them.

"Please, Moses, take us upstairs to fetch Betsy," said Robert.

Moses changed back to his usual self. "What will milady say?" he asked anxiously.

"It doesn't matter what she says," retorted Robert. "Whatever she says we storm the citadel for Betsy. Which way in?"

He flung the toga of a Roman emperor about his splendid torso and flourished a short but deadly sword. He could change from one person to another as rapidly as Moses but whereas Moses was only one man or another man, and both of them Moses, Robert could be any number of men, all of them quite unconnected with him until he had buckled them on. Whether they were still unconnected with him when he had taken them off, who can say? "Lead on," he said to his trusted Nubian standard bearer.

Moses smiled amiably and led the way toward the house. Hurt feelings were no part of the two men Moses was. One was gentle and humble and the other could be wild as a thunderstorm but neither was resentful.

A small door led from the house to the garden of the fountain and Moses took a bunch of keys from his pocket and unlocked it. "Milady uses this door when she walks in the garden in the moonlight," he said. They went in and Moses closed the door carefully behind them.

He led them down a long dark passage and then up a staircase. The stairs were not the stately ones that Betsy had climbed but narrow stone steps that went round and round. Then they went down more dark passages until they reached a door where a sunbeam was climbing through a keyhole and here Moses stopped and tapped.

"Come in," said the voice of an imperious old lady.

Moses, Lady Alicia's butler, threw open the door and announced, "Master Robert Linnet and Master Timothy Linnet." They went in, and he shut the door behind them and withdrew.

Lady Alicia, Betsy and Abednego were playing jackstraws. Each had a pile of delicate little ivory sticks and Abednego was winning. The entry of the boys caused him to drop the jackstraws and he chattered with annoyance.

"Where are your manners, Abednego?" asked Lady Alicia. "Remember it is now your duty to set a good example to the doll Gertrude." Then she turned to Robert and Timothy. "And to what do I owe the honor of this visit?" she asked. Her voice was very icy and her beautiful penciled eyebrows lifted themselves quite a long way up her forehead. It was obvious that she did not like being visited and Robert bowed very humbly indeed, sweeping his feathered hat from his head. Sir Walter Raleigh could not lay his cloak at the feet of

Gloriana, since she showed no signs of wishing to leave her chair, but his burning glance told her of his deep devotion.

"Is this histrionic gentleman your elder brother?" she asked Betsy.

"That's Robert," said Betsy. "And that's Timothy."

Lady Alicia lifted her right hand and held it out to the boys. "Since you are here, boys, we had better become acquainted," she said.

They advanced and Robert, since he was Raleigh until circumstances required of him that he should be somebody else, kissed her hand. Timothy, who was not anyone except a fair-haired small boy, merely looked up at Lady Alicia out of his intensely blue eyes and smiled. He did not know it yet but he had a devastating smile. Lady Alicia stared at him and suddenly appeared ten years older, and as she looked old already that was very old indeed. It would not have surprised Robert if she had suddenly fallen to dust before his eyes. Her voice, when she spoke to Timothy, was hoarse. "How old are you?" she asked.

"Eight," said Timothy.

"I told you he was eight," Betsy said. "Don't you remember? The same age as your little boy when—"

Lady Alicia silenced her with a gesture. "Children," she said sharply, "should not speak until they are spoken to. Abednego, stop chattering and serve these gentlemen the cupcakes."

On entering the room, Robert had seen out of the

corner of his eye the silver tray on a side table with its delicate cups and saucers of flowered china and a plate of little cakes. The jackstraw players had evidently finished their tea some while ago but there were a few cakes left, iced in pink, white and green with half a cherry on top of each. Robert and Timothy sat on the two footstools indicated by Lady Alicia, and Abednego handed the cakes to them. They ate in silent appreciation of Moses' skill as a chef and Lady Alicia turned to Betsy.

"Is there not another child?" she asked.

"Nan," said Betsy. "Robert, where's Nan?"

"She and Ezra and Absolom are looking for you in the wood," said Robert. "We've all been looking for you everywhere."

Lady Alicia now made the most surprising remark. "I should like to meet Nan," she said. "You must bring her to see me another day." Then seeing the children's astonishment she went on, "You have doubtless been told that I am an eccentric recluse. It's true that I don't like being visited but I believe in bowing to the inevitable and the Linnet family is, I think, inevitable as the sun and the rain. You have risen upon my darkness, fallen upon my drought, and it is just possible that you may do me good."

Quietness fell upon the room when she stopped speaking and for a minute or two the children did not like to break it. Then, just as Robert opened his mouth to make a chivalrous reply, a most appalling noise broke out somewhere below them in the house, yowling and caterwauling, shouts and bangs and bumps. Abednego, casting Gertrude to a place of safety on top of the bookcase, shot from the room, Robert and Timothy hard at his heels, and presently loud monkey screams and small-boy Red Indian yells were added to the din. Betsy would have gone too but for Lady Alicia's hand grasping the gathers of her frock at the back. It was a strange thing, Lady Alicia looked like such a very frail old lady but pull as she might Betsy could not free herself.

"Bow to the inevitable, Betsy," said Lady Alicia. "You do not leave this room except in my company. Find me my stick."

Betsy found it and they left the room together, Lady Alicia holding Betsy's hand extremely firmly. She was a little lame but with swishing silken skirts and tapping high heels she walked quite quickly along the passage. They were just turning to go down a short flight of steps toward the hubbub when suddenly they had to flatten themselves against the wall because a black shape leapt up at them from the passage below. They saw his blazing eyes as large as saucers as he sped by them, yet when they looked after him all they could see was a little black cat running away for dear life down the passage.

The pursuit was hard on the poor little creature's heels—Moses, Robert, Timothy and Abednego. "Come back!" Lady Alicia called after them. "You'll only make fools of yourselves. No one ever catches a cat." She might not have spoken for all the notice they took and the noise of the pursuit died away in the distance. She and Betsy went sedately back to the boudoir and ate the last two cupcakes to steady their nerves.

And presently the four males came back and they did look rather foolish. "Explain yourself, Moses," said Lady Alicia.

"That's a bad cat, milady," said Moses. "Comes into the house but don't catch the mice. What he come for? Timothy, he thinks he sees him in the little empty room halfway up the stairs. Moses goes to look. Cat there. Moses goes to make an end of that cat. Moses gets his hand on the cat's throat, milady, but the cat swells and Moses' fingers go down and down through fur like deep moss, and no throat. But the cat yowled and caterwauled, and then he grow small as a mouse and run away through Moses' legs. But the smaller that cat got, milady, the louder he yowled."

"What ridiculous nonsense, Moses," said Lady Alicia. "And how very wrong of you to try and kill a cat. Poor little creature. I'm glad he got away."

Abednego began to chatter in a manner which though incomprehensible was obviously in support of Moses' ideas, and Robert said, "Please, it is true. We saw what Moses saw." And Timothy said, "It happened like that before in the shop."

"Lack of balance in the male mind," said Lady Alicia.

Betsy opened her mouth to remind Lady Alicia of how she herself had leaned back against the wall as

Frederick went by. Then she shut her mouth again for she had become very fond of Lady Alicia and women must hold together.

The little clock on the mantelpiece suddenly chimed six and Robert looked at it in dismay. "I think we ought to go," he said. "Nan and I have to do lessons with Uncle Ambrose from six to seven and if we don't turn up we get no supper."

Lady Alicia thoroughly understood the seriousness of the situation. "Go at once," she said. "Present my compliments to your uncle and tell him from me that you were unavoidably delayed."

"Could you put that in writing?" asked Robert. His own diplomacy delighted him. What were diplomats worth a year?

"A very good idea," said Lady Alicia. "Abednego, my inkpot, pen and paper." He brought them to her from her writing table and she wrote the note and folded it into an elegant cocked hat. "Here you are," she said. "Come again and bring Nan. Abednego, show them the quickest way out. Moses, clear away the tea things. Good-bye, my dears."

She held out her hand and Robert and Timothy kissed it and Betsy kissed her cheek, and then they followed Abednego. He ran at tremendous speed and they tore at his heels down several passages, flew down the great carved staircase, across the hall, through an archway and down a long echoing passage. They came to the kitchen and through it to the yard where Ezra, Nan and

Absolom were putting Rob-Roy back into the cart and fastening the straps.

"Betsy!" cried Nan, opening her arms wide, and instantly there was such a touching scene of family reunion that if Abednego had not had Gertrude waiting for him upstairs he would have been affected to the point of tears. As it was, jumping onto the parapet of the well, he did sniff a bit, wiping his nose with the back of his hand. Moses, arriving in the kitchen with the tea things at this point, came out to the back doorstep, beamed at them and most surprisingly began to sing. He had a wonderful voice, deep and strong like thunder rolling in the hills. The rollicking tune was the same to which Ezra had sung in the middle of the night, but the words were different.

"Glory, children, glory alleluja,
Praise to the Lord.
Great glory for sun and moon and starshine,
And for his Word.

"Glory that wells, streams and flowing fountains
Sing to his praise,
That the snows laud him, frost, fire and rainbows,
The nights and days.

"Glory, children, glory alleluja
For birds and bees,
For shepherd and sheep upon the mountains,
Valleys and trees."

To the sound of his singing they piled themselves up on top of the beds and things in the cart and drove away. As the distance grew between them they could no longer hear the words of his song, but Ezra lifted up his voice and caroled forth a last verse.

> "Is it glory for the gift o' children
> To guard an' keep?
> Varmints an' scoundrels, I love 'em only
> When they're asleep."

Driving home, Betsy and the boys chattered to Nan and Ezra of their adventures, but Nan said nothing about Daft Davie. In a very short time she had become very attached to him and she did not want to talk about him to hilarious children in a bumping cart. Later, perhaps, when they had quieted down. Going through the shrubbery did not seem to take so long as it had before and it did not seem quite so dark. All the same they were glad to get out of it and be back again on the green, though a little alarmed to see a huge ugly bulldog, like the one on the sign, sitting in the inn doorway, and Frederick sitting outside the shop washing behind his ears. Frederick, looking small and innocent, did not even look up when they drove past him but the bulldog growled.

"That's the second time today we've seen Frederick washing behind his ears," said Robert.

"Andromache was washing behind her ears this morning," said Timothy.

"It's going to rain," said Ezra.

It was half-past six when they reached home and in

spite of Lady Alicia's note they felt apprehensive. They washed their hands and faces in the kitchen and presented themselves before Uncle Ambrose in the library. Timothy and Betsy came too, for though they were not involved in this the Linnets always presented a solid front in time of trouble. Trouble was certainly present in the person of Uncle Ambrose sitting at the table with a back like a ramrod and a face like a stone gargoyle on a cathedral, Hector on his shoulder growing taller and taller as the children crossed the miles of carpet which separated them from the door and Uncle Ambrose. Just as Hector's head appeared to touch the ceiling the journey ended at last and they stood before their uncle.

"Half an hour late," he said in a voice of thunder. "Explain yourselves."

Without going into the rather peculiar details Nan explained that Betsy had got lost and they had spent a long time looking for her in the wood and in the garden before they finally found her with Lady Alicia. Then Robert presented Lady Alicia's note and Uncle Ambrose put on his spectacles, read it, said "Umph" and put it in his waistcoat pocket. Hector said "Hick" and a pellet flew out of his beak and landed on top of the dictionary in the center of the table. It flew open, disclosing beaks and claws and a boot button. Uncle Ambrose tipped them into the wastepaper basket.

"Hector, having expressed your displeasure, you may now return to the Parthenon," he said, and Hector flew to the top of the picture of ruins and a thunderstorm. "Timothy and Betsy, go to Ezra, get your supper and go to bed. Nan and Robert, sit down. I am tonight instructing you in the rudiments of English grammar in preparation for tomorrow."

Everyone did as they were told but it was difficult for Nan and Robert to concentrate upon grammar with the delicious smell of Timothy's and Betsy's cocoa and baked apples creeping under the study door. Robert scarcely tried. His eyes kept slipping around to the clock. Six-forty now. In another twenty minutes it would be his and Nan's turn for supper.

"Attention, Robert!" thundered Uncle Ambrose.

The grammar lesson was difficult and dry as dust. When the library clock struck seven, Robert sighed with relief but Uncle Ambrose went on talking. The church clock struck seven but still Uncle Ambrose went on talking. Robert and Nan exchanged anxious glances but still Uncle Ambrose went on talking and Robert was so dreadfully hungry that he was obliged to interrupt.

"Uncle Ambrose!" His relative paused and glanced at him over the top of his spectacles. "Nan had no tea. The rest of us had tea with Lady Alicia, though there wasn't much of it, just some tiny cupcakes, but Nan was looking for Betsy in the wood and she didn't have anything."

"Robert," said Uncle Ambrose in a terrible voice, "do you remember what I said would happen to you if you interrupted the process of education with conversa-

tion upon irrelevant matters?" Robert remembered the little switch and he blinked. "Ah! I see that you do. This time, since your concern is for your sister, I will pass it over but next time I shall not do so. You thought, I fancy, that this lesson would cease at seven o'clock. You must remember that the time of preparation each evening was agreed upon as one hour. This hour commenced at half-past six." He glanced at the clock. "Resign yourself, Robert, to a further twenty-five minutes of education."

Robert resigned himself. There was nothing else to do. Seven-thirty came at last and he closed his exercise book with a sigh of relief.

"Nine o'clock tomorrow," said Uncle Ambrose. "Sharp. Collected any snails today, Robert? No time? I humbly suggest early rising as the perennial answer to that perennial difficulty. Well, get to bed both of you. No supper of course." Robert choked but said nothing, for fury choked him. A slight twinkle appeared in Uncle Ambrose's eyes. "The agreement between us, by which if you remember you were to go supperless to bed if not home by six o'clock, is in no way affected by Lady Alicia's note. An agreement is an agreement. Good night."

"Good night, Uncle Ambrose," said Nan gently. Even she thought he was being a bit hard but she trusted him. Robert bowed with great irony, turned on his heel and followed her from the room with measured tread. Falsely condemned to death he would not falter on the scaffold.

When the door had closed behind them Uncle Ambrose's eyes continued to twinkle and a smile softened his grim face to tenderness. The children would have been astonished if they could have seen him at this moment. He said to himself that they must be home by six. He did not consider it safe for them to be out later.

When Nan and Robert went upstairs they found Timothy and Betsy already asleep and their faces wore that smug look of satisfaction which the faces of the well-fed so often wear in sleep, provided they are not having indigestion. Timothy in particular was looking so very smug that Robert shook him awake to hear how he himself had been treated. "The old brute!" he said angrily. "I won't wash tonight."

"Why not?" asked Nan, for they had opened the door between their rooms so that they could talk to each other.

"Because the old beast likes us to wash and I'm not going to oblige him," said Robert. "And because hunger and dirt go together." He sagged pitifully at the waist and his eyes had a hollow look. "If you're starving you're too weak to wash. I wish we had gone to Uncle Edgar at Birmingham. At least he would have fed us."

"Uncle Ambrose does feed us," said Timothy. "Betsy and I had raisins inside our baked apples. They were jolly good."

"Hold your tongue!" said Robert angrily.

"What did you wake me up for then?" demanded Timothy.

"Don't quarrel, please," said Nan peaceably. "Don't you realize, Robert, that Birmingham is all trolley lines, shops and streets? No woods, no moors, no sheep, no pony and no bees. No Lady Alicia, or Ezra or Abednego or Moses. And would you really like to have no Uncle Ambrose?" Robert made no answer but she could see he had washed his ears. "And no adventure," she went on. "Don't you realize that we have started on a big adventure? Today something very exciting has begun to happen. We're going to do something very important here. Don't you know that?"

Robert grunted and put on his pajamas. His ears were the only part of himself that he had washed, he could bring himself to oblige Uncle Ambrose no further, but he was smiling as he got into the little bed lent by Lady Alicia, snuggled down into the feather mattress and pulled the patchwork quilt under his chin. "Good old Nan," he said. "You're right."

There was a tap at the door and Ezra entered with two steaming bowls on a tray. "The Master says," he informed them, "that he don't want yee to go to bed hungry and gruel, he says, made without sugar, is not supper. Now sup it up, me dears. 'Tis nasty but nourishin'."

They supped it up, Nan for love's sake but Robert because he was starving.

7

Nan's Parlor

The next day was Saturday and, as the cats had foretold, it rained. The children, accustomed to the wet seasons and dry seasons of India, weather as predictable as the layers in a sandwich cake, couldn't get used to this mixed-grill English weather when you didn't know what you were going to bite into next. Yesterday had been warm and sunny and today the southwesterly gale from the sea was emptying buckets of water over a drowning world. Robert, with a heroism that astonished no one more than himself, got up early, put on his wet weather outfit of mackintosh, boots and sou'-wester, and went out into the garden to collect snails. He had a very special reason for wanting to earn a lot of money rather quickly and he remembered what Uncle

Ambrose had said about early rising. But once he was out-of-doors he found it was fun collecting snails in the wet. There was so much water around that it was like being a diver at the bottom of the sea. It would be fun to be a diver and he was willing to bet the threepence he was likely to earn from the snails that they earned a good deal more an hour than he was doing.

The three other children, their faces pressed against the streaming windowpane in the intervals of dressing, saw his dripping figure against a background of trees lashed by the wind, but the moors and the distant hills had disappeared behind curtains of rain. Their world had contracted and Lion Tor and Linden Manor seemed very far away. It was almost as though they had dreamed the adventures of yesterday.

"I suppose we'd all better earn our livings today," said Timothy, watching Robert. "No more sweets till we do."

Breakfast in front of the kitchen fire with Ezra was a cheering experience but when they went into the library for lessons Uncle Ambrose was in such an extraordinarily sunny mood, as he waved them to their chairs, that their hearts sank. Their forebodings were correct for he worked them hard that morning. It was ghastly and yet at moments it was briefly rather glorious, like toiling up a mountainside with your lungs bursting and your legs aching but now and then being confronted with a wonderful view. Years later they discovered that Uncle Ambrose in his working days had been

considered one of the greatest educators in England,
and they knew how privileged they had been to be
taught by him. But today their future sentiments were
unknown to them and the grounding seemed awfully
gritty. But when it was dinnertime they were astonished, for the hours had flown. Never had hash and
treacle tart tasted so good. They all helped Ezra wash
up and then Robert put on his mackintosh and went
down to the stable to polish Rob-Roy's harness, Timothy sat on the kitchen floor cleaning shoes, Nan sat
on the settle darning socks, and Betsy helped Ezra pre-
pare the fruit for a plum cake for Sunday. Upon this
domestic scene Uncle Ambrose, his afternoon nap accomplished, entered. The seat of the settle was high
and Nan's feet, he noticed, did not touch the floor.
Nor was the light in her corner good enough for darning.

"Nan, my dear," he said gently, "will you come with
me? Bring your work with you."

She put the socks into her workbasket and went with
him with that feeling of trust and peace that the very
sight of him inspired in her. Halfway down the dark
cobwebbed passage that led from the kitchen to the
library he stopped and she saw to her surprise that there
was a door there that she had not noticed before. The
passage was paneled with dark wood and the door, made
of the same wood, was invisible unless you knew it was
there. Uncle Ambrose lifted the latch and she followed
him in. The room inside was a small paneled parlor.

There was a bright wood fire burning in the basket grate and on the mantelpiece above were a china shepherd and shepherdess and two china sheep. Over the mantelpiece was a round mirror in a gilt frame. A rug lay on the polished floor, colored blue and pink like a pigeon's breast. There was a little armchair, a small writing desk with drawers in it, a shelf of books above and a chair with gold legs in front of it. The latticed window had a windowseat and looked out on the terrace in front of the house, but the climbing rose outside grew around it so thickly that Nan had not noticed it when she had been in the garden two days ago. The curtains at the window and the cushions in the armchair were sprigged with carnations and forget-me-nots.

"Ezra lit the fire for you this morning," said Uncle Ambrose.

"For me?" whispered Nan.

"This is your parlor," said Uncle Ambrose.

"My parlor?" whispered Nan.

"My dear," he said, "you are the lady of the house. Every mistress of a household has her parlor. It's an odd thing but when I came here, having no wife or daughter, I yet furnished this little room. It cried out to me that I should furnish it. I am not a man of whims and fancies and I was slightly ashamed of myself, even alarmed, feared a softening of the brain, but I am ashamed no longer. I had, I think, a premonition of your coming. Your temperament, my dear, is reflective, as mine is, and as you grow older you will increasingly need somewhere to go when you wish to be private. I suggest that the younger children and myself enter this room only with your permission." Nan knew that if she were to try and speak she would cry, which Uncle Ambrose would dislike intensely. Dropping her workbasket and darning on the floor she turned to him impulsively and he bent down and permitted her to hug him briefly. "Lady Alicia used this room, I fancy," he said.

"Lady Alicia?" asked Nan, astonished.

"She is a daughter of a previous vicar," explained Uncle Ambrose. "He was a widower and she was an only child. When she was eighteen she married the squire of Linden Manor and thereafter her father kept bees to comfort him. I am the third vicar in succession to maintain his bees. You are wondering why I fancy that Lady Alicia used this room as a girl. To the right of the fireplace, hidden in the paneling, there is a cupboard and in it I found some children's books with her name in them. She must have forgotten to take them to the Manor with her when she married. They are now on that shelf above your desk. Well, my dear, I will leave you to the enjoyment of your parlor." He bowed to her as though she were Lady Alicia herself and left the room.

Nan sat down in the little armchair and folded her hands in her lap. A parlor of her own! She had never even had a bedroom of her own let alone a parlor. It was quiet in here, the noises of the house shut away, the sound of the wind and rain outside seeming only to intensify the indoor silence. The light of the flames was reflected in the paneling and the burning logs smelled sweet. Something inside her seemed to expand like a flower opening and she sighed with relief. She had not known before that she liked to be alone. She sat still for ten minutes, making friends with her room, and then she got up and moved slowly around it making friends with all it held.

The shepherd had a shepherd's pipe in his hand, the shepherdess had a crook wreathed with flowers and a pale blue frock looped up over a flowered petticoat, and the sheep had blue ribbons around their necks. The little mirror over the mantelpiece was so old that when she looked in it the face she saw seemed not her own. It smiled at her from a long way away, a much older face, making her think of Lady Alicia when this had been her room. Nan moved on to the desk, sat down in the chair and let down the lid. Inside was a row of little pigeonholes and they contained pale pink notepaper and envelopes, a crystal inkpot with ink in it, a pen and two small keys on a ring. Fastened to the inside of the lowered lid was a sheet of pink blotting paper and across one corner of it Uncle Ambrose had written in his beautiful pointed handwriting, "Nan Linnet," and at that, since he was not here to see her, Nan did cry. She cried out all her longing for her father, the burden of being the eldest and responsible for the other children, the relief of having found a home at last, and her love for Uncle Ambrose, and when she had finished she blew

her nose and felt marvelous. The three little drawers
below were empty, and she was pleased, for she wanted
to keep her workbasket in them, and her darning, and
the few little treasures she had, such as her mother's
fan and coral necklace, that she was always afraid Betsy
would borrow and lose. Then she looked at Lady Alicia's
books in the shelf on top of the desk. They were *Hans
Andersen's Fairy Tales, Gulliver's Travels, The Fair-
child Family* and *Pilgrim's Progress*. She took them
up one by one, turned the yellowing pages and looked
at the old-fashioned pictures. Lady Alicia had written
her maiden name in them, *Mary Alicia Trumpington,*
in a large young hand. Nan could not imagine how she
could have borne to leave them behind when she married and went away. Only five of them. Were there any
more in the cupboard that Uncle Ambrose had not
taken out?

It took her quite a long time to find the cupboard,
it was so well hidden in the paneling, and she would not
have found it at all had not her exploring fingers felt the
small keyhole. The cupboard was locked but she remembered the two keys on the key ring in her desk and
fetched them. One of them, not the bright one that
was the desk key but the other, unlocked the cupboard
door. It seemed empty but kneeling down Nan felt
with her hand inside it, and her fingers touched something in the darkest corner. She took it out and looked
at it. It was a notebook with covers of hard marbled
board and inside, the yellow pages were covered with

fine clear copperplate handwriting. On the flyleaf of the book was written, *Emma Cobley. Her book.*

Nan got up and her instinct was to drop the book as though it were a snake, but she held on. On the floor by her chair was her workbasket and the darning but they would have to wait while she looked at this book. As she turned to sit down she found herself looking in the glass again for Lady Alicia but the far-off smiling face was not the same, it was that of a dark-skinned girl with bright eyes like Emma Cobley's. Nan sat down in the armchair with shaking knees but nevertheless she opened the book and began to read.

Uncle Ambrose went back to the kitchen where Timothy was still laboriously cleaning shoes, but he did not know how to do it and he was not getting on very well. There were black lines under his eyes and Uncle Ambrose's heart smote him. This child, he feared, was not as strong as the others and would need special care. "We'll finish these in my library," he said. "I'll help you." Timothy could not believe his ears and neither could Ezra, for as far as he knew the Master had never cleaned a shoe in his life. He watched with his eyes nearly dropping out of his head as Uncle Ambrose scooped up an armful of boots and shoes from the floor and left the room with his dignity unaffected, Timothy scurrying after with the box of brushes and polishes.

But in the library, with newspaper spread on the table and the boots and shoes arranged in rows, it transspired that Uncle Ambrose had cleaned shoes as a boy and had not forgotten the trick of it. He showed Timothy exactly how to set about it and he cleaned away himself with great concentration. Hector paced up and down the table like Napoleon on the deck of the *Bellerophon*, the cover of a can of polish in his beak.

"Manual labor," said Uncle Ambrose, holding up his right-hand Sunday boot and admiring the shine he had got on it, "can be of great assistance in the development both of intellectual and spiritual powers."

"Yes, sir," said Timothy dutifully, rubbing away at Betsy's indoor strap shoes.

"The Cistercian monks are agriculturists," continued Uncle Ambrose, "and all great saints either dig or cook according to sex or temperament."

"We aren't digging or cooking," said Timothy.

Uncle Ambrose looked at him over the top of his spectacles. "Do you consider that you and I are great saints?"

"No, sir," said Timothy.

"I am glad to find you possessed both of humility and observation," said Uncle Ambrose. "Pass me the brown polish."

Both of them worked so hard that the work was soon done and Uncle Ambrose, rising, held out his hand. "We deserve a respite," he said, and seating himself in his armchair by the fire, Hector on his shoulder, he took Timothy on his knees and reached for a book on the shelf beside him. For one awful moment Timothy thought he was to be educated in the middle of the afternoon, then he saw that the book was full of pictures and knew that Uncle Ambrose would never be so mean. It was to be another of the wonderful storytelling times, and he was to have it all to himself. He leaned back against Uncle Ambrose's shoulder and abandoned himself to the enjoyment and honor of the occasion, but twenty minutes later he gave a little gasp of surprise and sat up gazing at the new picture on the page. For there he was again, terrible yet wonderful, sitting this time not on a rock in the middle of an empty fountain but among the roots of a great tree in a forest glade. He was not now listening in sadness for the dying echoes of vanished music but making the music, his musical instrument held to his lips, his strong fingers spread on the reeds. Nor, in this picture, was he lonely, for woodland creatures were creeping out of the forest to be near him, drawn by his music, and the trees were full of singing birds. For a whole minute Timothy could hear the music, beautiful, thin and unearthly, and the singing of the birds. Then he whispered, "The goat man!"

"You know the picture?" asked Uncle Ambrose.

"No, sir," said Timothy. "But I saw the goat man yesterday."

"You surprise me," ejaculated Uncle Ambrose. "Where did you see him?"

"In the garden of the fountain at Linden Manor," said Timothy. "He sits there on a rock."

"Ah!" said Uncle Ambrose. "A fountain perhaps."

"But he isn't playing anymore, only listening to the echoes, and he's sad."

"No doubt," said Uncle Ambrose, and he sounded sad too. "Turned to stone. Silenced by men's unbelief."

"Who is he, sir?" asked Timothy.

"The Great God Pan," said Uncle Ambrose. "The spirit of nature. Men worshiped him in ancient Greece."

"Don't they now?" asked Timothy.

"No," said Uncle Ambrose. "They don't believe in him now."

"Is he real?" asked Timothy eagerly.

"Not now."

"Was he ever real?"

"When men believed in him he was real to them."

"Not now?"

"Not now."

"Not now," echoed Timothy sadly, and the echoes were like a bell tolling.

There was a long sad silence and then Timothy asked, "Is he the goat in the poetry?"

"What poetry?" asked Uncle Ambrose.

"The poetry you taught us. 'Star of evening, bringing all things that bright dawn has scattered, you bring the sheep, you bring the goat, you bring the child back to its mother.' "

Uncle Ambrose looked at Timothy with affection and he said, "He might be. We'll say he is."

"Shall we believe in him?" suggested Timothy.

Uncle Ambrose's eyes twinkled. "That, Timothy," he said, "is a most unsuitable suggestion to make to a clergyman of the Church of England. I am no longer permitted to believe in the ancient gods. You of course can do as you wish."

Timothy, with shining eyes, closed the book. "I wish," he said.

"Take the boots and shoes back to the kitchen," said Uncle Ambrose. "It is nearly time for tea. Robert has not appeared. I'll fetch him."

Robert, having swept out the stable and made everything neat and tidy, was lovingly polishing Rob-Roy's harness and talking to Rob-Roy, who answered him with soft conversational sounds that he thought were peculiar to Rob-Roy, for he had never heard a horse or a mare talking to its foal. If he had he would have recognized the low-toned consolation and endearments. They talked of a dream Robert had, a dream of galloping over the moors before breakfast, the two of them alone together, and then long outings when they would be out from the first cry of the bird of dawning until the star of evening brought them home. It struck Robert that since they had come to England he had never felt more comforted than he did now. The sound of the rain drumming on the roof only seemed to make the warm stable safer and warmer. He did not want his afternoon with Rob-Roy ever to end and when he had finished the harness, rubbing away at it until he had the leather shining like satin and the metal buckles winking like diamonds, he tackled the cart and made that spick-and-span too. Then he set to work on Rob-Roy himself, combing his mane with a curry comb and stopping now and then to lean his cheek against Rob-Roy's neck and tell him how he missed Father. Because he was the elder son, Father had talked to him a good deal and had, he knew, felt special about him. One of his ears buried against Rob-Roy, and the other filled with the noise of the rain, he did not hear Uncle Ambrose come into the stable, and did not know he was there until he felt a hand on his shoulder and looking up saw the tall figure draped in a dripping mackintosh and wearing the most extraordinary head-gear he had ever seen. Once it had been Uncle Ambrose's best top hat but now, having become his third-best, it had shut up like a concertina beneath the weight of water that had descended upon it during the years that Uncle Ambrose had lived in Devonshire, and it was not what it had been.

"You miss your father?" asked Uncle Ambrose.

"Yes, sir," said Robert.

"Time passes," said Uncle Ambrose, his grip tightening on Robert's shoulder. "You'll be surprised at the way it passes. Before you know it your father will be home again. Robert, would you like to ride Rob-Roy?"

Robert looked up at him with shining eyes. "Yes, sir," he said. "I could ride him bareback, couldn't I, until I'd saved up enough to buy a saddle?"

Uncle Ambrose's eyes twinkled. "Ah, that explains that pailful of snails." He glanced around the stable. "You've worked well this afternoon, Robert, you've worked very well indeed. I'll give you the saddle and you can save up yourself for the bit and bridle." Robert was speechless with shock, joy and adoration, and also shame. How could he ever have thought Uncle Ambrose a beast? His uncle gave his shoulder a friendly shake. "Come along now. It's teatime. If I can teach you to construe a few simple Greek sentences as well as you polish harness I shall live to be proud of you."

They went back to the house together most amicably and found that Ezra had made buttered toast for tea, and after tea, while they were still sitting around the dining room table, Uncle Ambrose said, "This question of pocket money. The sums owing to you all should, I think, be paid on Saturdays. Shall we see what is owing today?"

He took his gold pencil and a notebook from his pocket but it was unnecessary, for Robert had already totted up the total while the others were washing their hands for tea. He now laid the piece of paper before his relative. Uncle Ambrose adjusted his spectacles, his mouth twitching a little at the corners. Nan was already coming to recognize this twitching as amusement on the part of Uncle Ambrose, amusement which it was necessary to control lest Robert get too great an opinion of himself. Uncle Ambrose read aloud the information Robert had inscribed upon the grubby piece of paper.

Robert. Rob-Roy 6d. Snails 3d. Washing-up 1d. Total 10d.
Nan. Darning socks 6d. Washing-up 1d. Total 7d.
Timothy. Boots and shoes 6d. Washing-up 1d. Total 7d.
Betsy. Washing-up 1d.
Total 2s. 1d.

"Not correct, Robert," said Uncle Ambrose. "The sixpences are, if you remember, for a week's labor on Rob-Roy, socks and shoes. Only one day's labor on Rob-Roy, socks and shoes has actually taken place."

"Don't we start with something in hand?" asked Robert, slightly outraged.

"You do not," said Uncle Ambrose.

"I only darned for five minutes," said Nan shame-facedly. "I didn't do any more work after I went into my parlor."

"Quite understandable," said Uncle Ambrose. "A ha'penny out of the sixpence for you. A penny for Robert, a penny for Timothy. And what about Betsy? Didn't I see her helping Ezra make the Sunday cake? If she's to be assistant cook, a development which I did not anticipate, she must earn her sixpence a week too. A penny of that for today." He made calculations with the gold pencil. "The totals for this week are therefore,

Robert fivepence, Nan a penny-ha'penny, Timothy tuppence, Betsy tuppence."

He took a handful of change from his pocket, handed out tenpence-ha'penny and immediately changed the subject. "Time for preparation. This evening, Nan and Robert, you will work in here, not in my library where I shall require to be in privacy for the preparation of my sermons for tomorrow which is, you will recollect, Sunday. And you will do work of a different nature. You will study the collect, epistle and gospel for tomorrow, learning the collect by heart and also such portions of the epistle and gospel as I shall choose for you. Timothy must learn the collect and some verses of a simple hymn, Betsy the verses only. I shall require you all to repeat what you have learned to me tomorrow. Robert, fetch the pile of books which you will find on my library table." Robert did so and they were each handed a large prayer book and hymnbook of their own, and shown what they must learn by heart. The amount which Robert and Nan had to learn was shocking. They dared not look at each other while Uncle Ambrose remained in the room but after he had said good night and left them they did, their jaws dropping in dismay.

"We'll never do it," said Robert. "Not in an hour."

"We will," said Nan. "If it couldn't be done in an hour Uncle Ambrose wouldn't have given it to us. He knows. We'll all four hear each other."

It was just as she said. It took Betsy, with Nan's help, only ten minutes to learn two verses of "All things bright and beautiful," and Timothy took a quarter of an hour over the same two verses and the collect, and then they went off to Ezra for their supper. Nan was a quick learner and at the end of forty-five minutes she was able to concentrate on helping Robert. As the clock struck seven he groaned and removed the wet towel he had wrapped around his head. But he was word perfect.

"Though will I be by the morning?" he asked anxiously.

"I'll hear you again before breakfast," Nan promised him.

"Do you suppose we shall have to listen to both Uncle Ambrose's sermons tomorrow?"

"I think only one to start with," said Nan. "He lets us down lightly."

"It's heavy going when he has us at the bottom," sighed Robert.

But Nan perceived he was no longer thinking that Uncle Ambrose was a beast. Something nice had happened between them, she was quite sure, something almost as nice as her parlor. Or as nice as her parlor would have been if she had not found the book in it. She pushed the thought of the book away from her and raced Robert down the passage to the kitchen, to the marvelous supper Ezra had prepared for them to make up for last night's gruel. But later, in bed in the dark, she remembered it again, for the sound of the wind and rain was eerie and she was scared. But then she remembered something else and she was no longer afraid. The

spells in Emma Cobley's book might be wicked, and
Emma Cobley herself, and Frederick the cat, and perhaps old Tom Biddle across the way was not all he
should be, but ranged against them was the goodness
of Uncle Ambrose, Ezra, Moses Glory Glory Alleluja,
Daft Davie and Lady Alicia, and the wholesomeness of
the animals, Rob-Roy, Absolom, Abednego, Andromache
and her kittens, and of course Hector and the bees, and
good spirits whom she could not see but of whom she
was aware at this moment, holding over her in the dark
a sort of umbrella of safety. She would not be afraid to
finish Emma's book tomorrow. The wind, she realized,
was dropping and it was no longer eerie, and the rain was
no more than a soft murmur at the window that sang
her to sleep.

8

Sunday

Breakfast was later than usual next morning because Uncle Ambrose went to church before it. They used the extra time in getting themselves what they hoped was word perfect, and it was a mercy they did for Uncle Ambrose had no sooner folded up his napkin after breakfast than he said, "Now then!" and marched them into the library. Under his severe eye, and Hector's, they acquitted themselves fairly well. Nan and Timothy made no mistakes but Robert stumbled twice and Betsy got so mixed up in the second verse of her hymn that Hector said, "Hick!" and shot out two mouse tails and a coffee spoon. Uncle Ambrose made no heavy weather over Robert's and Betsy's failures, merely remarking benignly that he would hear them again after dinner, and if they failed again, after tea, but not after supper because if they failed after tea they'd get no supper, but he did not, he said, anticipate that misfortune, and now they must get ready for church.

The storm had passed and white galleons of clouds were sailing across a brilliant blue sky, but there was a morning chill in the wind and Ezra advised blue serge sailor suits, not white linen, for the boys, and coats over the girls' cotton frocks. Nan's Sunday coat was pink and Betsy's was blue. Nan had a straw hat wreathed with roses and Betsy's bonnet was trimmed with forget-me-nots. They wore gloves for in those days children were very dressy on a Sunday. Grown-ups also. Uncle Ambrose wore a top hat of marvelous height and a coat with long tails. Yet they only had to walk up the back garden and across the churchyard to the church.

Uncle Ambrose went first and the children followed behind in single file like ducklings following their parent to the pond, holding their large prayer books and hymnbooks and the pennies that Uncle Ambrose had given them; for to his everlasting honor he was not expecting them to put their own hard-earned pennies in the collection. Uncle Ambrose carried a large Bible bristling with pieces of paper that marked the places. When they reached the beehives they bowed and curtsied, and he raised his top hat and said, "Good morning, madam queens and noble bees. It is the first day of a new week and we wish you well." Then he replaced his hat and they went on into the churchyard where at this season the grass was long, rippling in the wind and full of moon daisies and sorrel.

The children had not been in an English churchyard before and they were fascinated. The very old graves had headstones that leaned this way and that and were so weathered that the lettering on them was worn away, but the not so old ones had stones with names on them that one could read, and carved cherubs' heads. There were several big tombs overgrown with ivy and surrounded by tall railings. Up the main path from the lych-gate came a stream of villagers in their Sunday best and among them, the children saw to their astonishment, was Emma Cobley in a black bonnet tied beneath the chin with black velvet ribbons, a black shawl and black mittens. She carried a very large prayer book, her eyes were on the ground and she looked very good indeed.

"I'm going in by the vestry door," said Uncle Ambrose, "but you must go in through the west door under the tower. Nan, lead the way. Do not be alarmed. The sexton will show you the vicarage pew. I trust you will set a good example to the congregation." Then he removed his top hat, opened a little door under a low arch and vanished.

Holding Betsy's hand, Nan led her little flock around to the west door. The villagers smiled at them very kindly, and that was nice, but they also drew back respectfully to let them go first, and that was alarming, but with the tremendous clamor of the bells over their heads they went into the old church that was like a cavern under the sea lit with dim green light, with an uneven stone floor, shadows and pillars, and sunbeams here and there that had pierced down through miles of water from the world above. A strange little figure in a cassock, with the face of a grave and reverent gnome, moved toward them and to their intense relief they found that the sexton was Ezra. Without moving a muscle of his face, or making any sign whatever to show that he had set eyes on them before, he led them up the aisle and ushered them politely into a pew exactly beneath the pulpit. They trembled, for not only would they be exactly under Uncle Ambrose's eye when he preached, but the congregation behind them would be able to see what they did. And they would be sure to do something wrong, kneeling down when they should be standing, or dropping their pennies or saying amen in the wrong place.

Sitting very upright on the edge of the hard seat they glanced furtively at the front pew across the aisle, a much grander pew than theirs with cushions on the seat and hassocks with tassels at the corners, instead of just plain hassocks with sawdust bursting out as theirs did, and even as they looked a small door in the north wall of the church opened, letting in a burst of sunlight, and through it there stalked a most majestic figure. He was tall and stately, dressed in green velvet livery, with knee breeches and buckled shoes, and his white hair must have been washed last night for it was like snow above his black face. He carried a tall cane with a silver top, such as majordomos carry in pictures, yellow gloves, and an enormous prayer book with brass clasps. Closing the door behind him, he advanced with immense dignity, looking directly at the children but giving no more sign than Ezra had done that he had ever seen them before. Entering the grand pew he sat down, said a prayer with one large hand over his eyes, then laid his cane and gloves on the seat and his prayer book on the shelf in front of him, placed his hands one upon each knee and gazing straight ahead turned into an ebony statue. Nan, who was nearest to the aisle on her side, gave a sigh of relief. Moses, she knew, would do everything correctly and out of the corner of her eye she would be able to watch what he did and do the same.

The bells stopped and the choir filed in, eight little boys and four men, all with well-scrubbed faces and wearing starched white surplices, and Uncle Ambrose bringing up the rear in a surplice the size of a tent, looking taller than ever and most alarming, and the service began. The choir was accompanied on a wheezy organ played by a stout lady in a purple dress and hat and brown button boots, a little boy with a scarlet face blowing a sort of bellows behind the organ. She played with zeal but no talent and the singing though hearty was not musical, for Uncle Ambrose himself was not musical nor was anyone else. Except perhaps Moses. Nan had a feeling that Moses suffered during the sing-

ing, for though his wonderful deep voice kept the rest
of them more or less within reach of the right note its
vibrations were full of sadness. And so was Moses himself. He was a tragic figure in the Manor pew, looking
at times frozen with sorrow, aware that he was all that
was left now of the departed glory.

When the time came for the sermon Uncle Ambrose
towered above the congregation like one of the prophets
of the Old Testament. He gave out his text in a voice
like a trumpet and never had he looked more magnificent, yet it was strange to see him without Hector growing taller and taller on his shoulder. He looked as in-
complete as the children felt without Absolom at their
heels. "I wish," Timothy said to Nan, "that animals
and birds could come to church."

"*Sh!*" whispered Nan in anguish, and Timothy was
aware of a chasm of icy silence opening between
text and sermon, and of Uncle Ambrose's terrible eyes
fixing them over the top of his spectacles. He blushed
crimson and straightened himself. All four sat as though
they had swallowed pokers, hands folded in their laps
and eyes fixed on their prayer books on the shelf in front
of them, and so they remained for thirty-five minutes
while Uncle Ambrose's incomprehensible sermon rolled
out like thunder over their heads. When it was over and
he gave out the last hymn Betsy was so stiff that she
nearly fell over when she tried to stand upright, but the
last hymn made up for everything because it was "All
things bright and beautiful" and she was quite sure, and

so was Timothy, that Uncle Ambrose had chosen it to please them because it was the one they were learning by heart. No one dropped a penny. All four landed safely in the bag that Ezra carried around.

Sunday dinner was splendid, roast beef and Yorkshire pudding and trifle, and Ezra waited on them in his shepherd's smock and apron. Nan wondered how he managed to combine being sexton with being everything else that he was. His quick changes were magical and she suddenly wondered whether he was entirely human. Was there perhaps a strain of fairy in him? He had looked like a gnome in church. Were his ears pointed? To stare would have been rude but as he turned to go out of the room she gave a quick glance, and they were. Her heart missed a beat.

After dinner Uncle Ambrose heard Robert and Betsy once more and this time they were word perfect. He handed around peppermint lozenges and said, "Next Sunday, and on subsequent alternate Sundays, Ezra will drive you to take tea with your grandmother, at her request." He glanced with amusement at their startled faces. "Well may you look astonished. I myself could scarcely believe my ears when I heard that magnanimous old lady express a desire for occasional visits from you. The excellent Miss Bolt would also feel deprived if she were not occasionally in your fatiguing company. But not today. Both the admirable ladies require a short period of convalescence. Today you may do what you like until bedtime but"—and his eyes burned through them—"you must not go beyond the Vicarage garden. Tea is at five. You are not required to attend the six o'clock evensong with Ezra and myself but I shall expect to find you in bed when I come back. Ezra goes out on Sunday nights but he will have a cold supper ready for you. One further point. It is the Sabbath and you must therefore employ yourselves in docility and silence. In the cupboard under the stairs you will find a few aids to these two excellent virtues. I am now going to my library for a period of repose."

He went. They helped Ezra wash up and then ran to the cupboard under the stairs. It was full of parcels which must have arrived by mail yesterday when they were being educated. They brought them into the hall and opened them on the floor. Inside the boxes were jigsaw puzzles, stamp albums with packages of foreign stamps to stick in them, painting books, paint boxes and brushes, plasticine, books to read about pirates, birds and animals, bees, kings and queens. And there was a rubber bone for Absolom. They gasped. They couldn't believe it. Uncle Ambrose was marvelous. Apart from Father he was the first grown-up they had met who understood that you couldn't be good without something to be good with.

"And I said he was a beast!" said Robert.

"Let's go and thank him," said Timothy.

"At teatime," said Nan. "He's asleep now."

"I'm going to paint pictures in the garden," said Betsy.

"I'm going to stick stamps in," said Robert.

"I'm going to read about pirates in the cedar tree," said Timothy.

Timothy, Robert, Betsy and Absolom grabbed what they wanted and ran out to the front garden, Nan stopping behind to put the other things away in the cupboard and then following with a jam pot of water for Betsy's painting. They had, she found, made by common consent for the cedar tree. Betsy was spreading out her painting things at its foot, Absolom beside her with his rubber bone. Robert was on a broad branch a little way up; Timothy was still climbing. Nan gave Betsy the water and sat on the grass by her for a little while until she saw they were all settled, then she went back up the lawn to the terrace where the window of her parlor stood open among the green leaves of the rose tree. Before she climbed through it she looked back and saw that Timothy was now right at the top of the cedar tree, his book under his arm, looking out over the countryside like a sailor in the crow's-nest of a pirate ship gazing out to sea.

Nan sat on the windowsill and opened Emma Cobley's book. When she had opened it yesterday she had thought it was a recipe book, for each page contained a paragraph of instructions beginning, "Take . . ." But instead of being, "Take 4 eggs and a pint of milk," these recipes began with things like, "Take a boiled frog and the feathers of a black cock," or, "Take a root of hemlock digged in the dark," or, "Take wolf's-bane and cinque-foil and mix with the blood of a dog." It was when she had read this last one that she had abandoned the book in terror, for Absolom was distinctly plump and Emma Cobley the witch only lived at the top of the hill. Nan knew about witches for there had been people called witch doctors in India and everyone had been very frightened of them. But now, having seen Emma going to church and looking so good, she wondered if there was some mistake. Perhaps Emma had been a witch when she was a girl and now in old age she had seen the error of her ways. Yet Emma in her shop had not looked like a woman who had seen the error of her ways, whatever she might look like in church. And then there was Frederick. No one could say Frederick was an ordinary cat. Moses disliked him as much as Ezra disliked Emma, and Moses and Ezra were good men. Perhaps if she went on reading she would find the spells changing to recipes, and Emma from someone nasty to someone nice.

But she didn't. The spells went on being spells. There were a few nice ones such as the one, "For making a man dote upon a woman. Take the petals of seven scarlet flowers picked at midday under the sun, red rose, carnation, geranium, according to the season, and infuse them together with vervain and endive seed and well water drawn up at midnight under the full moon. Bottle and use in secret, the back of the beloved being turned, pouring a teaspoonful into his ale or wine, preferably his wine, especially if it be a red wine. Continue until his love be at the desired heat." But the nice ones were few and far between and the rest were all horrible. There was one for making a person go blind, and another for making him dumb. The one for "binding the tongue" said, "At the dead of night take a root of mandrake, shape it to the figure of the person standing with tongue thrust out, pierce the tongue with sharp pins and put the figure secretly aside."

And there was another nasty one "For causing a man to lose his memory that he wander away and be lost, even when the man is at a great distance from you. Take a mandrake root and form of it an image of him. Then pierce the head and feet with pins, take the image to some far place, even as he is in a far place, and hide it there. The place must be very secret for if the image be found the man also will be found. Do this at a time of great darkness, either when there be thunder in the air or when the moon is hid."

The last spell in the book was "For making a coolness and a strangeness come between a man and woman that love each other. Take nine snail shells and crush them. Then take seven foxglove bells from a place of shade, also the feathers of a black cock and the blood of the same, and . . ."

This spell went no further. There was a spatter of ink as though the pen had been flung down, and no more. It looked as though someone had suddenly come in and interrupted Emma Cobley. She had written nothing more in the book. The remainder of the pages were blank.

Nan had been reading for a long time. She was cold and stiff and scared and did not know what she ought to do. There seemed nothing she could do at present, except wait and see. She was glad when Ezra banged the big gong for tea and she could go and be with the others and push Emma Cobley to the back of her mind. It was easy to do this because during tea they were busy thanking Uncle Ambrose for their presents, and there was the cake that Ezra and Betsy had made to be eaten, and then Andromache came in with her kittens staggering after her, giving them their first Sunday outing, and Absolom had to be restrained and Hector pacified while the six round balls of prickly fluff were nursed and Andromache was given milk in a saucer. Then tea was washed up and the rest of the day passed according to plan, Uncle Ambrose's plan. They ate the cold supper that Ezra had left ready for them and they were in bed by the time Uncle Ambrose came back from church. But only just. Robert took the final leap and pulled the sheet up under his chin when he heard steps on the stairs. It was the first time Uncle Ambrose had come to their rooms to say good night to them after they were in bed and they wondered what he would do. He did not kiss them as their father had been accustomed to do but he stood very upright beside their beds, Hector growing taller and taller on his shoulder, adjusted his spectacles, looked at them benignly and said, "Ha." Then he patted their shoulders and stalked away and they heard the library door close behind him. Now he was going to write his book. Nan believed that he stayed up very late writing his book. His days were not as leisured as they had been and she realized suddenly that the education of children is not a process in which the children alone are the sufferers.

Nan woke to find the moon shining on her face. She got up and went to the window and looked out on the back garden. The full moon had just come out from behind the tower of the church and the scene was lit up as brightly as though it were day. She could see the beehives and the strange bunchy little figure standing near them. It was Ezra in his best coat. She slipped out of bed, put on her shoes and her warm dressing gown, ran downstairs, through the kitchen and up the garden. As well as the full-skirted beech-brown coat, Ezra was wearing his mustard waistcoat and scarlet neckerchief. His trouser leg was pulled up to show the beautiful bee on his wooden leg and in one hand he held a bunch of herbs and flowers.

"Ezra," she whispered.

He turned around and saw her. "Miss Nan! What be doing here? 'Tis close on midnight."

"What are *you* doing here, Ezra?"

"Come the first night of the full moon I talks to the bees at midnight."

"May I stay with you while you talk to them?"

"Aye."

He had scarcely spoken when midnight began to boom out over their heads. Nan stood beside Ezra until the last reverberation had died away over the moors and then she followed him close to the hives. Handing her the bunch of flowers and herbs to hold he took from his pocket a bag containing preserved sugar plums and pieces of barley sugar. At the entrance to each hive he laid a little offering of these sweet things, and at each hive he bowed. "Madam queens and noble bees, you sleep," he said, "but in your dreams you will know that the offerings be laid upon the threshold. For this moon more, madam queens and noble bees, extend your protection over your domain."

He stopped and listened intently, and Nan listened too, and she thought she heard a faraway unearthly music as though an army of little people the size of her thumb were singing on the other side of the world. Ezra nodded his head, as though in satisfaction, and taking the bunch of herbs and flowers from Nan he touched each hive once with it, bowed again and turned away down the garden path. Nan curtsied and followed him.

"Did you hear it?" she whispered when they were halfway back to the house.

"What, maid?" he asked, and he stopped and fixed her with his intensely bright eyes.

"The faraway music," she said.

"You heard it?" he asked in astonishment. "You heard the singing of the bees?"

"Was it the bees?" she asked. "But they were asleep."

"Bees sing in their sleep," he said. "But 'tis not often mortal ears can hear 'em. Maid, you be one of 'em."

"What do you mean?" asked Nan, a little scared.

"I thought as you had it in your heart the moment I set eyes on yee," said Ezra. Then, a little shamefaced, he corrected himself. "The moment I set eyes on yee and me sober."

They had walked on and reached the well and paused there and Nan asked, "What have I in my heart?"

"The gold, maid," he said. He stretched out a horny forefinger and laid it gently on her chest, to the left-hand side. "In your heart there be a nugget of pure gold and if you could see it you would see a shining like a flame. There's not many have it but them what do have it can hear the bees singing, and call the birds to their finger. And they can lay down their life for another."

"Birds don't come to my finger," said Nan.

"You must call 'em to yee," said Ezra. "You call 'em, maid, and I reckon they'll come."

"They come to you?" Nan asked, and then added, "But of course they do. You have the gold."

"Maybe," he said soberly. "But maybe 'tis only the silver in my blood. You see, maid, there be three sorts of men and women in this world, the gold-hearted and the black-hearted and them what's descended from the silver ones."

"Who are they?" asked Nan.

"They lived on this earth before ever the good God thought to make men and women. They was the elves and the gnomes and the giants, the fairy folk. That's to say in England we call 'em the fairy folk, but the Master tells me that in other countries they was called the gods and that the Greeks gave 'em names, Pan, Orpheus, Persephone and other names I don't call to mind. But gods or fairies, maid, 'twas the same breed, and all of 'em with silver in their blood. Then, if so be you've read your Bible, you'll know there was war in heaven, the good angels fighting the bad angels. The bad angels was cast down to earth and a few of the good 'uns, them that was that angry they couldn't loose their hold, fell down to earth too, holding to the throats of the bad 'uns. So then there was three breeds, the golden-hearted angels, and the black-hearted, and the fairy folk with the silver in their blood."

Nan had sat down on the parapet of the well. She thought a moment and then said, "I don't think that's quite true, Ezra. I've known people, especially children, who could be both black-hearted and gold-hearted. One on Monday and the other on Tuesday."

"That be true, I reckon," said Ezra. "That old battle between the dark and light, it do be going on in every heart that ever beats. But as life goes on, maid, either one wins or t'other, you'll notice. Miss Betsy, now, she'll be good one day, bad the next, but the Master, well, I've never known 'im have a black-hearted day." Ezra's voice sunk to a low growl. "And I ain't never knowed Emma

Cobley to have a gold-hearted day. And I've knowed Emma all me life. Her father was a black warlock, and he taught her his wicked spells, and my old mother, she were a white witch and she taught me her good 'uns. So Emma and I, we just about have the measure the one of t'other."

There was a long pause and then Nan said, "So the silver in your blood is fairy power?"

"That be right, maid," said Ezra. "And it be the power to make music and paint pictures and write poetry."

"You and Moses Glory Glory Alleluja both make music," said Nan.

"Aye."

"And Daft Davie paints pictures," said Nan.

Ezra, who was busy doing something at the back door, swung around. "Do he?" he asked. "I ain't never been in the place where he bides. Can't climb there. And other folks won't go near the place. They be scared of 'im. Were you scared?"

"I wasn't scared," said Nan. "Daft Davie lives in a cave and he has painted splendid pictures all around the walls."

"Lady Alicia painted when she was a girl," said Ezra. "Not with a brush. With a needle. Needlework pictures. Ever so pretty."

"Did you know her when she lived in this house?" asked Nan.

"Aye. I was garden boy here then."

"Betsy says she lost her little boy Francis when he was eight years old," said Nan. "Is that true?"

"Aye," said Ezra. "The squire had just gone away to foreign parts and Lady Alicia and the child and his nurse went up to the moors for a picnic, to take the child's mind off fretting for his father. The little boy rode his pony, and Moses, who was a young footman then, came with 'em to carry the picnic basket. He hadn't been with 'em long at the time, Moses hadn't. The squire brought him back from foreign parts when he was just a young boy in his teens. They say he bought him in a slave market."

"Poor Moses!" said Nan. "Go on, Ezra."

"What I be telling yee now, Moses told me," said Ezra, "so I know 'tis true. 'Twas a fine day, Moses said, but misty and he felt a bit anxious-like, for he'd not been up to the moors afore and the French nurse was a flighty young woman who couldn't get her tongue round any decent language, only her own jabberwock what Moses couldn't make head nor tail on. Well, they had their picnic tea, right up on Lion Tor under the Castle Rock, and then the nurse and the little boy went off to play games together and Lady Alicia sat and did her picture embroidery. Moses hobbled the pony and then sat on a rock at a respectful distance with his hands on his knees till he should be wanted. It got mistier, and the voices of the nurse and the child seemed further off, and Moses he felt uneasy and kept looking at Lady

Alicia, but she were stitching her picture and did not notice the mist till she started to feel cold. Then she says to Moses, 'Where be nurse and my son?' And Moses says he didn't know but had he her permission to go and look for 'em? And she told 'im to go." Ezra stopped suddenly. "The Master would not like yee to be out here at night, maid. You might catch cold. And he'd not like me to be telling yee such a sad story."

"It's warm and bright as day," said Nan. "And you *have* to tell me this story."

"Aye," said Ezra. "There's something tells me as I do. You be young but it's always the goldens what puts things to rights, and things ain't right up at the Manor."

"Couldn't Moses find the nurse and the little boy?" asked Nan.

"He found the nurse, lost and going round in circles, poor silly thing. She'd played hide and seek with the boy, of all the daft things to do in such a place, and he'd vanished. Moses called Lady Alicia and they hunted all ways, crying the child's name, but there weren't no answer, and then Lady Alicia sent Moses down to the village as fast as he could go on the pony to fetch help, for the mist was coming on thicker. All they ever found was his little hat, caught in a thorn tree beside Weepin' Marsh. They thought as he'd drowned in the marsh. Lady Alicia believed that. Yet maybe the gypsies took 'im."

Nan felt cold and shivery in spite of the warmth and brightness of the night, and she was so sorry for Lady Alicia that she wanted to cry.

"Lady Alicia never went out of the house by daylight again," Ezra went on. "And she wouldn't be visited. The squire he took to going to foreign parts more than ever, finding it dull at home. He went to look for some lost city out in Egypt and no one never heard of 'im again. It's a sad story, maid, and you'd best come in and have a hot posset."

Looking toward the back door as she got off the well, Nan saw what it was that Ezra had been doing there. He had been fastening his bunch of greenery over the lintel.

"To protect the house from the evil eye," he told her. "I puts a fresh bunch there each full moon. There's honesty there, Saint-John's-wort, rosemary and rowan. That's rowan, maid, that there with the white flowers. Come the autumn it has a berry as bright as holly. It grows in the woods and it grows on the moor and witches and bad folks can't abide it. They'll run from it, so great be its power for good. So any time you children be in trouble in the woods or on the moor keep your eyes open for a rowan tree. And when you've picked a branch of it use it like a sword. Rosemary too, that always brings a blessing. 'Tis a real holy herb. With a sprig in your pocket not much harm can come to yee. Now come and have your posset."

In the kitchen he lit the lamp and stirred up the fire.

Into a small saucepan he put sugar, ginger, rosemary and dried lime blossoms, poured water on them and brought the concoction slowly to the boil, all the while murmuring something in a strange language. Then he strained the liquid into a mug and brought it to Nan.

"Drink it up, maid," he said, "and come the morning you'll be neither sick nor sorry."

Nan was drowsy long before she had finished her drink. She was vaguely aware of Ezra carrying her up to bed and the next thing she knew it was the morning, and in spite of Emma's book and the sorrowful story of the little boy, and not as much sleep as she was accustomed to, and the fact that it was once more pouring rain, she felt splendid.

9

Hugo Valerian's Library

It rained solidly all the week, it rained as though it would never stop, and the weather came down like a curtain between the children and the queer things that happened at the top of the hill, and the separation did them good. Uncle Ambrose said that such rain was designed by meteorologists for the encouragement of intellectual labor, which is why the wettest parts of England produce the best brains. The children were skeptical but to please him they did work very hard, and when they were not engaged in intellectual labor they cooled their hot brains by collecting snails in the rain. The only person who had any adventures was Robert, for Uncle Ambrose bought a saddle for Rob-Roy from one of the farmers, Ezra made a bridle of rope to do duty until Robert could save up enough to buy a real one, and whenever the rain let up a little, Robert rode Rob-Roy not up the hill to where it was queer but down the hill, over the bridge and away onto the great healthy moor beyond. What he and Rob-Roy did there he did not say but he came home again with his wet face rosy and his eyes very bright. He became older during that week and somehow nicer. Nan in her free time forgot about the book of spells and withdrew into her parlor like a snail into its shell, and Timothy and Betsy painted pictures and made little figures out of plasticine under Ezra's tuition. He could make the most wonderful little figures, of birds and beasts and people. He made figures of Uncle Ambrose, the children, himself and Absolom. He seemed to have magic in his fingers.

But on Sunday it was fine again and Ezra drove them to have tea with Grandmama and Miss Bolt. It was a queer visit for though they had been with Uncle Ambrose for only a short while so much had happened that it seemed like years. But the queerest thing was that they found they now liked Grandmama and Miss Bolt, and they rather thought that Grandmama and Miss Bolt liked them. Uncle Ambrose, when asked to explain this, said briefly that distance lends enchantment to the view.

And the next day it was still fine and the top of the hill called them like a distant trumpet call. After they had helped Ezra wash up (a penny each, fourpence all told) they assembled in the yard and sat on the well swinging their legs. Absolom swung his tail.

"Today we're going up the lane that leads between the Bulldog Inn and the manor-house wall," said Robert. "We're going to the wood."

"Not yet," said Nan. "We're going to see Lady Alicia."

"But we've seen her," objected Timothy.

"*I* haven't," said Nan. "And you told me she asked you to bring me to see her."

"Not today, Nan," said Robert. "I want to do something new today."

"And I want to see Lady Alicia," said Nan. It was not like her not to want to do what other people wanted and Robert looked at her in surprise. She looked very determined and Betsy took her part. "So do I want to see Lady Alicia," she said. "And I want to see Moses Alleluja again, and Abednego and Gertrude."

"And I want to go to the wood," said Robert obstinately. "And so does Timothy. And what's more we're going. We don't want you girls."

There was a silence and Nan felt as though Robert had stabbed her, because they always did everything together. Then because she knew she had to see Lady Alicia, and because she did not want to have a row with Robert, she gave in. "Very well," she said, "you and Timothy go to the wood. But you must each have a sprig of rosemary in your pockets. Ezra says rosemary

is a holy herb and not much harm can come to you if
you have it in your pocket."

"What rot!" said Robert.

"Nothing Ezra says is rot," said Nan. "We'll go up
through the garden and through the churchyard so that
we can pick rosemary. Come on."

They trooped up the garden and Robert pulled Nan's
hair to show he was sorry he'd said he didn't want her.
She pinched him gently to show she understood and
when they reached the rosemary bush near the beehives she gave him an extra large sprig to put in his
pocket. Pausing to bow and curtsy to the bees they went
through into the churchyard and today, as they were
not following Uncle Ambrose like ducks going to the
pond, they were able to stop and look aboout them.
One of the ivy-grown tombs behind iron railings
attracted them because a wonderful show of red flowers
was growing inside the railings and they went over to
look at it. They found it was not a regular-sized tomb
but a square pillar about five feet high. The bees were
hovering over the flowers.

"They aren't wallflowers," said Nan, "and they aren't
hyacinths. What are they?"

"Don't know," said Robert. "Look, there are words
carved on one side of the pillar under the ivy."

He put his hand through the rails and pulled the ivy
away and underneath was a carved crest, a gloved hand
with a falcon on the wrist, and below it the words, HUGO
FRANCIS VALERIAN. *Born July 12, 1846. The date of his*

death is known to God. And below that again, *They sought for a city.*

"Valerian!" exclaimed Robert. "That's the name of the red flowers. I saw them in a book of flower pictures at Grandmama's."

"That's a nice bird," said Timothy, regarding the falcon with keen interest.

"It's a falcon," said Robert.

They stared at the pillar for a long time, feeling deeply concerned with it but not knowing why. Then Timothy moved around to the other side and pulled the ivy away and cried out to the others, "Here's another falcon. And more words." They ran to join him. The inscription had the same crest and the same name, Hugo Francis Valerian. But the dates were different. They showed that this Hugo had lived for only eight years. And the text below was, *All flesh is as grass.*

"Only eight years old," said Nan, and then suddenly, "Why, it must be Lady Alicia's little boy!"

"Then the other Hugo must be Lady Alicia's husband," said Robert.

"But Betsy said that Lady Alicia said that her husband lost himself in Egypt," said Timothy.

"Yes," said Betsy. "He was looking for a city and he vanished."

"Then there's no one in the tomb," said Timothy.

"Then they aren't dead," said Betsy.

"Yes, they are," said Robert. "But not in here. That's not a tomb. It's what's called a memorial."

"They're not dead," repeated Betsy obstinately.

"Yes they are, silly, it says so," said Robert.

And Nan, in spite of the story that Ezra had told her, heard her own voice saying in loud firm tones that matched the brilliance of the flowers behind the railing, "People are not dead because they've vanished."

They went on through the churchyard and came out on the green. There was no sunshine so far today. It was gray and very still. When they came to the lane that led into the wood between the Bulldog and the manor-house wall, and stood looking up it, the wood looked very dark and not a leaf moved.

"Good day, young maids an' masters," said a voice behind them, and they all looked around. The inn door had opened and on the threshold stood Tom Biddle propped on his two sticks, nodding and smiling. In the shadows behind him was the bulldog and it growled at Absolom. "Surprised to see me 'ere?" he asked. He glanced up at the Bulldog sign over his head and pointed with one stick to the words, *Eliza and William Lawson. Licensed victuallers.* "Me daughter and her husband," he said. "Be going to the wood?"

His eyes were bright with inquiry but just as Robert opened his mouth to reply, Nan said quickly, "Good-bye, Mr. Biddle," and turned away toward the manor-house gates, pulling a reluctant Robert with her.

"Linden Manor?" Tom Biddle asked.

"Yes," said Nan.

He nodded, produced his clay pipe and became ab-

sorbed in filling it, but all the time they were struggling
to get the gates open Nan felt that Tom Biddle was
watching them; yet when she glanced back he seemed
to be still filling his pipe.

"What did you do that for?" complained Robert
when they were in the shrubbery. "Timothy and I
wanted to go up that lane into the wood."

"Not with Tom Biddle watching you," said Nan.
"Ezra doesn't like Tom Biddle. There will be another
way into the lane. Do you remember Ezra saying that
Moses and Abednego come and go over the wall? Let's
get through the shrubbery first."

The shrubbery no longer scared them now that they
were used to it and they pushed through it quite quickly
and came out into the sea of grass and docks and nettles
beneath the apple trees. Robert, who was quick at seeing the lay of the land, turned left and made his way
along the edge of the shrubbery, the others following,
and in a few minutes they reached the wall that divided
the manor-house garden from the lane and the wood.
The wall was high but full of crannies where good
climbers could cling with toes and fingers, and Robert
and Timothy didn't have any trouble climbing it. Absolom barked to go too, because he was Robert's dog,
and Nan handed him up to them when they were astride
the wall.

"Do you remember the branch of rowan over the
back door that I showed you this morning?" she said.
"Rowan trees grow in woods and on hillsides and Ezra

says that witches are frightened of it. He says if you are attacked by wicked people you can pick a branch of rowan and use it like a sword."

Robert nodded and disappeared from sight and Timothy, handing down Absolom, followed him, and suddenly Nan was scared. And then she saw three bees flying over the wall after the boys and she was happy again.

"Come on, Nan," said Betsy, pulling at her skirt, "we don't want to be late for jackstraws and tea."

Neither Moses nor Abednego was in the kitchen and Nan and Betsy decided that they would go straight up to Lady Alicia. The passage did not seem so long and dark now there were two of them holding hands, and Betsy enjoyed doing the honors of the place and showing it to Nan. "This is the hall," she said. "Aren't those cobwebs lovely?"

"Beautiful," said Nan with awe, as they climbed the staircase. "They are like lace curtains. But it's dark. Are you sure you can find the way to Lady Alicia's room?"

"Of course I can," said Betsy. "You go along a landing and up some steps and along a passage. And then you see a light shining through a keyhole and that's it."

They went along a landing and up some steps and along a passage but they didn't see any light shining through a keyhole. What they did see was a faint line of light showing under a door at the end of the passage. Four steps led up to the door.

"That must be it," said Nan. Betsy was puzzled because she didn't remember the steps and she did not think Lady Alicia's room had been at the end of the passage. But they went up the steps and Nan knocked at the door. There was no answer but thinking that perhaps she had not been able to hear an old lady's soft "come in" she opened the door and they went in.

"It's not Lady Alicia's boudoir," said Betsy.

It was a fairly large room, a shut-up room but with light in it because from one of the two windows the velvet curtains had been drawn aside. One window looked out on the terrace, and this was the curtained one; the other, on the garden of the fountain. "Oh look!" cried Nan, standing at the second window. "Look at that wonderful man!"

Betsy joined her and they stood together looking down at him.

"But he's got legs like an animal," said Betsy, and she slipped her hand into Nan's. "I don't like him," she went on in quavering tones.

"I do," said Nan. "Oh, I do! Listen, Betsy. He wants us to listen." She opened the window and they both leaned out. But Betsy couldn't hear anything and Nan could only hear the distant sound of a lark and mingling with it, very far away, the voices of the sheep on the moor.

"Why, he's only a stone statue in a fountain!" said Betsy, and was no longer afraid.

"So he is," said Nan slowly. "But all the same he wanted us to listen."

She closed the window again and turned back to the room. It gave her a shock for it seemed as though some man had left it only ten minutes ago. His cloak lay over the back of a tall carved chair and his gloves were on the kneehole writing desk. In one corner of the room were fishing rods, sticks and riding crops, and on the mantelpiece above the big empty hearth were racks of pipes and jars of tobacco. Three walls of the room were lined with glass cases containing ancient treasures, bead necklaces and pottery figures of birds and men, and bookcases full of books, and above these were pictures of ruined temples and cities, and fierce heads of wild beasts, snarling tigers and weird heads with horns. On the fourth wall, one on each side of the window looking on the garden of the fountain, hung two large maps, one of central Africa and one of Egypt.

"Egypt!" said Nan. "Look, Betsy. It's Egypt, where Father is." There was no response from Betsy and Nan did not look around, so intent was she on the map. Egypt, where Father was. It seemed to bring him here into the room with her. She stood close to the map, tracing the blue ribbon of the Nile with her finger and finding names that she knew. Then there was a sudden crash behind her and she swung around. "Betsy!" she said. "What have you done?"

Well might she ask. Betsy had pulled out one of the

drawers of the writing desk and pulled it a little too far. The whole thing had fallen to the ground, spilling papers and bundles of letters all over the floor. Betsy, a child not easily intimidated, was intimidated now and on the verge of tears. "The drawer has a brass handle like a lion's head," she said, "and I just wanted to see if it would pull out."

"Well, it has pulled out," said Nan and her voice was so dry that she sounded like Uncle Ambrose at his most sarcastic. It was bad enough, she thought, to walk into a room in a strange house without permission, even though it was by mistake, without pulling out drawers and scattering their private contents on the floor. "You ought to be ashamed of yourself, Betsy," she said. "Now we must pick them all up and put them back."

This was the first time in her life that Betsy had heard her dear Nan speak to her in anger and the shock of it, on top of the shock of the falling drawer, brought the tears over the verge. Seated beside Nan on the floor she wept like a cataract. Nan was too angry to comfort her. With grimly folded lips she began gathering up the scattered papers and putting them back in the drawer. One bundle of letters, tied with a scarlet silk ribbon, had burst open in its fall. The ribbon, frayed with age, had snapped and the letters were all over the floor. Picking them up she saw that they were in a handwriting she knew, and she went cold all over, for it was Emma Cobley's handwriting. Not knowing what

she did, drawn by that writing as a fascinated bird is
drawn to hop nearer to a snake, she began to read. They
were love letters, written by Emma to Hugo Valerian.
Nan had come across some gentle love letters in books
she had read but never anything like these, and the
wild and vivid language both fascinated and repelled
her. There was nothing gentle about this love. It was
like a tempest, all rolling protestations of undying
adoration shot through with fiery flashes of anger,
threats and reproaches.

Suddenly Nan dropped the letters and her face
turned scarlet with shame. What was she doing, reading
letters which were not hers? That was a dreadful thing
to do. It was far worse than what Betsy had done. She
was so upset that she began to cry too and her tears
dripped down onto the letters as she gathered them
together again, retied the red ribbon and put them at
the back of the drawer.

"And what, may I ask, are you two children doing?"

Nan scrambled to her feet and curtsied to a very dig-
nified and very angry old lady. She was so stiffened by
annoyance that she looked as though she would never
be able to bend again. One hand rested on her ebony
stick and the other on Abednego's shoulder, and the
rings on them sparkled like ice and her eyes flashed blue
ice-fire. Abednego, with Gertrude in his arms, shook
his head and chattered more in sorrow than in anger.
Nan's tears had been checked by shock and she wiped

her eyes and blew her nose and was done with it, but Betsy wept on. She did not weep often but when she did the thing was thoroughly done.

"Betsy was bringing me to see you and we opened the wrong door," said Nan. "I was looking at the map of Egypt because my father has just gone there . . ." She paused, partly because the children never told tales on each other and partly because Betsy's grief had now reached its crescendo.

"And Betsy pulled a drawer out too far," said Lady Alicia. She did not raise her voice to dominate Betsy's grief but she spoke with such icy sharpness that she cut right through it. "Betsy, stop crying at once." Betsy stopped instantly and sniffed. "Have you a handkerchief? Then blow your nose. I do not like a sniffing child. Is this the only drawer you have opened, may I ask?"

Betsy blew her nose on the handkerchief Nan handed her and gulped. "Only this one. It has a lion's head on it."

Lady Alicia's face softened a little. "Ah yes," she said. "Pleasant to pull. Abednego and I heard the crash but could not at first discover from which room the sound came. I did not expect to find you in my husband's library." She turned and glanced around the room with interest. "Moses keeps it swept and dusted by my orders but I have not myself entered it since my husband left home for the last time." She looked at the gloves on the desk and the cloak over the back of the chair. "How strange!" she murmured. "He has kept this room exactly as Hugo left it. Almost as though he expected him to come back. Very odd. Abednego, assist these young ladies to clear up this mess."

Abednego put Gertrude on the desk beside Hugo Valerian's gloves and in a few moments the papers had been packed neatly away in the drawer again. "Tea, I think," said Lady Alicia, and turning abruptly she led the way out of the room, down the passage, up another and then they were at the door of her boudoir, which Abednego opened for her. "Abednego, fetch the tea," she said and swept in.

Once more enthroned in her chair, with Nan and Betsy on chairs facing her, she said, "If I am to be often honored with your company you must have the exact position of my boudoir clear in your minds, my dears. I do not wish you to go blundering about in my house without my knowledge or permission."

"We are very sorry," said Nan humbly.

"Of that I am aware," said Lady Alicia graciously. "And we will say no more about it. So you are Nan." Her blue eyes scrutinized Nan very thoroughly. "Plain but pleasing," was her comment. "And so your father is in Egypt. To what part is he going?"

"He's going up the Nile to a place called Abu Simbel."

"Ah!" said Lady Alicia. "That is where the great temples are. My husband was last heard of at Abu Simbel."

This remark had for Nan a most ominous sound and

she was thankful to see Abednego come in with the tea. Gertrude was now on his back, hung around his neck in a little hammock made of string. He was looking quite a different person now that he had Gertrude. He was a cheerful monkey now.

It was while they were drinking tea out of delicate fluted cups like seashells, and munching cupcakes, that Nan looked up and for the first time saw the tapestry of the horsemen riding up through the wood with the falcons on their wrists. She put her cup down very carefully and stared and stared.

"Do you like my tapestry?" asked Lady Alicia, and Nan nodded, speechless. "It took me years to do. I began it on the day I became betrothed to my late husband and I only finished it just before he left on his last journey. My husband was a great traveler and so was his father before him. All the Valerians were restless men, never content to stay at home. And so with my needle I painted that portrait of them. A falcon is the Valerian family crest and so they all carry falcons on their wrists. They are riding to a city in the clouds. That is what the Valerian men have always done."

"The hill is shaped like Lion Tor," said Nan.

"Yes," said Lady Alicia. "My little boy was always wanting to be on top of Lion Tor. He called the Castle Rock a city. He was a Valerian like all the rest."

To Nan, Lady Alicia's voice seemed to come from far away because she was stunned with astonishment. For that picture on the wall in front of her was the pic-

ture that Daft Davie had painted on the wall of his
cave. She was glad that Betsy was chatting away to
Abednego, and he to her in his strange language, for the
noise they made covered up, she hoped, her confusion.

She was herself again by the end of tea and then
they played jackstraws, Nan keeping her eye on the
clock. "Because of having to be home by six for Robert
and me to do our lessons," she explained to Lady
Alicia.

"If they are late they don't have supper," said Betsy.
"I do because I don't have to do evening lessons."

"Youth has its blessings," said Lady Alicia. "Do not
worry, Nan. I will tell you when you must leave."

So Nan relaxed and enjoyed her jackstraws. She had
small, neat, steady fingers and she played nearly as well
as Abednego, but not quite. He beat her, to his great
delight, and Lady Alicia gave him a prize, a pink satin
ribbon to tie around Gertrude's waist. To Nan and
Betsy she gave consolation prizes, a blue velvet snood
for her hair to Betsy and to Nan a tiny green silk purse
on a green cord to hang around her neck. Nan was not
a conceited child but she couldn't help knowing that
during the course of tea and jackstraws Lady Alicia had
become very fond of her. When it was time to go she
came with them to the top of the great staircase and
she kissed them both and her hand lingered on Nan's
shoulder. "My compliments to your uncle," she said.
"And I trust he will permit you to visit me again. I am
sorry that Moses is not here to see you safely home. He

has gone to town to do the shopping. You know your way. Straight down the long passage. The front door is not in use at present."

"It was dull today," said Betsy as they walked home. "Nice but dull. There wasn't Frederick getting into the house and everybody chasing him and Moses getting angry. I wasn't frightened today but I was dull. I'd rather be frightened than dull."

"I think," said Nan, "that I'd rather be dull than frightened. But one can't choose, you have to take what comes, Father says. Do your legs ache? Shall I give you a pig-a-back?"

They were home in good time but there was no sign of the boys and Absolom, and Uncle Ambrose and Nan started work without Robert, Uncle Ambrose looking decidedly grim and Nan trying to work hard enough for two. But though she tried hard she did not cover herself with glory and presently Uncle Ambrose said, "That will do, Nan. Shut your book and tell me what you have been doing this afternoon."

Nan looked up at him. "Stop working?" she asked incredulously.

"Yes," said Uncle Ambrose. "Stop working and tell me why you have those unbecoming shadows under your eyes. Have you been crying? I dislike a weeping woman but I dislike even more not knowing the reason for her tears."

"I did something dreadful," said Nan, and she found she was thankful to burst out with it. "I read somebody else's letters."

"Most reprehensible," said Uncle Ambrose with interest. "Whose? And what was in them?"

"Emma Cobley's. And they were love letters written by her to tell the squire, Hugo Valerian, how much she loved him."

Uncle Ambrose's spectacles, that had been placed rather low down on his nose, fell off it onto the table and Hector, who was sitting on the back of his chair, uttered a loud derisive hoot.

"Hector," said Uncle Ambrose, "return to the Parthenon." Hector returned and Ambrose replaced his spectacles and looked at Nan over the top of them. "You had better tell me how these letters came into your hands," he said with severity.

Nan told him how they had gone into the wrong room by mistake and what had happened. "I didn't mean to read the letters," she said, the tears beginning to well up again, "and when I realized what I was doing I stopped."

"Then do not disturb yourself," said Uncle Ambrose, "and do not, I beg, weep. Sin, my dear Nan, lies more in the intention than the actual deed. A reprehensible action which is not premeditated remains reprehensible, and should not be repeated, but is not in the eyes of heaven a grave sin. Have a peppermint, my dear, it is difficult to cry while sucking." He took a screw of white paper from his pocket and handed her one and again there came that gleam of interest in his eye. "Do you recollect anything that you read?"

Nan shook her head. "I didn't read much. It was just that she said she loved him and that if he didn't marry her, as he'd promised he would, dreadful things would happen to him and his family."

"A woman's notion of love can be peculiar," said Uncle Ambrose. "In celibacy lies the only safety. So, it's true."

"Please, what is true?" asked Nan.

"A story I was told by a respectable old lady, now deceased, but once resident in the village. She liked a good gossip and I used to humor the old soul while lending little credence to her tales. Women are gifted with narrative power but I make it a practice to believe only one third of what they tell me, for their notions of veracity, like their notions of love, are not to be relied upon. The only exception, Nan, being yourself. I shall always believe, my dear, every word that you tell me and I place great reliance upon your affection."

Nan was so astonished and overwhelmed that she turned scarlet and was once more so near to tears that Uncle Ambrose had to hand her another peppermint.

"I think, my dear," he went on, "that I had better tell you the story as told to me. It will then be easier for you to put the whole thing from your mind and attend to matters more suited to your tender years, English grammar for instance, and the Greek alphabet." He leaned back in his chair and put his fingertips together. "Emma Cobley was the only child of a farmer who lived out on the moor, a strange man reputed to be a warlock. He died when she was sixteen years old and she came to the village to be housekeeper to a retired doctor who lived here. He became very fond of her and finding her clever and quick to learn, he educated her. She also appeared to pick up a good deal of medical knowledge. My informant thought it likely that she read his medical books after he was in bed at night, and that what she read became interwoven with the strange things she had learned from her warlock father. Be that as it may she made a good deal of money by concocting and selling medicines and ointments, love potions and such nonsense, quite unknown to the old doctor. When he died he left his house and most of his money to his sister, the old lady who told me this story, but he left money to Emma too. She purchased the cottage on the green where she lives now and with her legacy and her own earnings to support her she lived quite like a lady. She was, my informant told me, quite startlingly beautiful."

"She has twinkly eyes now," said Nan.

"Do not, I beg, interrupt me," said Uncle Ambrose. "Where was I? Ah yes. Hugo Valerian, a boy in his teens and six years younger than herself, fell in love with her and gave her his promise that he would marry her as soon as he was of age. His father was dead and his mother had little control over him so foolishness on his part was only to be expected. Then his mother also died, he came of age and to celebrate this event the uncle who had been his guardian took him abroad with him. The journey gave him the taste for foreign travel which later became a passion with him. It broadened his mind and in the course of it his passion for Emma Cobley became somewhat cool. When he came home he did not at once end his betrothal to her but he did not make it public, and he appears to have refused to fix a date for their marriage. At about this time the vicar's young daughter left her schoolroom, put her hair up, went to Paris to be finished and returned a very lovely young lady, wellborn, graceful and accomplished. She also, in the intervals of her duties in house and parish, was partial to foreign travel, having relations in Italy and France. When news reached home that she had married Hugo Valerian in Paris it gave much pleasure, for both the young people were held in affection."

"And Emma?" asked Nan.

"She was greatly enraged, so much so that for a time she quite lost the ladylike demeanor and genteel manners which she had been at great pains to cultivate. Then she calmed down and returned to her former way of life, winning a great reputation in the neighborhood for her cures, and when she got older she started her very successful grocery business. She apparently entirely forgave the squire and his wife but I fancy it must have been something of an embarrassment for them to have her living always at their gate." He paused and sighed. "Poor things!"

"Were they unhappy?" asked Nan.

"For some years they had no children," said Uncle Ambrose carefully, "and the squire was increasingly away from home. Lady Alicia must have been very lonely. Then at last she had a son. There was great rejoicing in the village and I understand that both parents drew together in their attachment to the child. But I regret to say that he died. And that, my dear, is the end of the story as I know it."

Nan did not tell Uncle Ambrose that Ezra had told her of the way in which the little boy had disappeared, for she was afraid he might be angry with Ezra for telling her such a sad story. Instead she said, "Uncle Ambrose, Emma Cobley is what in India is called a witch doctor, isn't she?"

"Something of the sort," Uncle Ambrose reluctantly agreed.

"Do you believe that witches and warlocks, the black ones and the white ones, can really harm people or help people with their spells?"

"I do not," said Uncle Ambrose forcibly. "And I trust that Ezra has not been filling your head with any of his nonsense. Ezra is a very excellent old man but he is devoid of education and shares the superstitions of this benighted countryside."

Nan fixed her clear eyes upon her uncle's face. "You bow to the bees," she said.

Uncle Ambrose looked at her and then suddenly threw back his head and laughed. "Yes, Nan, I do. I have the greatest respect for bees." He paused and then said very seriously, "And I am very deeply aware of the mystery of things."

"Do you think Emma Cobley could have harmed Lady Alicia and her husband?" asked Nan.

"Not by her spells, which are nonsense," said Uncle Ambrose, "but possibly the thoughts of an unloving mind can have power to do harm if they are not confronted by a corresponding power for good. But such considerations, my dear, are unsuitable for your age. It is suppertime and where are Robert and Timothy? You and I had better have supper together."

They did so while daylight faded outside the windows. Nan could see that Uncle Ambrose was anxious, and Ezra too. Hector also seemed uneasy and Andromache kept prowling in and out in a restless sort of way, trailing kittens in her wake. When supper was over and Ezra was lingering anxiously at the door, Uncle Ambrose said, "Nan, where did you say those boys had gone?"

Nan explained how they had climbed over the wall from the manor-house garden and to comfort him she said, "Three bees are with them."

"Three bees?" ejaculated Uncle Ambrose.

"Yes. I saw three bees fly after them over the wall."

Ezra smiled and relaxed but Uncle Ambrose seemed to find little comfort in the statement. He got up and turned to Ezra. "You've nothing to smile about, Ezra," he told him, "for you and I must now go and search for these boys. Fetch me my cloak, for it may be cold in the wood before we find these objectionable children. How intensely do I dislike children! Nan, you'd better wash up the supper things, that'll be another penny, let's say tuppence as you will be doing it alone, and then join Betsy in bed. Do not worry, my dear. Only good boys die young."

Nan saw them off at the front door, Uncle Ambrose looking very imposing in his cloak and his battered wet-weather hat, with Hector on his shoulder, and Ezra carrying his shepherd's crook. Nan had not seen his crook before and she found the sight of it reassuring. She washed up and then put herself to bed beside the sleeping Betsy. But in spite of the bees and the crook, and the sprigs of rosemary in the boys' pockets, she couldn't sleep. She lay awake listening.

10

Lion Tor

"It's nice not to have the girls," said Robert.

"Women slow one down," agreed Timothy.

They were certainly getting along at a good speed in spite of going steeply uphill through the marvelous wood. The trees grew thickly and below were ferns and brambles and moss-covered boulders. "Look!" said Timothy and they stopped, for they had never seen such a splendid tree. It was a giant beech with wide-spreading branches and platforms of green leaves that went up and up like clouds in the sky. The trunk was of polished silver and below it the great roots spread out as the branches did, with ferns growing between them, making a wonderful place for someone to sit and rest, or sit and make music, and Timothy thought he heard a faraway piping.

"Listen!" he said, and he and Robert stood and listened, while Absolom seized the opportunity to sit down and have a good scratch. At first they could hear nothing and then, distantly, the sound of a lark singing and the voices of sheep on the moor.

"Is that all?" asked Robert.

"That's all," said Timothy, but he wasn't disappointed for nothing could have been more beautiful than what they had heard.

They went on. The lane soon petered out into a cart track and then into no track at all, or rather into an invisible track, a sort of magic under the ground that held one's feet to something that had been here once but wasn't visible now. Timothy expressed it by saying, "Once the road went right up to the top of the hill, like in that picture."

"What picture?" asked Robert.

"The one of the men riding up through the wood in Lady Alicia's room."

"Oh yes," said Robert vaguely and Timothy wondered if he had even noticed the picture, for they didn't often notice the same things, Robert noticing useful things like saws and hammers and food and Timothy noticing pictures and birds flying and the patterns the clouds made in the sky. Then Robert brightened and said, "Weren't there horses in the picture?"

"Yes," said Timothy, "and men with birds on their wrists, birds like the one in the churchyard you said was a falcon. They were riding up through a wood to a sort of city in the sky." He stopped suddenly. "Look! There it is!"

Even Robert stood still and gazed in wonderment while Absolom once more seized the opportunity to sit down. Far up above them at the end of the invisible track there was a break in the dark trees. They could see where the wood ended and above it towered the shining silver sky. The city was built in the sky and that too leapt up and up, one steep gray roof climbing above another, with almost invisible silver towers rising at the summit and losing themselves in the silver of the sky. And then it seemed to fade and dissolve and then to reappear and it was the same and yet different.

"It's only the rocks on top of Lion Tor," said Robert.

"So it is," said Timothy, but again he was not disappointed, because nothing could have been more beautiful than what they were seeing, the wonderful mass of gray rock with towers of white cloud behind it, all built up against the silver sky. The sun was coming out, and over clouds and rocks and sky was a veiled sparkle of light that made them seem very far away. And below was the darkness of the silent woods. Without a word, and with their eyes on the beckoning city above them, they began to climb quickly up the invisible road.

Suddenly Robert gave a shout. "Look out!" he yelled. But he was just too late. Timothy, who was ahead of him, had crashed into a hidden ditch and instantly Robert, who was wonderfully good at doing the practical thing on the instant, flung himself on his face, pushed his arm down through the brambles and ferns that hid the ditch and grabbed Timothy by the back of his jersey. Then he thrust the other arm down and got both hands under Timothy's armpits and heaved mightily. Absolom was no help for he had dashed away into the wood growling and barking, but Timothy kept his head and in a moment or two Robert had dragged him up. They rolled over together, their jerseys torn and their faces scratched and bleeding.

They lay panting for a moment and then sat up and had a good look at the booby trap, for that was what it was. The ditch was only the bed of some stream that had now dried up but it was deep and there were some uncomfortably sharp stones down at the bottom. It was damp at the bottom too, and there seemed slimy things down there, worms and toads. The nasty thing about it was that it had been hidden by a mass of loose bramble and fern spread across it on light branches broken from the trees. Some man or men had deliberately hidden the ditch. And only a short while ago, because the ferns and the leaves on the branches were green and fresh.

"Where's Absolom?" asked Robert.

"I don't know," said Timothy. "But I heard him growling and barking."

They called and presently Absolom came back, still

very angry and with his hackles up, and he too was bleeding and torn. But not by brambles. It looked as though his ears and his face had been scratched by sharp claws. It was all very odd but one thing was clear.

"Someone doesn't want us to climb up to the top of the tor," said Timothy.

"Then we're going," said Robert. "I suppose they thought we'd be frightened by falling into the booby trap. We'll show them we're not."

"But how do we get over it?" asked Timothy.

"We jump," said Robert.

Timothy's heart missed a beat because though Robert might be able to jump that far he very much doubted if he could. But he would rather fall into the booby trap again than let Robert think he was afraid. "Come on," he said.

"It's the castle moat," said Robert, who had suddenly become an invading Norman knight before the besieged castle. "Who's for the drawbridge?"

"Swords," said Timothy, suddenly remembering what Nan had said about the rowan branches. "We need swords!"

He ran back into the wood where he had seen a rowan tree and broke off two flowering branches, and he picked a twig of rowan and twisted it into Absolom's collar. "Now!" he said. They went back a bit, brandished their swords, ran and jumped, and just at the most terrifying moment of the leap, when Timothy was quite

sure he would never do it, he saw three bees revolving
in a patch of silver light on the other side. He leapt
toward them, aware of Absolom leaping beside him
with ears streaming out like banners and Robert shouting, and then they were all three lying in a heap together
on the far side.

They picked themselves up and went on triumphantly
and gradually they climbed right up above the tops of
the trees, and as they came out of the wood the sun
broke through and they were dazzled by its light. Then
they began to run over the short springy turf, and
jump over the tufts of heather, and sing and shout, for
only so could they express their joy in this high cool
place full of wind and space and light. Then they
dropped breathless on the heather.

All about them were the rolling spaces of the high
moor, the rough grass full of the small flowers that
grow on the heights, patched here and there with fern,
heather and gorse. It was like the sea and the shadows
of the clouds passed over it as they do over the sea, and
islands of rock came up out of the green waves. Sheep
were cropping the turf and larks were singing overhead.
When presently they stood up again they could see for
miles. Quite close to them the ground sloped up to the
great mass of rock that was the summit of Lion Tor,
and at a little distance it fell away to a lower pile of rocks
among stunted trees that seemed growing on the edge
of a precipice.

"That's the Lion's head," said Robert. "We're looking at it from behind."

"There's breath coming out of it," said Timothy. "You can see the Lion's breath!" The faint curl of whiteness rose in the air as human breath does on a frosty day. Robert could not see it at first and when he did he had a practical explanation. "It's only smoke," he said. "There are people having a picnic there and they've lit a fire to boil the kettle. And perhaps they're cooking potatoes in the embers." He paused. "I feel awfully hungry," he added.

Timothy, who had sensitive feelings, was quick to interrupt Robert's train of thought. "You can't barge in on picnic people you don't know and ask for food," he said. "What about the besieged city? There may still be some food inside. There is a king inside the city, I know there is, and he will give us food. Come on!"

Robert caught fire again and brandishing their swords and shouting, Absolom racing after them, they stormed up the green slope toward the city. As they ran they could see clearly the battlements and the archers at their stations and hear their answering yells of defiance. Soon they were scaling the walls, climbing up and up, panting and excited. Then Robert dropped his rowan branch and was too thrilled to notice what he had done. "Pick up your sword!" cried Timothy below him. Robert stopped and picked it up and was aware again that they were climbing not walls but rocks, with here and there ledges of turf like miniature flower gardens sweet with thyme and thrift and yellow bedstraw.

"There's a cave up there," said Robert. "Perhaps that's where the king is." It was above them, a little to the right. Most of the entrance was hidden behind an outcrop of rock, but they could see the upper part of it and like all half-hidden things it was exciting. It was also frightening.

"We'll have to go around the rock to get to the cave," said Timothy. "And we can't see what's behind it. Stop, Robert!"

But Robert was already halfway to the cave and Timothy scrambled after him and Absolom after Timothy. They were under the rock, and with a few steps more Robert would have been around it, when Absolom growled.

And then suddenly it all happened. A vast and horrible black shape leapt to the top of the rock from the other side and around the corner bounded a big red-faced giant brandishing a knobbly stick over his head, his teeth flashing in his big black beard, and at his heels ran a bulldog the size of a calf, growling and snarling. There was no time to be terrified, no time to think what to do, and Robert, Timothy and Absolom acted by instinct only. Robert struck his branch of rowan straight in the man's face and Timothy hit out with his at the black shape, while Absolom, in the most superb action of his life, leapt for the bulldog's throat and held on. Then he abruptly let go again, bounding in the wake of Robert and Timothy as they turned and fled.

"The picnickers!" gasped Robert and Timothy nodded.

The picnickers would help them. Down and down they ran, somehow keeping their feet on the rocks and slippery turf, and behind them the noise of the pursuit, the shouts and growls and yowls, sounded very near. Then they were down below the tor and running like the wind for the wisp of smoke rising from the rocks and stunted trees below them. They ran and ran but the pursuit, they knew, was gaining on them. "Rowan trees!" gasped Timothy. "Rowan trees among the rocks!" They could see the white blossoms below them and they could also see something rising from the trees and coming toward them. A sort of cloud. A cloud of bees. The cloud sailed over their heads and away behind them and they were nearly there.

They were there. They leapt in among the rowan trees and fell behind a great rock, the three of them together in a heap, far too breathless to run any more but aware of safety. And also of howls of distress dying away in the distance.

As soon as they had got their breath they crept out and looked back through the sheltering branches. A man, a bulldog, both of normal size but still very large, and a poor little black cat were running for their lives in the midst of the swarm of bees, and to judge from their cries being stung as they ran.

"Poor things!" said Timothy.

"They're not poor things," said Robert. "They may go in and out like concertinas but whatever size they are they're wicked and deserve to be stung. Let's find the picnickers."

They found the smoke but it wasn't coming from a fire, it was coming from down in the earth, eddying up through a circle of piled stones.

"Look out!" said Robert. "It's a volcano!"

"It can't be active," said Timothy, "because of all the green ferns and the rowan trees. It's just smoldering." He looked at the stones and considered them. "That's a chimney. So this must be a roof. It's the top of the Lion's head and it's a roof. Let's see if there are any more chimneys."

They looked among the trees and rocks and ferns and presently Robert gave a shout and Timothy and Absolom joined him. Well hidden in a clump of rowans there was another hole, not a chimney this time but a slanting rocky tunnel like a ladder down into the dark.

"Let's go down," said Timothy.

"We don't know what's waiting for us at the bottom," said Robert. "Remember what happened when we tried to get into that other cave."

"Whatever is down at the bottom it won't be bad," said Timothy.

"Why not?" asked Robert.

"Because the bees came from here and because of all these rowan trees." He looked at Robert. "Do you want to go back the way we came?" he asked. "They will be waiting for us in the wood by that ditch that we had to jump over."

"They'll go home to have their stings attended to," said Robert.

"If they do," said Timothy, "William Lawson and his dog and Frederick aren't the only ones. There's still Emma Cobley and Tom Biddle and Eliza Lawson. And we don't know how many others are in the wood and coming here after us."

"We'll go down," said Robert, adding with courage, "I'll go first." He took Absolom under one arm and they went down carefully, feeling with their feet for each new foothold. Robert was not as sure as Timothy that this was a good place and at any moment he expected to feel his ankles gripped by a horrible hairy hand. But they were not and presently he said to Timothy, "I've got my feet on the rungs of a real ladder." After that it was easy going. They were soon at the bottom and lifting the curtain of hide, they stepped out into Daft Davie's cave.

He was not there. They looked around with beating hearts and then went outside and ran down the steps and found the workbench, and went a little way down the valley, and looked back and saw the Lion's splendid head and his extended paws, and they knew that the whole place was very good.

"We were in the Lion's mouth," said Timothy excitedly. "Right inside!"

"Let's go back," said Robert, and they raced back up the steps and explored the cave afresh. They found the bed of bracken this time, the pots and pans beside the fire and the bowls of apples and nuts. They walked around the walls pointing out the birds and beasts to each other and then they found the picture of the horsemen in the wood and looked at it for a long time.

"It's Lady Alicia's picture," said Timothy.

"Is it?" said Robert.

"Yes," insisted Timothy. "Not exactly but like it."

"I wonder who lives here," said Robert, suddenly losing interest in the picture. "Do you think he'd mind if we ate his apples?"

"No, he wouldn't mind," said Timothy. "Whoever he is, he's good."

They ate the apples and they were so hungry that they did not notice how hard and dry they were. And they found a pitcher of water and had a drink and they poured some water into a bowl and Absolom had a drink too, and then Timothy said, "I'm awfully tired."

Robert remembered that Timothy was supposed not to be strong. "Lie down on the bed," he suggested.

So Timothy curled up on the springy bracken and

he looked so comfortable that presently Robert began to yawn and lay down beside him. And then Absolom jumped up on top of them and curled himself around in the comfortable V shape behind Robert's bent knee, and in five minutes they were all three deeply asleep.

Robert woke up first and saw that the moon was shining through the cave's mouth and making a pool of silver on the floor. He gazed at it stupidly for a few minutes and then he sat up and shook Timothy and Absolom awake. "Wake up!" he said. "It's night."

Timothy sat up and rubbed the sleep out of his eyes. "So it is," he said with awe. "Is it midnight?"

"It might be," said Robert.

"They'll be anxious at home," said Timothy.

"We must get home quick," said Robert.

Timothy looked piteous and Robert knew that he was thinking not so much of enemies as of the long walk over the tor and down through the wood in the dark. "We'll go down that little valley," he said. "There must be a way out at the bottom and perhaps it will be a quick way home."

They ran down the steps and down the valley. It was almost as bright as day, for all the clouds had cleared away now and in the month of June, daylight lingers long enough to make love to the moonlight. When they reached the precipice they paused, wondering which of the Lion's paws they should climb over. The one to the right looked brambly and difficult and the one to the left easy as a flight of steps. "That's the way," said Robert and they climbed over and found themselves on the path up which Nan had climbed. They went down a little way and then Absolom growled and Timothy, who was in front, stopped and said, "Look!"

Down below them a terrifying figure was climbing slowly up the path. He looked very big but he wasn't the black-bearded giant who had pursued them on the hill above. He looked all white like a ghost and he seemed hunchbacked. He raised his head and they saw his terrible white face with great pits for eyes. He saw them and leapt upward, making extraordinary noises. How could they know that it was much earlier in the evening than they thought it was, and this was only Daft Davie coming home, his head and beard blanched by the moonlight and his clothes whitened by the sack of flour he carried on his shoulders? They had never heard of Daft Davie and they fled back in terror over the Lion's paw, jumped across the stream and ran across the little valley and up over the other paw, fighting their way through the thick brambles. Then they plunged down into the wood on the other side, where they struggled on and on through the undergrowth until at last they all three dropped down out of breath in a ferny dell. They listened but there was no sound.

"But a ghost wouldn't make a sound," said Timothy.

"Where are the rowan branches?" asked Robert.

"We left them behind in the cave," said Timothy.

"Then we've lost our swords," said Robert. "And we don't know where we are or which way to turn to get home."

"Listen!" said Timothy.

"I can't hear anything," said Robert.

"I can," said Timothy, and he listened intently. He could only just hear it, unearthly and far away, music like a bird, but not a bird. Absolom listened too, his head on one side, his ears cocked, the tip of his feathery tail trembling. Though the music was so faint it was irresistible and Timothy and Absolom did not try to resist it. They ran after it, Absolom going first but Timothy not far behind him. Robert could hear nothing and he thought they must have gone crazy but he followed them, and though the way may have been long it did not seem so. They felt no fatigue while they followed and they trod lightly; even Robert, who did not hear what Timothy and Absolom heard. But it was Robert who realized first that they had come back to familiar ground.

"There's the beech tree!" he said. "What's the matter, Tim?"

For Timothy had stopped dead and so had Absolom and they were trembling. "Look!" whispered Timothy. "Under the tree!"

The great tree stood full in the beams of the moon, so strong and glorious and yet so pale and unearthly in the strange light that Robert trembled too and for just a moment he thought he saw something under the tree, a man, strong and pale like the tree, but only a man to the waist. He blinked and saw only the moonbeams under the tree. But Timothy saw more. He saw the bent head and the noble bearded face, and the hand raised that they might listen to the echoes of the music. He heard the echoes fading away and when they vanished so had the man. Yet the three of them stood trembling for a full five minutes, looking at the place where he had been.

"Who was he?" whispered Robert at last.

"He was Pan," said Timothy.

"Who?" asked Robert.

"Pan. The man from the garden of the fountain," and he began to cry.

"What are you crying about?" asked Robert.

"He's gone!" sobbed Timothy.

"Crybaby!" mocked Robert. "And the man from the garden of the fountain is only a statue. It was just moonbeams we saw."

Timothy did not remind him of the music they had followed, because he was swallowing his tears and could not speak. He turned blindly away and Robert took his hand, not unkindly. "Come on," he said. "We know where we are now. We're nearly home."

They went slowly down the path, so tired that they could scarcely drag one foot after the other, and because they were tired they felt very dejected, and because they were dejected they ceased to be wary. If it had not been for Absolom's warning growl they would have fallen into the trap, but when he growled they looked up and stopped still in a sort of despair, for down below them in the lane that ran under the manor-house wall were Emma Cobley, Tom Biddle and the cat Frederick, coming to meet them.

"And we haven't got our swords!" whispered Timothy.

"Let's get away into the wood," said Robert.

They turned to the right and there in the moonlight was a big fat woman, Eliza Lawson, getting sticks, and the bulldog was with her. They looked to the left and there was William Lawson with his face bandaged up, as though he had been very badly stung indeed. He saw them and shouted and brandished his knobbly stick, and then pandemonium broke out. Eliza with the bulldog came running from one side of the wood and William Lawson from the other, and from down below came Frederick, Emma and Tom Biddle, and it was surprising how quickly these two old people moved, even Tom Biddle on his sticks.

"The beech tree!" gasped Timothy.

It was not far behind them and they ran back to it. They climbed over the great tree roots and scrambled up to the first low-growing branch, Robert handing Absolom up to Timothy. Then they climbed higher until they were well beyond a tall man's reach. And then they stopped, clinging to the trunk of the tree like limpets to a rock. They had been only just in time.

When they leapt in among the tree roots the bulldog's teeth had been only six inches from Robert's heels.

Looking down they knew they were safe. Their enemies were all around the tree but they could not get beyond the outer circle of the tree roots. The bulldog and Frederick kept leaping up and down furiously, but it was as though they leapt against some invisible wall which every time threw them back, growling and yowling with fury and frustration. The four humans went around and around and tried from every side but they could not get through either.

"You young varmints!" shouted William Lawson, shaking his stick at them. "Once let me get me hands on yee, and I'll give yee such a hiding as yee won't forget in a hurry! Setting them bees on me!"

Robert was feeling so brave that he shouted back, "And what were you doing, William Lawson, making that booby trap in the wood?"

"That weren't no booby trap," shouted William Lawson, "that's Devil's Ditch, what's been there as long as the wood itself."

"Not hidden with leaves and with sharp stones and slimy things down at the bottom," Robert shouted back.

They had to shout to be heard above the noise the animals were making, yet when Emma Cobley now spoke her quiet voice pierced through the din like a sharp knitting needle through paper and the dogs and

Frederick were suddenly silent. She had been standing with bent head, moving the point of the stick she carried thoughtfully here and there in the beech mast, but now she looked around. "Shame on you, Will, to scare little children," she said, and then she looked up at them. "Come down, pretty dears. We mean you no harm. 'Tis time you were in bed. Come down and Emma Cobley will show you the way home."

"We are very comfortable where we are, thank you," said Robert with dignity.

"We can't stay here all night, Emma," muttered Eliza Lawson. "What's around this tree?"

"Power," said Emma briefly.

"Ain't you got power, Emma?" asked Tom Biddle.

"Wait," said Emma, and she went on moving her stick in the beech mast. She was making triangles and circles with the point of her stick, weaving them in and out of each other in an invisible pattern.

"She's making a magic," whispered Robert, but his whisper was caught short by a yawn. Timothy was yawning too and rubbing his eyes. "Let's get down," he murmured. "Let's go to bed." And suddenly Absolom, half asleep already, slipped, and would have fallen out of the tree if Robert had not grabbed him.

"Hold on!" Robert whispered urgently to Timothy. "Don't go to sleep. Hold on."

They held on but their heads were rocking on their shoulders and whether the power of the tree would have proved stronger than Emma Cobley's magic, or whether Emma would have won, there is no knowing, for suddenly there was a shrill cry of *"Tuwhit tuwhoo!"* and a shout from the wood below.

The boys' heads jerked up, and down on the path they saw Uncle Ambrose with Hector on his shoulder, and Ezra with his shepherd's crook.

"Ah-h-h-h!" roared Ezra like an angry lion when he saw the boys and their plight, and he stumped up the hill at a great pace, brandishing his crook. Hector took off from Uncle Ambrose's shoulder with a great whir-ring of wings and came flapping down like an avenging angel upon the heads of the enemy. Uncle Ambrose neither shouted nor flapped but his stride lengthened and his face was very grim. "Ah-h-h-h!" roared Ezra again, laying about the legs of the enemy with his crook while they ducked and cringed to avoid Hector's great flapping wings and terrible beak.

Uncle Ambrose's strides had now brought him upon the scene of action and he plucked Ezra off William Lawson with as much ease as though he was lifting a coat off a peg on the wall. "That will do, Ezra. There is no need for violence. Hector, that will do. Return to my shoulder. Good evening, Miss Cobley. Good eve-ning, Mrs. Lawson. I fear you are suffering from tooth-ache, Mr. Lawson. I offer my condolences. Good eve-ning, Mr. Biddle. A nice evening for a stroll."

Then he walked straight through the invisible wall

that had kept out the others and standing among the tree roots looked up at his nephews and Absolom. "Come down at once," he said sternly.

"I've been telling the pretty dears to come down," said Emma Cobley sweetly.

She was the only one of the enemy who remained quite unabashed. The other three and the bulldog were slinking away but she stood where she was, her hands folded on top of her stick, her head a little to one side like a listening bird, her little face inside the black bonnet alight with respectful amusement.

"Good evening, Miss Cobley," said Uncle Ambrose again, and once more he lifted his hat politely. But he did not return it to his head. He stood with it poised while his deep fierce gaze met Emma Cobley's bright stiletto glance. For a full minute they fought with their eyes only and then Emma dropped a charming old-fashioned curtsy. Uncle Ambrose bowed and replaced his hat and she turned away with immense dignity. Her back view as she walked slowly down the path toward the lane was that of Queen Victoria.

11

Strawberry Jam

Twenty minutes later Uncle Ambrose, Ezra, Hector, Robert, Timothy, Nan and Absolom were together in the library. Nan had come running down in her dressing gown as soon as she heard them arrive. The room was bright and warm, for Ezra had put a match to the fire because Timothy was shivering. Sitting on Uncle Ambrose's lap in the big armchair he was still shivering.

"I wasn't afraid," he explained. "But I'm hungry."

Robert looked at Uncle Ambrose with desperate and pleading hope but his relative was not to be beguiled. "Gruel only," he said sternly to Ezra. "You may put sugar in it. Sugar, I understand, is good for shock." He turned to Robert as Ezra left the room. "Now then, Robert. I must know exactly what you have been doing this afternoon and why you are a good three hours late for preparation."

Robert began at first to tell the story rather haltingly, for he was almost as tired as Timothy, but after a few minutes he suddenly realized what a wonderful story-teller he was. Sitting there on a low stool, with his hands held out to the comfort of the wood fire, he thought he was like one of the French troubadours who went from court to court telling their marvelous tales. His tiredness vanished, his voice deepened to a fine vibrating musical note, and he lavished such a wealth of descriptive detail on the booby trap in the wood that he had got no further than their heroic leap across it when Ezra returned with the steaming bowls of gruel. Ezra's pointed ears were standing out almost horizontally from the sides of his head and noticing this phenomenon Uncle Ambrose said, "You may sit down, Ezra, and hear this story out to its conclusion."

"Thank you kindly, sir," said Ezra, and sat down on the extreme edge of the most uncomfortable chair he could find, his hands placed one on each knee and his blue eyes fixed on Robert's face.

The gruel was for the moment too hot to eat and Robert's clear voice once more took up the narrative. He, like all children, could use exquisite tact when telling a true story to grown-ups. He knew one must not ask too much of their credulity. Things are seen and heard by the keen senses of the young which are not experienced by the failing powers of their elders, but as powers fail, pride increases and the elders do not like to admit this. Therefore, when told by the young of some occurrence outside the range of their own now most limited experience they read them a lecture on the iniquity of telling lies. This can lead to unpleasantness all around, and so the tactful Robert did not tell Uncle Ambrose of the way in which Frederick, the bulldog and William Lawson had expanded to an enormous size when they bounced out of the cave, nor how they had concertinaed back to small stature when the bees were after them. Nor did he speak of the ghost they had seen climbing up to the valley beneath the Lion's head. Still less did he mention the music Timothy had heard or the man he himself had seen under the tree. He was also silent about the invisible wall around the tree and the sleepiness that had come upon them when Emma Cobley had drawn patterns with her stick. But everything else he related at length, even describing the wall painting in the cave which was like Lady Alicia's tapestry, and when he had finished he ate his gruel.

"Ah-h-h-h!" growled Ezra, low and angrily.

"Humph," said Uncle Ambrose and he looked very grim. Then he turned to Ezra. "This inhabited cave with the painted walls of which the boy speaks," he said. "Who lives there?"

"Daft Davie," said Ezra, and he told Uncle Ambrose the story of Daft Davie just as he had told it to Nan.

Robert and Timothy looked at each other, aware now that their ghost was not a ghost after all, and Nan looked down at her lap, uncomfortable because she had told no one of her own meeting with Daft Davie. Now she thought she ought to and looking up she bravely did so, looking only at Uncle Ambrose because she dared not meet the accusing eyes of Robert and Timothy. They always told things to each other if they could.

"I couldn't tell about it before," she said pleadingly to Uncle Ambrose. "I couldn't even tell Robert."

"Why not?" asked Uncle Ambrose.

"Because I don't think Daft Davie wants to be visited. He seemed frightened even of me. He's dumb, you see." She paused. "I liked him very much."

Uncle Ambrose raised inquiring eyebrows at Ezra. "I reckon there ain't no harm in Daft Davie," Ezra said. "He's goodhearted, and keeps his place tidy and clean, I'm told. No harm couldn't come to our children in that cave. But the other. My stars!"

"You hear?" said Uncle Ambrose to the children. "You must not again visit that cave on the summit of the tor. William Lawson is not a pleasant character and has the reputation of being a poacher. There are rabbits and pheasants in the wood, which is the property of the Manor. As for the booby trap I do not for a moment think it was intended for you, but it must have been intended for somebody and was a nasty piece of work. What those four were doing down by the beech tree at such a late hour I do not know, but I suspect they had come out to set traps or something of that sort. I sympathize with you in your flight up the tree but I do not suppose they would have done you any harm."

Hector said "Hick!" very suddenly and loudly, ejecting among other oddments some hairpins which he could only have culled from the head of Eliza Lawson.

"Go to the Parthenon, Hector," said Uncle Ambrose with annoyance. Then he leaned forward, his fingertips together, looked at the children very gravely over the top of his spectacles and delivered judgment. "Nevertheless," he said, "I am responsible to your father for your safety and I feel it my duty to put the wood, as well as the summit of the tor, out of bounds. You must give me your promise that you will not go to either place again."

There was an appalled silence. Not go to the wood anymore? Not to the top of Lion Tor? That meant no more adventures. And it meant no conclusion to the one big mysterious adventure in which they all felt themselves engaged. They looked at each other in horror and then they looked at Ezra, to find him looking at Uncle Ambrose.

"Our children would be safe with me, sir," he said. "There won't no harm come to 'em neither in the wood nor on the tor if I be with 'em."

Nan knew already that Uncle Ambrose and Ezra had not only a great affection for each other but also great respect for each other's judgment. They looked at each other now steadily and gravely for a few moments and then Uncle Ambrose said, "Very well, Ezra. You hear, children? You may go where you choose in Ezra's company."

There was a great sigh of relief. Adventures were likely to be slowed down by Ezra's wooden leg but they would at least be possible. Then Uncle Ambrose's eyebrows suddenly beetled alarmingly. "But woe betide you," he said, "if you are ever again late for preparation. Now go to bed."

The next day was a warm blue day with the smell of hay and flowers coming on a light wind, for in the churchyard and the fields around the village the grass was ready for cutting and the hedges were festooned with roses and honeysuckle. Uncle Ambrose entered the kitchen as they were having breakfast and surveyed the heavy-eyed children languidly spooning porridge from their bowls. Only Betsy was bright-eyed and alert, but even she did not appear quite so attractive as usual because as the only one not suffering from a hangover she was looking very smug. " 'Morning, Uncle Ambrose," she said. "Lessons?" Smiling at him with her head on one side she took off her bib and folded it up, as though yearning to run to the library instantly.

But Uncle Ambrose, surveying her over the top of his spectacles, did not allow the twitch at the corners of his mouth to develop further. "If there's one thing I dislike more than a child it's a roguish child," he said

sternly. "Your milk is not finished I see. Replace your
bib. There will be no lessons this morning."

There was a silence of utter stupefaction.

"No lessons?" gasped Robert.

"No lessons," repeated Uncle Ambrose. "But not a
holiday. By no means. What have you done to deserve
a holiday? I wish you to assist Ezra in the picking and
hulling of the strawberries, which are now ripe." He
looked at Ezra. "You have, Ezra, I understand, dedicated this day to the making of strawberry jam for these
undeserving children. I do not wish you to labor alone."

Actually Ezra had dedicated this day to the bliss of
lonely gardening, but his understanding always kept
pace with that of Uncle Ambrose whenever it could. A
moment's consideration showed him that a day spent
in the safety and fresh air of the garden would be better
for the children in their present state than either lessons
or adventure. "Very good, sir," he said cheerfully. "The
strawberries it shall be."

"No cooking will be required today," said Uncle Ambrose airily. "Merely cold meat and salad and so on.
I hope to spend the day writing in my library but shall
be available for consultation if required."

He left the kitchen with a light and happy tread, for
it wasn't often these days that he could devote many
consecutive hours to writing, but Ezra sighed. The gen-
try always seemed to think that cold meat and potato
salad and orange jelly fell already chilled from heaven.
They failed to grasp the fact that meat has to be hot

before it is cold and jelly liquid before it solidifies. Nan saw his worry. "Hard-boiled eggs and lettuce, Ezra," she said. "I'll boil the eggs. And then strawberries and cream. We can't need them all for jam."

"The Master don't hold with hard-boiled eggs," said Ezra.

"He can't always have everything he likes," said Nan. "He's lucky to have anything at all on a jam-making day. And whose idea was it that we should make jam today? I could see in your eye that it wasn't yours. And he won't help with the jam."

Nan really loved Uncle Ambrose just as much as ever but she was tired and cross after anxiety and the late night. When one is tired it is always one's nearest and dearest who fall under one's heaviest displeasure.

"How much are we paid for picking strawberries?" asked Robert.

Nan transferred her displeasure from Uncle Ambrose to her elder brother. "You dare ask to be paid for picking strawberries!" she said. "You mean wretch! Can't you do *anything* for love?"

Robert opened his mouth to make a nasty retort, Betsy upset the sugar on purpose because no one was taking any notice of her and Timothy trod on Absolom by accident. Absolom, usually so sweet-tempered, snapped and snarled, Andromache leapt for the safety of the drainboard and the kittens swarmed up the roller towel.

Ezra perceived that this sunny morning was likely to

develop into one of those days when even the nicest
children and dearest animals appear to be possessed
with demons. "Now then!" he said. "I won't have no
nasty tempers in my kitchen. Let alone they scare away
the bees. Bees won't stand no nasty words in their
dominions. You have to be proper careful with bees.
No more now or when us gets to the top of the garden
to pick them strawberries we'll find the hives empty."
Four pairs of eyes gazed at him in horror. "I'm not
saying as it will be so," he consoled them. "But it might
be so. Now us'll clear away the breakfast things and
wash up and boil them eggs and while we work us'll
sing, just to show the bees all unpleasantness is now
past. 'Rule Britannia' now. You all know that. Here
goes."

To the clashing of cymbals, as the crockery and
saucepans were flung pell-mell into the sink, Ezra lifted
up his voice and sang and the children joined in at
the tops of their voices. The noise was wonderful and
in his library Uncle Ambrose sighed and laid down his
pen. His powers of concentration were great but not
quite great enough to render him entirely soundproof
against uninhibited juvenile enjoyment. But all things
pass, he told himself, and presently a slight lessening
of the din suggested that the singers were passing out
of the kitchen and up the garden with their baskets.
With a sigh of relief he took up his pen again.

Ezra and the children sang the last verse for the sixth
time not far from the beehives, and when they had fin-

ished they bowed and curtsied to the bees. But there wasn't a single bee to be seen. Usually on a fine morning they were going in and out to fetch and store their honey but today stillness and silence enveloped the hives and the children looked anxiously at Ezra. He was looking grave but not despairing. He bowed again and stepped forward, motioning to the children to come with him.

"Madam queens and noble bees," he said, "these children be good children and if they have offended you they be sorry for it. They be proper grateful for your protection and guidance. Madam queens and noble bees, us do beg yee to show us you ain't offended."

They waited anxiously and then a brown body appeared at the entrance to the first hive, and then another and another and another from the other hives. Four brown bees, their heads crowned with antennae and many gleaming eyes, winged like the seraphim, sheathed swords in their tails, the four royal and angelic warriors seeming to hover there as though for the children to look at them.

"Don't yee touch now!" whispered Ezra.

But the children knew better for they remembered about the sheathed swords. "What does it feel like to be stung by a bee?" asked Timothy.

"It's as though the fire of the sun pierced you," said Ezra. "The whole limb burns. Ah, there they go!"

The four bees zoomed up, then dived joyously into the scented air like swimmers diving into the sea. Then the airy traffic began once more, bees coming and going in ones and twos and threes, the returning ones gold-dusted with pollen and with their honey bags weighed down with treasure.

"They comes and goes all the while," said Ezra, "they likes to be with each other. A lost bee will die of loneliness. There be as many as sixty or seventy thousand bees in a hive, children. 'Tis a regular city in there with houses and streets and nurseries, and thousands of larders for the honey and bee-bread, all built of sweet-smellin' wax. There be workers and nurses for the children, guards at the gate and ladies-in-waiting for the royal family. At the heart of it all be the queen on her throne and the princesses in their cradles singing the song of the queens. There's nothing more wonderful in all the world, children, than a beehive."

"Isn't there a king?" asked Robert.

"For a short while," said Ezra. "He be one of the drones, but only king for a moment. The drones are the bee-men and they don't never go out to work. In the bee world 'tis t'other way round from what it be in our world, for 'tis the women, the worker bees, what gathers the honey and the men what stays indoors. Fine roisterin' fellows they be, wearing helmets of glittering eyes and forever drunk on honey. On her marriage day, and she chooses a fine sunny morning, the queen leaves the hive for the first time in her life and darts up into the blue sky. Up and up she flies, beyond the flight of the birds, beyond the tops of the tallest trees, up toward

the sun, and the bee-men in their glistening helmets
fly after her. But her flight is that swift that one by one
they falls away and only the strongest among 'em, the
best and noblest, follows toward the sun. Right up in
the sky, beyond sight of every livin' creature, the larks
far below 'em, they dance together, king and queen for
a moment. Then his small brown body falls down and
down to the earth below, all his sparkling eyes dark in
death."

"Poor king!" cried Nan, nearly in tears. "Why must
it be like that?"

"How should I know, maid? 'Tis the way of it."

"And the queen?" asked Timothy.

"She comes lonely down from the sky, and lonely
she goes to her palace in the middle of the city. Unless
she leaves the hive with a swarm she will never see the
sun again." Ezra stepped back. "Our reverence to you,
madam queens and noble bees," he said, and the children bowed and curtsied.

Strawberry picking began in an awed silence, until
Timothy asked, "Why do the bees swarm, Ezra?"

"If not frightened away by quarreling children, 'tis
hard to tell," said Ezra. "It seems that when they've
brought the city to perfection they grows restless and
leaves it. Some of the workers stay behind to look after
the children but the rest flies away after the queen to
find a new home. 'Tis a sort of adventure, this seeking
for a new city. When the bee master catches up with
'em, with his skep in his hand, he'll find 'em all hangin'

from some tree in a cluster together and they be singin'
for joy. They don't mind when he shakes 'em into the
new hive. They settle down there and they build a new
city as contented as can be. That's enough for now,
children, but there ain't no end to the wonder of the
bees and I'll tell yee more another day."

When the others were absorbed in their strawberry
picking, chattering and singing, Nan said to Ezra, "I've
a lot to tell you."

"You have indeed, maid," said Ezra severely. "You've
kept a lot to yourself that you should have told me." He
straightened himself. "Robert, Timothy and Betsy,"
he said loudly above their uproar, "I can't stoop well
with this here wooden leg so I be going to sit outside the
kitchen door and hull the berries as you bring 'em to
me. An' I shall need Nan to help me. Keep at it, children, keep at it."

He stumped off down the garden path and he and
Nan settled themselves on two chairs outside the kitchen
door. "Now, maid," he said, "what's worrying yee?"

"A book I found hidden in the cupboard in my
parlor," said Nan. "Uncle Ambrose said he'd found
Lady Alicia's books there so it must have been with
them. But it isn't one of hers. It's Emma Cobley's. It's
a horrid book, Ezra. It's full of spells and they are nearly
all nasty."

"Fetch it out here," said Ezra and Nan fetched it.
But Ezra, it appeared, had never learned to read and he
asked her to read the spells aloud to him.

Nan began to tremble. "I can't read them out loud, Ezra," she said. "They're too nasty."

"How be I to know what they be if yee don't read 'em?" asked Ezra. "They won't seem so bad read out loud in sunshine."

So Nan read them and with Ezra beside her and the smell of warm strawberries in her nose they did not seem so bad.

"Ah," said Ezra when she had finished. "Two can play at that there game."

"How do you mean, Ezra?"

"I mean, maid, that I know a spell or two meself. Now read again that spell for making a person dumb, and the one for causing a man to get lost in a far place."

Nan read them again and when he had heard them twice Ezra repeated them word for word. "How you remember things, Ezra!" she said admiringly.

"Ah!" said Ezra. "I ain't never wanted to learn to read. Book learning destroys the memory."

"Ezra, how do you think Lady Alicia got hold of Emma's book?" asked Nan.

"How should I know, maid? Better ask Lady Alicia."

"Ezra, the day I found the book I thought I saw Lady Alicia in the little mirror. And then I thought I saw Emma. First one and then the other and they both looked young. Could I have seen them, Ezra?"

"Likely," said Ezra. "Both after the same man, they was, and hating one another like poison. Now don't you worrit no more, maid. Leave Emma to me."

"What are you going to do, Ezra?"

"Tomorrow I be taking you children in the pony cart to Pizzleton. There be a nice little shop at Pizzleton and I mean to do a bit of shopping."

"But why, Ezra?"

"I said, maid, leave it to me."

"Pizzleton," said Nan. "Isn't that where Daft Davie lived when he was a little boy?"

"Yes, maid. Now don't yee ask no more questions. You get on with hulling them berries."

At dinnertime Uncle Ambrose adjusted his spectacles and regarded the hard-boiled eggs with disfavor. "Ezra, you know my personal abhorrence of hard-boiled eggs. Have you nothing more palatable to offer me?"

"No, sir," said Ezra, and moving to the dining room window, which he always kept shut now because of Tom Biddle opposite hearing what they said, he opened it wide. "There be nothing in the larder," he said loudly. "These children eat us out of house and home. Have I your permission to go shopping in town tomorrow? I could take the cart, sir, and the children. Get 'em out of your way. And maybe, sir, for one more day they could be excused their preparation? They will have worked in the morning and they be still peaky-looking. Also, sir, we be that low in victuals that the shopping is likely to take some time."

"Very well," said Uncle Ambrose testily. "I shall never get these children educated, but anything to deliver me from a diet of hard-boiled eggs. And shut that window, Ezra. If there's one thing I dislike more than hard-boiled eggs it is a draft down the back of my neck."

Ezra complied with the request, left the room and returned with one sardine on a plate which he placed before Uncle Ambrose. "Hector's, sir," he said, "and the last."

"I do not wish to deprive Hector," said Uncle Ambrose. But actually he did not get the chance, for Hector on his shoulder said, "Hick!" very loudly, shot out a pellet in Ezra's face, leaned over and grabbed the fish.

"Pass me the lettuce," said Uncle Ambrose. "I doubt if Diogenes ate anything but grass and who am I that I should fare better than one of the greatest philosophers of all time?"

"Was Diogenes a Greek?" asked Timothy.

"He was," said Uncle Ambrose. "Pass me the salad dressing."

"I've heard of him," said Robert. "Didn't he live in a tub?"

"He did."

"Why, Uncle Ambrose?"

"He desired peace and quiet," said Uncle Ambrose. "Possibly he had nephews and nieces. Pepper and salt, please."

He seemed put out and after dinner, disappeared into the library. But after tea he and Hector entered the kitchen, where Ezra, watched by the children, was stirring the jam. "I shall be obliged, Ezra," he said, holding out a letter, "if you will take this to the Manor. I shall continue stirring the jam in your place. Be so good as to lend me your apron."

It was Ezra's turn to be put out. "Could I take your letter later, sir?" he asked.

"Why later?" asked Uncle Ambrose.

"The strawberries, sir. At any moment now they will become jam."

"And do you think I have not sufficient intelligence to know when strawberries become jam?" asked Uncle Ambrose haughtily. "My eyesight and my olfactory organs are as yet unaffected by old age. I shall be obliged, Ezra, if you will hand me your apron."

Reluctantly Ezra took off his apron and Nan tied it around Uncle Ambrose.

"You try it on a saucer, sir," said Ezra.

"Try what on a saucer?"

"The jam, sir. When the jam jells 'tis jam."

"I am obliged to you for the information," said Uncle Ambrose. "The fresh air, Ezra, will do you good."

Ezra left looking rather worried. Uncle Ambrose straightened his shoulders, adjusted his glasses and gripped the wooden spoon. Hector, on his shoulder, leaned over to regard the bubbling jam. The children gathered around. "Don't let it stick to the bottom," whispered Nan.

"Is your letter to Lady Alicia, Uncle Ambrose?" asked Robert.

"Is there anyone else at the Manor with whom I should be likely to communicate?" asked Uncle Ambrose shortly. He sniffed. "Nan, should you say there is a subtle change in the aroma of this mixture?"

"Not yet," said Nan.

"Then oblige me by telling me once again of this likeness which the boys fancied they observed between the tapestry in Lady Alicia's boudoir and the wall painting in the cave of—what was the unfortunate gentleman's name?"

"Daft Davie," said Nan. "And they didn't fancy the likeness. I saw the painting too and it's the same picture."

"A most remarkable coincidence," said Uncle Ambrose. "Thank you."

Hector, who had been all this while peering into the jam, suddenly reared up and flapped his wings. "Whoo!" he shouted warningly.

"The jam's jammed!" yelled Robert.

Uncle Ambrose hastily pulled the saucepan off the heat and Timothy leapt for a saucer. They dropped a little liquid into it and it set like glue.

"A little overcooked?" asked Uncle Ambrose anxiously.

"That's a fault on the right side," said Nan soothingly. "Let's pour it into the pots quickly while it will still pour."

They did so and then because it was a whole holiday today they went into the library and Uncle Ambrose

read to them and told them stories until they heard
Ezra come back. The others went out to welcome him
but Timothy lingered behind, laying a hand on Uncle
Ambrose's knee. "I saw him," he said.

"Saw whom?" asked Uncle Ambrose.

"Pan," said Timothy, and he told Uncle Ambrose
about the marvelous music, and the man he had seen
sitting under the beech tree in the moonlight. When
he had finished he trembled because he was so afraid
that Uncle Ambrose would say "nonsense." He was
taking a risk which Robert last night had not dared to
take. But then Uncle Ambrose was not like other grown-
ups. He rumpled Timothy's hair and then most surprisingly he kissed him. "Now go along and have your
supper," he said.

They all had their supper in bed, so that they would
get to sleep early, and it was a very good supper, but
Ezra seemed a bit glum when he brought it up.

"I'm sorry I said this morning that Uncle Ambrose
wouldn't help us with the jam," said Nan. "He did, and
he looked wonderful while he was doing it."

"Huh," said Ezra. "Handsome is as handsome does
and come the morning there'll be no way of getting that
jam out of them pots without taking a hatchet to 'em.
Be there anything more that you fancy?"

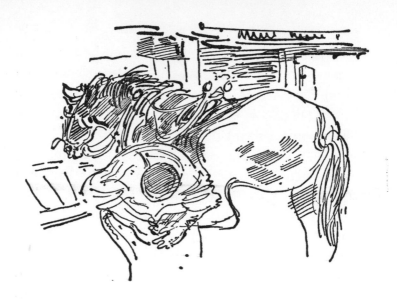

12

The Little Figures

Next day after dinner Ezra left the children to do the washing up by themselves while he went, he said, to tog himself up. This they thought was mean of him. Didn't they have to tog themselves up? They did a very sketchy wash-up, changed into clean frocks and sailor suits, brushed Absolom and then found to their astonishment that Ezra, Rob-Roy and the cart were already waiting for them outside the front door. Ezra was wearing his bunchy coat and the mustard waistcoat, but a little awry as though he had got into them in a hurry, and carrying on quite a friendly conversation with Tom Biddle, who was sitting on his Windsor chair as usual, just as though there had been no unpleasant occurrence in the wood two days ago.

"Going to town?" asked Tom Biddle. But it sounded like a rhetorical question, as though he knew the answer already.

"Aye," said Ezra. "Us'll be back late, I shouldn't wonder, shopping and that."

"The children will want to see their grannie," said Tom.

"Aye," said Ezra.

"Pretty little dears!" said Tom, as the children and Absolom took their places in the cart. "Nice little dog that be."

Absolom growled and the little dears, with the exception of Nan, glared in silence, and Nan's smile, bestowed upon Tom Biddle because if he was wicked he was also old, was not as friendly as usual. Ezra said, "Come up, lad" to Rob-Roy, and they went off down the hill at a spanking pace.

"I was going to harness Rob-Roy," said Robert crossly to Ezra. "And why did you bring him up the hill to the front door? We always start off from the yard."

They crossed the bridge and were out of sight of the village and then suddenly Ezra turned off the road and swerved to the left along a cart track that led across the moor.

"This isn't the way to town, Ezra," said Robert.

"No need to teach your grandmother to suck eggs,"

said Ezra. "We ain't going to town. Us be going to Pizzleton."

"But, Ezra, you told Uncle Ambrose we were going to town," said Timothy, and he looked very grave because he had not thought that Ezra would tell a lie.

"Pizzleton means pixies' town," said Ezra. "And it weren't only your Uncle Ambrose I were telling. What for did yee think I opened that window so wide?"

"So that Tom Biddle would hear," said Nan. "Ezra, you're very clever. They won't be keeping watch at Lion Tor today. Are we going there?"

"Pizzleton is below Lion Tor on t'other side from High Barton," said Ezra.

"I needn't have put on my clean sailor suit," said Timothy, who hated being clean.

"Nor I needn't have put on me mustard weskit," said Ezra. "But 'tis all in a good cause."

The drive was long and bumpy but glorious. The heather and ling were beginning to color and the gorse smelled like peaches in the hot sun. They saw the moorland birds, falcons and snipe and curlews with their wonderful curved beaks, and heard the larks singing and sometimes the rush of a moorland stream. The way they followed circled around the great sweep of Linden Wood and they never lost sight of the towering mass of Lion Tor, though as they came around behind it they no longer saw the Lion but only the crags of the Castle Rock. Presently the track entered a lane which turned and twisted between windblown hawthorn trees until

it brought them out into Pizzleton. It was a bigger village than theirs but it had the same cottages of cob and
thatch grouped around another church on a hill, with
a tower so tall that the cottages looked like mushrooms
about its feet.

The shop was bigger than Emma Cobley's and was
kept by a very respectable-looking lady, apple-cheeked
and wearing a blue print dress sprigged with roses. But
even so the children had a good look through the window before they followed Ezra into the shop in case she
kept a cat. All they could see was a canary, so they
trooped in to give Ezra the benefit of their suggestions
and advice. They were in the shop for half an hour
and there wasn't anything left of the money Uncle Ambrose had given Ezra by the time they'd finished, even
though food was cheap in those days, and the big shopping basket was nearly overflowing with parcels. The
respectable lady was looking very happy when they
left the shop. After that they went to the forge where
Daft Davie had worked when he was a boy. The man
who had been cruel to him was of course dead long ago
and the present blacksmith was a distant cousin of
Ezra's, a very charming man, Jake Barley by name. Rob-
Roy had a shoe loose and Jake allowed Robert to help
him put it on again. It was marvelous in the forge with
the clang of iron, the roaring fire and the flying sparks.
If they hadn't had an adventure on their hands the children would have liked to stay there till bedtime.

"Come along now," said Ezra, when Rob-Roy was

shoed. "I brought the saddle along, and the rope bridle, so us'll leave the cart here, and take Rob-Roy with us for the littl'un to ride when she's tired. And we'll leave our basket here too. Jake shall take it to his missus to mind and us'll pick it up when us comes back. That right, Jake?"

"Right," said the blacksmith. "Where be going?"

"A picnic," said Ezra.

"What about a picnic tea?" asked Robert.

"Take what you like from the basket."

Robert took ham and ginger cookies from the basket and stowed them away in Ezra's capacious pockets and they set off. Beyond the village a stony road climbed up toward the tor. It was creepy here on the north side of the great hill, dark and strange. The larks did not sing here and the cry of the curlews was sad and wild. It was such a long climb that Ezra made Nan and Timothy as well as Betsy take turns on Rob-Roy's back. The pony picked his way up bravely and nimbly and so did Ezra on his wooden leg, with his crook to help him, and so did Absolom though his tongue hung out nearly to the ground. In the face of their perseverance Robert could not for very shame ask to take a turn on Rob-Roy's back too, though he felt very sorry for himself until he suddenly remembered that he was leading his band of heroes to the summit of Everest, and then he strode ahead with no fatigue at all.

The road ended on a grassy plateau beneath the great pile of rocks and Ezra called a halt. They flung themselves down on the sweet-smelling turf, gazing out over the great and glorious view, and when they were rested they drank water from a stream and ate ham and ginger cookies, which contrary to what you might expect are excellent when eaten together. Then Ezra loosely hobbled Rob-Roy so that he could go on cropping the turf, and led the way up the rocks, up and around to the left, and very soon they were on the other side and could see the Lion's head and Linden Wood down below them.

"Now where be this here cave?" asked Ezra.

It was so well hidden that it took a little while to find it, but presently they saw the big rock on which Frederick the cat had leapt. "You children stay here," said Ezra. "When you hear me call 'Hi there!' come and join me, but if I should yell like a screech owl then you take to your heels and run back to Rob-Roy and get along home as quick as you can."

He left them standing together in an apprehensive bunch, climbed doggedly up to the big rock and disappeared around it. After a pause which seemed long to the children they heard a hail of "Hi there!" and scrambled up to join him.

There was the width of a doorstep between the rock and the narrow entrance to the cave, hardly more than a long crack through which a big man could squeeze with difficulty. Ezra was standing in the entrance. "All except one, come in," he said. "But one of you must keep watch. You, Robert, for a start. Don't yee climb to the top of the rock where you'd be seen. Stand at the side and look around and call out if you see anything you don't like the looks of. Keep Absolom with yee. Don't fret, lad, you shall take your turn inside later."

Robert scowled a bit but he did what he was told and the others followed Ezra into the cave. It was not quite dark inside, for a crack in the roof let in some light, and when their eyes grew accustomed to the dimness they could see quite well. At first there seemed nothing to be seen; just rock and ferns, for rainwater came in through the roof and the cave was damp. But Ezra went nosing around like a dog after a rabbit, examining the rocks and feeling behind the clumps of ferns and presently he gave an exclamation, took his jackknife from his pocket and opened it. "Hold up them ferns, Nan," he commanded.

Nan lifted up the curtain of green that he had pointed out to her and he set to work with his knife on the rock behind it. Then he drew out a loose stone that had been shaped to fit, like the stopper of a bottle, into the hole behind, a roughly circular hole about the width of a man's hand.

"Be careful, Ezra," Nan said anxiously, "there might be snakes inside."

"Must risk that, maid," said Ezra with a grin and he plunged his hand and arm into the hole. "No snakes," he assured her, "but plenty else. Quite a sizable little cupboard inside. I'll hand 'em out to yee one by one, maid, and yee can put 'em down on that ledge of rock there."

One by one he handed out a number of objects about the size of small dolls, queer knobbly little figures stuck with rusty pins. Nan put them down on a shelf of rock and they were just looking at them when Robert appeared at the mouth of the cave. "Come quick," he said.

"Who is it, lad?" asked Ezra sharply.

"It isn't a person," said Robert, "it's a thing."

Ezra swept up the little figures, put them in his pockets and followed Robert, the other children at his heels.

As they rounded the rock they shivered, for in the short time they had been inside the cave the weather had suddenly changed. The Lion, facing south, was still in full sunshine, and he looked warm and peaceful and good, but when they turned and faced the other way the sunlit moor had vanished in a moving pall of gloom. There was no wind but the air that touched their faces was clammy and cold.

"The sea is coming in over the moor!" gasped Nan.

"And there are devils on horseback riding over the waves," said Timothy. He spoke calmly but with a sort of despair, as well he might, for the sight was truly frightening. The waves that were rolling in were the high gray waves of storm but they made no sound and the terrible tossing riders made no sound either. It would have been less terrifying if they could have heard the crash of the waves or the neighing of the horses.

"Don't yee be feared, children," said Ezra. " 'Tis naught but mist rolling in over Weepin' Marsh. It can come very sudden and take queer forms. But us'd best be going and quick too. Us have a long ways to get home. Come on now."

They scrambled back to Rob-Roy, unhobbled him and put Betsy on his back, and they got down the steep way to Pizzleton in double-quick time. Jake Barley and his wife were looking out for them and no time was wasted in conversation. Rob-Roy was put into the cart, the basket was stowed inside and they were off, going quickly down through the village and along the lane beyond with the mist at their heels. Facing the sunlit south, and with the cheerful rattling of the cart in their ears, the children forgot to feel afraid.

"I never saw the inside of the cave," said Robert, aggrieved.

"We'll tell you about it when we get home," Nan consoled him.

"If we'd been half an hour later climbing up the tor the mist would have got there first and we wouldn't have found the cave," said Timothy.

"Nearly got us," growled Ezra. He was looking very grim and Nan thought he spoke as though the mist were a savage beast that had been set on them by somebody. Weeping Marsh, she thought, was where the little boy was lost. She began to shiver and pulled Betsy closer to her, for it was growing colder, and Ezra took the old torn rug and a couple of sacks from under the seat and made the children wrap themselves up. The sun was veiled now, as though a bonfire had been lit below the horizon and was sending up smoke across its face. Presently they left the lane for the track across the moor and they could now see only a few yards in front of them.

"Don't be afeared," said Ezra. "Us've but to follow the track, and if presently us can't see it Rob-Roy will take us home."

Rob-Roy neighed and tossed his head in confident pleasure and when later they found themselves traveling blind, thickly wrapped in cotton wool and unable to see a yard in any direction, Ezra let the reins go slack and the pony went slowly but steadily forward on his own. All the same it was rather alarming traveling in this strange chilly no-man's-land of nothingness, and Ezra struck up Moses' song of the wind and the sea and the bees and they all sang the chorus. When they paused for breath Timothy asked, "Ezra, did you make up the tune, or Moses?"

"Moses," said Ezra. " 'Tis his song but I makes up fresh verses to it to suit meself."

"What words were you singing that first night?" asked Nan. "We hummed and stamped in the chorus but we didn't catch the words."

The children could not see Ezra's face but they fancied he was looking a little sheepish. "I weren't what you would call dead sober that night," he said. "Mind you, I weren't drunk but I weren't dead sober."

"Come on, Ezra," said Robert. "Tell us what you sang. Come on!"

"I sang a drinking song and now I don't drink no more it ain't suitable as I should sing it," said Ezra obstinately.

"Why don't you drink anymore?" asked Timothy.

"The Master said I had to set an example to you youngsters," said Ezra gloomily. "Aye, it were a black day when you come to the house."

Though they could not see his face they knew he was smiling and they laughed and said, "Come on, Ezra! Sing us the song."

"Only this once, mind," said Ezra, "for it puts such a thirst on me as yee wouldn't believe." And he lifted up his voice and sang.

> "Glory for the foamin', brimmin' tankard,
> Good ale an' beer,
> Champagne in the polished crystal glasses
> Sparklin' an' clear.
> Glory glory alleluja!
>
> "Glory for the rich an' purple vintage,
> Grapes in the sun.
> Glory for the red wine freely flowin'
> When summer's done.
> Glory glory alleluja.
>
> "Glory for the juice o' cider apples
> At autumn's end.

Glory for the stirrup cup o' winter
Quaffed with a friend.
Glory glory alleluja.

"Glory for the punch that's drunk at yuletide
Spiced, strong an' hot,
Glory for plum puddin' soaked in brandy,
Thanks for the lot.
Glory glory alleluja."

The children sang too. They were roaring out the last chorus when Rob-Roy suddenly swung left into the stableyard and they found they were at home.

They stabled Rob-Roy and groped their way up the steps to the garden, Ezra carrying the basket. The lamp was already lit in the library and they could see Uncle Ambrose pacing up and down the terrace with his hands behind his back, his tall figure sometimes blocking out the light and sometimes revealing it again, like a cloud passing backward and forward over the moon. They gave a shout and saw him straighten himself with relief. Then he came down the terrace steps and caught Betsy up into his arms. He appeared to be extremely annoyed but they remembered that Father had always lost his temper when he had been anxious about them and then suddenly wasn't, and they were not alarmed.

"This child is chilled to the bone," he said angrily. Actually it was only Betsy's face and hands that felt cold, because she had been well wrapped up, but she put on the shivering act she had learned from Absolom and vibrated in Uncle Ambrose's arms for all she was worth, leaning her head against his shoulder. Absolom shivered against Uncle Ambrose's leg and Timothy produced a perfectly genuine sneeze.

"I'll poke up the kitchen fire and give 'em supper round it, sir," said Ezra. "Mutton broth and baked apples and a hot posset each when they're in bed, and then there won't no harm come to 'em. I'm sorry, sir, if you've been worried."

"Worried? Who said I was worried?" snapped Uncle Ambrose. "Had you gone across the moor I might have suffered some slight anxiety but on the main road from town you were in perfect safety."

They trooped indoors and he drew the curtains, shutting out the mist. "It came up with remarkable suddenness," he said.

"Took me by surprise, sir," said Ezra. "Never known it come up quite like this afore."

"Where were you when it caught you?" asked Uncle Ambrose.

"Looking the other way, sir," said Ezra. "If you'll excuse me I'll see to that fire. And the children had better come with me." He glanced at the pages of manuscript littering the library table. "You're at work, sir, I see. Come on, children, don't disturb your uncle."

Some while later, with Betsy already in bed and asleep, Ezra, Nan, Robert and Timothy sat on the settle by the kitchen fire, with the lamp burning on the mantelpiece, and Nan had the book of spells on her lap.

"Now then," said Ezra. "There ain't no time to be lost."

"It seems a shame to be doing this without Betsy," said Robert.

"She's young yet," said Ezra. "Might be scared. It's best it should be just the four of us."

His coat was hanging over the back of a chair and he took from the pockets the little figures they had found in the cave and put them in a row on the kitchen table. "They be carved from mandrake roots," he said. "Well carved, too. I will say for Emma, she can get a good likeness. Mandrake be an evil root. It's likely to bring bad luck to folk by itself, let alone having pins stuck into you."

"But they aren't real people," said Robert. "They're just little figures."

"They be figures of real people, lad," said Ezra. "And what Emma did to these figures she did to the people. She has the power. It be all in the mind, lad, the mind and the will, and Emma she's strong-minded and strong-willed. Now, maid, you read out of that book the spell for binding the tongue."

Nan found the place and read it out and Ezra picked up one of the little images and brought it to the light. Held in his hands it seemed almost to take on life. It was of a little boy about eight years old and he had his tongue out.

"He's showing it to the doctor!" said Robert.

"That he's not," said Ezra. "Look closer."

They looked closer and saw that pins pierced the tongue. They had been thrust in while the mandrake root was still supple and now it was like hard wood and they were rusted in firmly.

"You'll never get them out!" cried Nan in distress.

"I shall," said Ezra. "Hand me the pincers from the kitchen drawer, Robert."

Robert gave them to him and gripping the head of one of the pins he began gently moving it to and fro, murmuring as he did so:

> "Pins, come you out! Do no more harms,
> Spell, unwind to good from evil.
> Now all good spirits work your charms,
> Save the sinner from the devil."

And while he spoke all the pins came out as smoothly as though they had been stuck in butter, and Ezra handed the little figure to Nan. "I'll say the next verse, maid," he said, "and when I finish and clap me hands, throw it in the fire."

"Burn the little boy!" cried Nan. "It would hurt him."

"Once I clap me hands," said Ezra, "the real boy and the image of him ain't any more one person than soul and body be when a man dies and goes to heaven. Fire be a grand thing, maid, it destroys what's evil and liberates what's good. Now then.

"Flames, leap you up! Red fire and gold.
Now, freed spirit, dance in gladness.
Dance your way homeward to the fold,
Turn your back on grief and sadness."

Ezra clapped his hands and Nan threw the little figure into the fire. The flames roared up and they were
of marvelous colors, red and gold and pink and green
and purple.

"He ain't dead yet!" said Ezra in satisfaction.

"How do you know?" asked Timothy.

"Had he gone to heaven the figure would have burnt
quietly, happy but gentle, but when the flames roar up
with all them lovely colors, you know the man or woman
be still on earth."

"Let's do another," said Robert.

Ezra took a second figure from the table. It was a
tall bearded man, whose figure seemed to take on grace
and elegance when Ezra took it into his hands. There
were pins through his feet and his head.

"What do they mean?" asked Nan.

"Don't yee call to mind the spell for making a man
lose his memory and wander away and be lost?" asked
Ezra. "Find it, maid, and read it."

Nan found it and read it, the two rhymes were repeated, the pins removed and the little figure cast in
the fire. The flames leapt up as before, very bright and
gay. "So they're both alive still," said Nan, and they all
sighed with relief.

"Who are they?" asked Robert.

"I can't say, lad," said Ezra, adding, "Not yet."

"Why were they hidden in that cave?" asked Nan. "The spell said to put the figure of the lost man in a far place, but why was the little boy there too?"

"Might be for convenience sake," said Ezra, "if the two of 'em was made at the same time. But there could be another reason. It helps on a wicked spell to put the images in an unlucky place. The Castle Rock, though it can look fine when the sun be on it, 'tis an unlucky place. The Lion be good but not the Castle. 'Tis too near Weeping Marsh to be lucky. And a king was found buried there at the top, some old king who died hundreds and hundreds of years ago. That's not lucky neither."

Robert and Timothy glanced at each other, remembering the king they had imagined living in the Castle when they stormed it. Then Robert said, "There are more little figures, Ezra."

"Let's look at 'em," said Ezra, and Nan noticed that his eyes were twinkling. "Stand 'em in a row on the hearth."

Robert picked them all up and stood them in a row. There were seven of them, a tall man with a top hat, a little man in a bunchy coat, four children of varying sizes and a dog. Each figure had a pin in the chest. The faces were not recognizable but the figures were.

"It's us!" gasped Timothy.

"That's right, lad," said Ezra, and he roared with

laughter, slapping his knee. "But there ain't no harm come to yee, for about the same time Emma made her figures I made mine. Do yee recall me making figures out of Timothy's plasticine?"

The children laughed too, and Timothy asked, "Where are they now, Ezra?"

"In a good and lucky place," said Ezra. "They be in the church in a hidy-hole I knows behind the altar. But don't yee tell your uncle. He'd say it were superstition. I reckon the cleverest men be ignorant at times."

"Let's burn ourselves!" said Robert.

"You can if you've a mind but there ain't no need," said Ezra.

"It would be better to burn ourselves," said Nan a little anxiously.

So they roared out the rhymes and burned the seven figures, and the flames were like rainbows leaping up the chimney.

"Just one thing more," said Ezra. "There be a spell in that there book I didn't take to, a spell for making a coolness come between a man and a woman. I have a feeling as Emma used that spell and I'd like to undo it." He got up, went to the dresser and came back with two little figures fashioned out of Timothy's plasticine. "I made 'em last night," he said. They were of a man and a woman, not recognizable as anyone in particular but beautiful as a pair of young lovers on a valentine. He took a piece of red wool out of his pocket and handed it to Nan. "Now hold 'em together, maid, breast to breast,

and wind the wool round 'em while I says me rhyme,"
he said. Nan did so and he repeated,

> "Thread of my song,
>   Heart to heart binding,
>   Thread of my faith,
>   Haste the heart's finding.
>
> "Thread of my hope
>   Heal the heart's smarting,
>   Thread of my love,
>   End the heart's parting.
>
> "Thread of my prayer,
>   Send shadows fleeting,
>   Let journeys end,
>   In lovers' meeting."

Ezra took the figures from Nan and put them back
on the cupboard. "Tomorrow," he said, "they'll go in
me hidy-hole with t'others I made. Now children, we'll
burn the whole nasty book and be done with it forever."

They put the book on the fire and the pages writhed
like snakes in the flames and then were consumed to
nothing but glowing ash. Ezra raked them away and
they were gone. "Now up you goes to your beds," he
said, "and when you be there I'll bring yee your hot
possets."

They ran upstairs, undressed and washed and then
curled up in bed, waking up Betsy, who was already
asleep with Absolom beside her, so that she could enjoy

hot milk too, and presently Ezra came in with four steaming cups on a tray. It was the same sweetened milk that he had given Nan and it tasted wonderful. They were buried in their pillows again and already half asleep when Nan asked, "Is everything coming right, Ezra?"

"Everything be coming right, maid," said Ezra.

"But what is it that's coming right?" asked Robert.

"When 'tis come right you'll know," said Ezra. "Now I be off to make a hot drink for your uncle. He's properly shook up with worrit. Good night, children."

"Good night," they murmured drowsily and they were asleep by the time he reached the door.

13

Singing in the Wood

Next day at breakfast there were letters from the children's father, one for each child and one for Uncle Ambrose. Breakfast was much prolonged while they read them aloud to each other, even Uncle Ambrose reading aloud parts of his, which was very long. One part said that Father was glad that the children were living at the Vicarage. Knowing his brother's desire for solitude and frequently expressed dislike of children, it was not an arrangement he would himself have dared to suggest, but now that it had come to pass he was delighted, and he looked forward to the day when he would retire from the army and they would all six of them live together. The more the merrier, wrote Father, and at this there were loud cheers from the children, not dampened by Uncle Ambrose's voice announcing in trumpet tones above their clamor, "With no proverb do I more profoundly disagree."

"Now here's an interesting part," he continued when the noise had subsided. "Nothing to do with us but interesting. Your father says, 'I am as you know in the valley of the kings, among the tombs and temples of ancient Egypt, and deeply interested in all the discoveries that are being made here. And also in the discoverers. To one man in particular I am much attracted. I am told he has lived here for years, earning his living as a worker in the excavations but a man of considerable intellect, for he speaks several languages and is a fine Egyptologist. But he suffers from a curious form of amnesia.' "

"What's amnesia?" asked Robert. "Is it measles?"

"Certainly not," said Uncle Ambrose. "Amnesia is loss of memory and you should know that at your age. Where was I? If there is one thing I dislike more than a boy it is an interrupting boy. Ah, here we are. 'He does not know who he is or where he came from. Memory for him begins when, a young man, he found himself sailing down the Nile in a native boat. He had no luggage with him and nothing in his pockets that could give him any clue to his identity, or even to his nationality, for he found he could speak English, French, Italian and the lingo of the Egyptian workers with equal ease. A most curious case and a most interesting man.'" Uncle Ambrose folded the letter and put it away. "Well, we must get to our lessons. Come along, children. Hector, come to the Parthenon."

Lessons that morning seemed to the children, and possibly to Uncle Ambrose too, little more than an interlude. They were all glad to find themselves once more in the dining room, especially as it was beefsteak and kidney pie and treacle tart. After a moment of silent and happy repletion between courses Uncle Ambrose drew breath and said, "Nan, I have received Lady Alicia's permission to visit her this afternoon and I shall take it very kindly if you will give me the pleasure of your company."

Nan flushed with delight. "Just me?" she asked.

"Just you. The entire family would, I think, be somewhat overwhelming for an old lady. Robert and Timothy will take great delight in entertaining Betsy in the garden while we are out."

He fixed his stern eyes on his nephews and such was his authority that their glowering glances were fixed on their plates only. Betsy, looking very smug, kicked them under the table. They did not dare kick back lest she yell but Timothy glanced up briefly with such a *you just wait* expression on his face that Ezra, passing the potatoes, sighed. It would be his part to keep the peace.

"Until now I have respected Lady Alicia's wish to

live unvisited," said Uncle Ambrose, "but I asked her in my recent note if once only I might do myself the honor of waiting upon her. I do not feel it right that her kindness to you children should remain unacknowledged on my part."

Uncle Ambrose sounded pompous and Nan privately thought there was more in this than met the eye. She believed he was burning with curiosity to see Lady Alicia and her picture. Especially the picture. Then she saw that he was also a little embarrassed. He cleared his throat and Hector on his shoulder cleared *his* throat and scratched behind his ear in a self-conscious way. "Boys," went on Uncle Ambrose, "I may possibly be late home for preparation."

His nephews lifted their transformed faces and fixed their eyes on his face in bright and wicked glee. Their mouths trembled but they did not laugh.

"Don't worry, Uncle," said Robert in winning tones. "If you're very late and we get anxious we'll come and fetch you."

"Thank you," said Uncle Ambrose dryly.

After his nap he and Nan set forth, Uncle Ambrose in his Sunday frock coat and top hat and carrying a silver-headed walking stick, Nan wearing a clean pink linen smock and her Sunday hat wreathed with roses, for this was an occasion. When they reached the green they saw William Lawson lounging in the door of the Bulldog, smoking his pipe. When he saw Uncle Ambrose he straightened himself and touched his cap.

"Good afternoon, Mr. Lawson," said Uncle Ambrose. "I trust your toothache is less troublesome?"

"Yes, sir, thank yee," said William Lawson. Eliza and the bulldog were not to be seen, and neither was Emma, or Frederick. Nan thought to herself, If they've gone up to the cave to see if the little figures are still there and when they find they are gone, what will they do?

The iron gates into the shrubbery were difficult to open and William Lawson came over and helped them, swinging them wide with one great brawny arm.

"Thank you, Mr. Lawson, I am much obliged," said Uncle Ambrose, and he stalked through into the shrubbery without looking back. Nan did not look back either but all the way through the shrubbery she had a shivery feeling up and down her spine for fear William Lawson had slipped through after them. But when they were out in the wild garden she forgot her shivers because Uncle Ambrose was so interested in all he saw. The japonica flowers and the apple blossom had long ago drifted away on the wind but there were tangles of roses everywhere and foxgloves growing in the grass.

"What a very beautiful house," said Uncle Ambrose, and he stopped still to look at it where it stood deep in the wild overgrown garden, shuttered, lovely and blind.

"The front door is open!" exclaimed Nan. "It hasn't been opened for years and years, and now, look!"

It was wide open and under the gracious portico stood Moses in his Sunday livery. When Uncle Ambrose and Nan reached the terrace he stood aside and bowed, and the visitors walked in. He was, Nan realized, in a state of trembling happiness, as though he longed to believe the old days were coming back and yet dared not believe it. His hands were shaking as he took Uncle Ambrose's hat and stick but he was smiling from ear to ear.

"This is an auspicious occasion, Moses," said Uncle Ambrose. "I am honored that her ladyship is willing to receive me."

"Her ladyship is waiting, sir," said Moses. "Will you be pleased to come this way?"

He led the way up the stairs with his bowed shoulders straightened and his head held high. The glory of the swinging cobwebs had disappeared and Nan felt a pang of sorrow, realizing for the first time that every gain carries with it corresponding loss. Moses was happier, but he had swept away the cobwebs.

Lady Alicia received them in her boudoir in a very gracious and queenly manner. The weight of her years seemed to be weighing less heavily on her. She looked so much younger that Nan suddenly wondered if she was as old as she had thought she was. There was a sparkle in her eyes that matched the sparkle of her diamonds. It was wonderful to watch Uncle Ambrose bowing to her and kissing her hand, and to hear the exchange of elaborate old-fashioned courtesies that flowed between them.

Then a marvelous and ceremonial tea arrived. Moses entered first carrying a large silver tray shoulder high, and Abednego, with Gertrude slung in her hammock on his back, came behind with another, also held shoulder high. Abednego was very much smartened up. He appeared to have brushed his face and was wearing his footman's livery of worn green velvet. On the silver tray were not only iced cakes but delicate sandwiches with lemon curd filling, scones and sponge cakes. While the tea things were being set out under Lady Alicia's critical eye Uncle Ambrose looked about him, not with vulgar curiosity, and not really appearing to do it, but doing it all the same. Nan watched his hawk's nose turn here and there, and noticed the gleam in his eyes. He wasn't missing much, she thought. His glance lingered long upon the tapestry.

But when Moses and Abednego had left the room he did not comment on it and somehow or other he led the conversation around to his youngest brother, the children's father. "An army man but an amateur Egyptologist," he said. "He is now in Egypt for a while before going on to India."

"My husband traveled a great deal in Egypt," said Lady Alicia. "Before you leave I will take you into his library. There are some Egyptian treasures there that you might like to see."

"I should be honored," said Uncle Ambrose.

"Since my husband left home for the last time," said Lady Alicia, "Moses alone had entered the room until Nan and Betsy went there by mistake the other day." She smiled at Nan. "As they have seen it, I find I do not mind you doing so too." She turned her bright glance to Uncle Ambrose. "These children, sir, are working havoc with my habits."

"With mine too, ma'am," said Uncle Ambrose with deep sympathy. "But I hope you feel the benefit?"

"I believe that I do," said Lady Alicia, and laid her hand on Nan's while she continued her polite inquiries into the welfare of the children's father. Uncle Ambrose told her about the man whom his brother had met, with his vast knowledge of Egypt and his complete forgetfulness of his own past.

"Egypt affects the brain," said Lady Alicia. "I hope your brother will not stay there too long. My husband was more fatally bewitched by Egypt than by any other country in which he traveled. He was susceptible to witches. Is Emma Cobley still alive?"

Her question shot out so suddenly that Uncle Ambrose was actually taken aback. It was a moment or two before he answered, "Very much alive."

Nan had been sitting quiet as a mouse all this time but now to her own astonishment she heard herself say, "Lady Alicia, Uncle Ambrose has given me the little parlor that was yours. There were some of your books in the cupboard."

"Some of my childhood books no doubt," said Lady Alicia. "I hope you enjoy them, my dear."

"Yes I do," said Nan. "But there was another. A book of spells."

Lady Alicia withdrew her hand from Nan's and was

silent for a moment, and then she said with horror, "That thing? I thought I had burned it."

"It was hidden way at the back of the cupboard," said Nan.

"Perhaps I couldn't find it to burn it," said Lady Alicia, and she put her hand over her eyes. "I forget. It is so long ago."

"Nan," said Uncle Ambrose sternly, "this is a painful topic of conversation for our hostess."

"No," said Lady Alicia with sudden vigor. "This must be explained. One day when I was a girl my father sent me to see Emma about some parish matter. She was young too, then. The front door opened right into her little sitting room and it was ajar and I saw her sitting writing at her desk in the corner. I knocked and she closed what looked like a diary and pulled her workbag over it before she came to the door. We talked and she went upstairs to fetch some magazine my father had lent her. For my father, I must tell you, was fond of Emma and would never believe the stories told about her in the village."

"Did you believe them?" asked Uncle Ambrose.

"I believed the few harmless stories of her cures that had been told to me, but I was not afraid of her. Perhaps if I had been afraid I would not have done the naughty thing I did now." She smiled at Nan. "I was a young and giddy girl at the time and I was as naughty as Betsy was in the library the other day. What was Emma writing in her diary? I wondered, and I took her workbag off the book and opened it, and it opened at the page on which she had been copying out a spell for making a coolness come between a man and a woman. Then I *was* afraid. I was already very much in love with Hugo Valerian and I knew that village gossip said Emma was too. I guessed she was trying to separate us and the wild idea came to me that without her book she would be powerless to do so. I hid it in my muff and when Emma came downstairs I was standing at the front door. I took my father's magazine from her, said good-bye and went quickly away. When I got home the mail was in and there was a letter from my aunt in Paris asking me to come to her as quickly as I could, for there was a ball to which she wanted to take me. I knew Hugo Valerian was in Paris and in wild excitement I packed and went. At that ball he proposed to me and we were married in Paris. I was so happy that I forgot Emma's book and when I came home, if I remembered it again, I expect I thought I had destroyed it before I left for Paris, and Emma's power with it."

"So you read no more of the book than that one spell?" asked Uncle Ambrose.

"And only part of that," said Lady Alicia. "She had only just finished copying it. It was only later, much later, when I knew more about Emma, that I realized I had done something she would never forgive. There Nan, that is the explanation of the book in the cupboard. I beg you, my dear, to destroy it now."

"It is burned already," said Nan.

"I am glad to hear it," said Lady Alicia.

"In these enlightened days,' said Uncle Ambrose politely but firmly, "we have learned that spells and charms and so on are mere superstition. Those who fear them fear no more than a bad dream."

"How fortunate we are then that we now live in days in which bad dreams have lost their power," said Lady Alicia, but she said it dryly and changed the conversation to mushrooms, which she said she had loved to gather in her youth in the fields near the Vicarage.

After tea they went to the library, where Hugo Valerian's cloak still lay over the back of the chair and his gloves and riding crop on the desk. Lady Alicia picked up the gloves and drew them through her hands caressingly. Her face looked suddenly as soft and bright as a girl's. The room felt quite different today. It seemed alive and so full of a sense of expectancy that for a moment or two no one said anything, and Uncle Ambrose half turned toward the door, as though ready to bow to someone who would come in, but no one came in and he turned his attention to the Egyption treasures in the glass cases. These fascinated him, and so did the pictures and books. He and Lady Alicia discussed them together while Nan stood at the window looking out on the garden of the fountain.

The sweet-smelling flowers of June were in bloom now, bergamot, lavender, roses and honeysuckle. She opened the window and leaned out and the voices of the two elderly people in the room behind her died away.

The man in the fountain was grave, serene and still, but not sad today, and she listened as he bade her to the sharp staccato cries of delight made by the little brown bird who was sitting on his hand and talking to him. Other birds were flying around, sometimes perching on his knee or shoulder and all singing their special songs of delight, but it was the little eager sharp-voiced bird in which he was particularly delighting at this moment, and wishing her to delight. But she could not at this distance see what sort of bird it was and he wanted her to see. He leaned a little forward and lifted up the hand on which the bird was perching, and she leaned forward too and held out her hand, and the bird flew up and came to her finger with soft whirring wings. It was a very small speckled bird, cheeky-looking, with a very bright eye, a sharp beak and a perked-up tail. It chatted to Nan in a high, trilling voice which matched its appearance, and Nan and the man in the fountain looked at each other across the sun-warmed space of blue that separated them and laughed to hear it. Then they were both silent, listening. And then the bird flew away.

"I am sorry, my dear," said Lady Alicia, in the room behind Nan. "I moved."

Nan drew back from the window and saw that Lady Alicia and Uncle Ambrose were close to her, and looking at her lovingly. To her surprise she saw that Lady Alicia had tears in her eyes. Uncle Ambrose took out a large clean handkerchief, unfolded it and trumpeted loudly. But in mid-trumpet he suddenly paused, peering over the top of his handkerchief. Then with rather shaky hands he polished his spectacles with the handkerchief and stared again. And then he smiled and nodded as though to a friend.

"A beautiful statue, is it not?" said Lady Alicia. "Very lifelike. My husband bought it in Italy but the sculptor was a Greek."

Uncle Ambrose struggled for composure, cleared his throat and began to discuss the statue with Lady Alicia. But he did not stay much longer after that. They went back to the parlor and he and Lady Alicia bade each other a protracted Edwardian farewell, the silver bell was rung and Moses and Abednego were summoned. They were conducted down the stairs and seen off with all proper ceremony.

But at the corner of the house, instead of turning toward the garden to go home, Uncle Ambrose stopped and said, "Nan, will you take me to call on the gentleman whom you call Daft Davie?"

Nan was very much taken aback. "But it's up through the woods and then a long climb," she said. "Ezra can't manage that climb."

"I retain the use of both legs," said Uncle Ambrose severely, "and am less aged than I appear."

"But he may be out," said Nan.

"In that case I shall leave my calling card," said Uncle Ambrose. "Whether the gentleman's cave is within the boundary of my parish or not I am not quite sure, but in any case I reproach myself that a human creature in

his unfortunate condition has remained unvisited all
these years. I may be able to be of assistance to him."

Full of misgivings Nan led the way up through
the woods. She went first up the rock, glancing anxiously
behind her every now and then to see how Uncle Ambrose was managing. Each time it was very well, for his
long legs made light of the steep steps that nearly de-
feated her. Sometimes indeed he gave her a shove up
from behind and always his tall hat remained in position. Right at the top, looking out over the murmuring
sea of green leaves below them, she found that he was
as moved as she was by this mounting up and up from
floor to floor of one of the mansions of the world.

"To have the clouds lapping against one's feet, as
the leaves do now, wouldn't it be wonderful?" she said.

"I have experienced that on mountaintops," said
Uncle Ambrose. "These ascents are not only physical,
Nan. The world of the spirit too has many mansions.
We live upon a staircase."

They climbed on over the Lion's paw and down into
the little valley beyond. Uncle Ambrose looked about
him and seemed to have no words for his delight.
Dragonflies were darting over the stream and foxgloves
with speckled bells grew in the lush green grass as tall as
Nan herself. The Lion's head was golden and glowing
in the sun.

"Who's that singing?" asked Uncle Ambrose.

They stopped and listened. It was Moses' song but
it was not Moses who was singing. Moses had a deep

voice like rolling thunder but this man sang like a tenor bell, every note ringing out clearly above the sweeping rhythm of some strange musical accompaniment. Nan began to run and Uncle Ambrose strode after her and in a moment or two they saw a tall bearded man sawing wood and singing as he worked.

"It's Daft Davie," gasped Nan. "Davie! Davie!" she cried.

He put down his saw, shaded his eyes against the sun and then saw who it was. He strode a few steps down the valley and held out his arms. Nan jumped into them and he lifted her as though she weighed nothing at all, holding her up at arms' length and laughing at her round eyes of astonishment. He's not old as I thought he was, Nan thought, he's quite young. And how can he sing? Is it a miracle? She had heard of miracles but she had not met one before, and when Daft Davie set her down on the grass again her knees nearly gave way. But it steadied her to hear Uncle Ambrose saying, "Good afternoon, sir," and to see him raising his hat and holding out his hand just as though this were a perfectly ordinary afternoon call.

"Good afternoon, sir," said Daft Davie in a clear voice. "Will you come up into the house?"

"Thank you," said Uncle Ambrose. "But first I must offer my apologies for having been so long in calling upon you. The fact is, sir, that I have only lately become aware that you are resident here."

"I have been something of a recluse," explained Daft Davie courteously. "Shall I lead the way?"

"Lead on, sir," said Uncle Ambrose.

Daft Davie led on and Nan whispered to Uncle Ambrose, as they climbed up the steps at some little distance behind him, "He isn't dumb anymore."

"So I perceive," said Uncle Ambrose.

The cave, when they reached it, seemed full of light, for the westering sun shone straight into it. It was also full of color for there was a pot of foxgloves and honey-suckle on the table and a wooden dish of red cherries, and best of all the sun shone straight onto the painting on the wall. Nan saw Uncle Ambrose look at it atten-tively, but he did not yet speak of it for Daft Davie was delightedly doing the honors of his home. Uncle Am-brose and Nan were already full up with Lady Alicia's cakes and sandwiches but they could not refuse the spring water and cherries he offered them, or the thin biscuits baked on a red-hot stone, because he was so happy that he had them to offer. They sat on wooden stools and ate and drank and the painting on the wall grew brighter and brighter as the sun's light upon it grew more deeply golden.

"That was a charming song, sir," said Uncle Ambrose.

"I learned it from an African servant who used to play with me as a child," said Daft Davie.

"Indeed?" asked Uncle Ambrose calmly. "You were born in these parts?"

"I do not know," said Daft Davie. "You see, sir, I have two sets of childhood memories, divided by a pit of darkness, and the first belonged to a place and time of which I have no knowledge."

"I see," said Uncle Ambrose. "Can you tell me of the time when your memories became consecutive?" And then, as Daft Davie seemed puzzled by the long word, he added, "When they ran together like beads on a thread."

"When I was living with my foster parents at the forge at Pizzleton," said Daft Davie. "They told me they had rescued me from gypsies who were ill-treating me. But I only remember the gypsies as a vague nightmare."

"And the black pit of which you spoke?"

"It was an illness which I suffered while living with the gypsies. I remember nothing of it except fever and distress and trying to speak and finding I could not. My illness, they told me, was the cause of the dumbness from which I have suffered for a number of years." His intensely blue eyes suddenly blazed like lamps. "But not now," he said with joy. "Now I speak as easily as though I had always spoken."

"And the first set of memories?" asked Uncle Ambrose.

"I remember the African servant who played with me and taught me to sing," said Daft Davie. "I remember my father and mother, and my mother's room is bright as a picture in my mind, and the picture in my mother's room is a picture within a picture. I remember, I think, what I loved, but nothing else. I should have thought those memories to be a dream but for that love, and for the song. Can you carry love and music away with you from a mere dream?"

"Hardly," said Uncle Ambrose, "nor so vivid a memory of a picture as you have painted on that wall. For I imagine that that is the picture you loved?"

"Yes, sir," said Daft Davie.

"I fear you must think my questions impertinent," said Uncle Ambrose.

"I am glad to answer them," said Daft Davie, "for words taste like honey on a tongue that once was bound and now is free."

"Their sound too has sweetness," said Uncle Ambrose. "They come to you, I think, from the time of your early memories, not from the forge at Pizzleton. Sir, I am deeply interested in your history and that must be my excuse for asking you one more question. Was your tongue bound for long?"

"It was freed, sir, only last night. I was sitting by my fire at evening. It was a dying fire but suddenly the flames leapt up like the fires of spring and they were all the colors of the rainbow. The sight was of such marvelous beauty that I cried aloud, 'Glory glory alleluja!' "

"You might well do so," said Uncle Ambrose, "for your recovery is remarkable. May I look more closely at the pictures around your walls?"

He got up, adjusted his spectacles and walked around the cave with Daft Davie, giving Nan time to recover from her dizziness. For she had felt like an acrobat at a circus all the time Uncle Ambrose and Daft Davie had been talking. Sometimes the ceiling of the cave had seemed over her head and sometimes it had seemed under her feet. But she had come right end up again when Daft Davie had spoken of the rainbow flames leaping up and his speech coming back, for it had been at the time when they had been sitting around the fire and Ezra had been pulling the pins out of the little boy's tongue. The little boy and Daft Davie were the same person, Lady Alicia's son Francis, who hadn't been drowned in the Weeping Marsh after all. Nan wondered why she had not known they were the same when she first saw that the picture in Lady Alicia's boudoir was like the picture on the wall of the cave. Uncle Ambrose, she realized now, had had his suspicions just from hearing about the two pictures, let alone seeing them. But then Uncle Ambrose was very clever. She got up and joined the two men and slipped her hand into Daft Davie's, and he looked down at her as though she were Helen of Troy and the Sleeping Beauty rolled into one.

"Nan, you are the most wonderful little girl in the world," he said.

"She will not remain so if you cause her head to swell," said Uncle Ambrose severely. "Your drawings of birds and animals are excellent. You have, I see, a great love for them."

"I love all creatures," said Daft Davie simply. "I go

around the woods destroying the traps and snares set for them." Then his voice became thick with anger and his face crimson. "If I could catch the man who snares my rabbits and pheasants I'd fling him over the roof of the Manor."

He looked so tall and strong and angry as he spoke that Nan believed he could and would do just what he said, but Uncle Ambrose, looking suddenly just as tall and strong and angry, eyed him with beetling brows. "Vengeance, sir," he said severely, "is cruel, stupid, useless and vulgar. Remember that when you return to the world. Well, Nan and I must bid you farewell. I will, if I may, do myself the honor of waiting upon you again tomorrow morning."

"May I come down to the woods with you, sir?" asked Daft Davie, as meek now as a scolded child. "Then I can go on talking," he added happily.

So the three of them went down the valley together, climbed over the Lion's paw and stood looking down at the rustling sea of green leaves below them, and up into the unendingness of the golden sky above, where invisible larks were singing. Suddenly Daft Davie began to sing again, his song ringing out over the treetops. When the song ceased, echo answered from down below the green leaves, a deep echo like a voice singing under the sea. Uncle Ambrose and Daft Davie listened in amazement but Nan said, "It's not echo, it's Moses singing in the yard by the back door."

"Moses?" asked Daft Davie. "Moses?" He looked so

bewildered that Uncle Ambrose changed the conversation.

"Sir, you must be much attached to these woods," he said.

"They are mine," said Daft Davie simply, "and all the creatures in them."

Uncle Ambrose hastily led the way down the rocks. They were nearly at the bottom before Nan said, "Look!" They stopped and looked and down in the wood below was William Lawson, bending down and doing something at the foot of a tree. He was setting snares. Daft Davie flung back his head and roared like a lion. He looked like a lion too with his tangled mane of hair, a terrible infuriated beast whose roaring turned to a flood of furious words that made William Lawson look up and then stare as though turned to stone, terror and amazement on his face.

Uncle Ambrose had hold of Daft Davie by his lion's mane. "Stop that!" he commanded. "Don't swear. Sing!"

With a tremendous struggle Daft Davie strangled his roars and sang. And from below came the deep rumble of Moses' singing, and from the woods the voices of children.

"Down with all hard-hearted naughty scoundrels,
   Their traps and snares.
   Down with those who plot the death of squirrels,
   Rabbits and hares.

"Shame on those who harm the stripy badger
And hunt the fox.
Shame on all ill-wishing jealous witches
And black warlocks.

"Run from our green lanes and hills and meadows,
From moor and wood,
Or else speak truth, be affable and kindly,
Harmless and good.

"Glory for the fleeing of the shadows,
The rising sun.
Glory, children, glory alleluja,
For night is done."

Glory, glory seemed to ring from every corner of the wood and William Lawson turned and ran. And from hidden places in the woods came Emma and Frederick, Eliza and the bulldog, and they too were running for their lives. Yet not one of the unseen singers had moved, or did move until the woods were free. Then they appeared through the trunks of the trees, Moses, Abednego, Ezra, Robert, Absolom, Timothy and Betsy.

"I said these children were to stay at home," said Uncle Ambrose severely to Ezra.

"I be sorry, sir," said Ezra. "I feared some harm might come to you. And the children had the right to be here." Then he looked up at Daft Davie. "Glad to hear your voice, sir," he said.

But Daft Davie was not listening to him or even looking at him. He was looking first at Moses and then at Abednego and his face was working strangely, as though he were trying to remember something. Uncle Ambrose put his hand on his shoulder. "Go back to your house, sir," he commanded. "Go back to the cave and possess your soul in patience. Tomorrow morning I will come to you and all that now seems strange will be made plain." Daft Davie turned around and went slowly back, for when Uncle Ambrose commanded, everyone always obeyed. Then Uncle Ambrose turned to Moses, who was staring at Daft Davie's retreating back with as much bewilderment as Daft Davie had stared at him. "Moses, take me back to Lady Alicia. I have a great deal to tell her, and to tell you also. Ezra take the children home. Confusion is at present great but undoubtedly it is a happy hour."

They all tramped joyously down through the woods, parting at the stableyard. Uncle Ambrose, Moses and Abednego went into the house and Ezra, the children and Absolom went singing through the garden and the shrubbery. They did not stop singing until they reached the green.

"My stars!" ejaculated Ezra.

"What is it?" asked Nan.

"Look there," said Ezra. "And stand back. Keep out of sight."

They obeyed him and looked in the direction of his pointing finger. The Bulldog sign outside the inn had disappeared and the bar from which it had hung was empty, with an equally empty stepladder standing beneath it. As they gazed in stupefaction William Lawson came out of the inn carrying a brightly colored picture, followed by Emma and Frederick the cat. It was Emma who nimbly mounted the ladder and William handed the picture up to her and she hung it where the Bulldog had been. Then she came down the ladder again and William carried it back inside the inn. Emma and Frederick remained where they were, looking up at the new inn sign.

It represented a magnificent peregrine falcon with creamy speckled breast, night-dark wings and curved scimitar beak. Behind him was a sky of brilliant blue and the hand that held him up into the sunshine was gloved in scarlet.

" 'Tis the old Falcon!" whispered Ezra in fierce tones. "The sign that was there afore Squire Valerian went away. William Lawson took it down, blast 'im! 'Tis the old sign come back."

Emma turned around and saw Ezra and the children standing by the gate. She looked at them with a most charming expression on her face, smiled sweetly and curtsied to them. Then she walked slowly and serenely to her shop with Frederick, a very meek little cat, trotting at her heels, went in and closed the door quietly behind her.

Ezra breathed a great sigh of relief and said, " 'Tis gone!"

"What's gone?" asked Timothy.

"The wickedness," said Ezra. "All the badness

that's been in this village for many a long year. And sorrow and parting with it. 'Tis gone.''

"Emma's still here," Nan reminded him.

"She won't do no more harm," said Ezra. "Her spells be burnt and she won't do no more harm. Hanging up that falcon was her sign to us that she knows she's beaten. She won't do no more harm. Glory glory alleluja!''

They went singing down the hill to the Vicarage and then straight up the garden to the beehives, where they stood in a row and bowed and curtsied. The marvelous light was now so brilliant that they all turned gold while they did it. "Madam queens and noble bees," said Ezra, "we offer thee our humble thanks for all your help in driving badness and sorrow away from our village. And I, old Ezra, in your presence, bless the day that brought these troublesome varmints to live at the Vicarage. Varmints they may be but with your help they've done a good work that won't never be forgotten. Clothed in gold, they be, gold as yellow as your honey. Golden be their future, and gold be in their hearts forever.''

The children, at this magnificent tribute, grew rosy and shyly ducked their heads and bobbed their curtsies once more, while behind the church the sky began to unroll the first bright banner of a sunset that was the most magnificent of any ever seen in those parts, a sunset that was spoken of for years to come.

Deep inside the hives the bees could be heard singing.

14

Happy Ever After

Uncle Ambrose arrived home very late that night, after spending a long time telling Lady Alicia that she had a son, and he went off very early the next morning and spent an even longer time telling Daft Davie that he had a mother. And then he took him to the Manor and left him there, with Lady Alicia and Moses, and no one knew what happened within the Manor during the following week. All they knew was that Moses was very busy in the overgrown shrubbery with a hatchet and saw, clearing the old driveway, and also that he went out shopping several times looking very pleased with himself and that on the second occasion he bought two dappled-gray horses.

Then, at the end of the week, the village had the surprise of its life, for Lady Alicia and her son Francis Valerian went out for a drive. It was the milkman, taking the morning's milk to the Manor, who saw the ancient carriage, all polished and furbished, issuing out of the stableyard with Moses on the box. Moses was very much furbished too, and there was a large rosette of scarlet ribbon on the whip which he was brandishing over the backs of the two dappled-gray horses. The milkman did not wait to see any more. He dumped the milk behind a bush and he ran as though for his life, though actually he was not afraid, he was merely running to rouse the village and bring it to its doors.

They were all at their doors when the gates were opened by Moses and the Valerian carriage rolled through. It paused for a moment on the green to allow Moses to climb back to his place, and a great cheer went up from the villagers, and louder and louder cheers as more and more people came running up the hill to the green. Uncle Ambrose and Ezra and the children and Absolom came racing from the Vicarage; or rather the children and Absolom raced while Uncle Ambrose and Ezra strode and stumped as fast as was compatible with adult dignity, and Hector flapped his wings and hooted with joy on Uncle Ambrose's shoulder. Men came running from the fields and the women from their washtubs. The village school broke up in confusion and all the children came tumbling out. Only the older people in the village had ever seen Lady Alicia or her carriage, and though a few had seen the recluse who had lived in the Lion's cave they did not know what he would look like transformed into Francis Valerian.

He looked magnificent in a suit of fine cloth that had once belonged to his father, with his father's cloak about his shoulders and his father's tall hat on his head. His beard and his lion's mane of hair had been trimmed and cut and he looked now a man in the prime of life. And Lady Alicia, in a beautiful lavender silk dress and a bonnet trimmed with violets, looked no longer old but merely elderly. She was smiling and happy and so was her son. The old carriage, with the Valerian crest painted on the panels of the doors, shone almost as brightly in the sunshine as the coach of glass in which Cinderella drove to the ball.

With cheering people lining the way they drove down the hill past the Vicarage and then over the bridge and up the hill beyond. The people did not follow up the hill for they thought that Lady Alicia would want to be alone with her son and her faithful servant when after so many years she saw the moors again. So the strange old carriage rolled away unattended to where the larks were singing in a cloudless blue sky, and the wind was warm and honey-scented and the bees were humming in the gorse. They were gone for quite a long time and when they came back they looked happier than ever.

The people did not cheer this time, for too much cheering can be trying for the people who are cheered, but when they heard the carriage wheels they came to their doors and waved and smiled. And Tom Biddle stood at his door and waved and smiled, and Emma Cobley stood at her door and curtsied and smiled, with Frederick beside her, and as the carriage passed the shop Lady Alicia turned and smiled at Emma and because she was so happy, and wanted everyone else to be happy, she forgave Emma all her wickedness from the bottom of her heart. Yet as she drove back through the shrubbery to the Manor she was weeping a little because in the last few days all her old love for her husband had come back again and she was very sorry indeed that he had lost himself.

The only people who were not at their doors to smile at Lady Alicia were Eliza and William Lawson. They were not there because they had gone away. William had never been happy at High Barton; he thought it rained a lot in the west country and he thought they would be happier somewhere else. So they went and they were not missed and the village settled down to enjoy the finest summer anyone could remember, with no more rain than was necessary for the gardens and the crops.

But Emma and Tom did not go away and they became quite nice old people. Their change of heart was astonishing at their age and the villagers were at a loss to explain it. Of course they did not know what a hard fight the goodwill of the children and Uncle Ambrose and Ezra had put up against the ill will that had opposed them, and they did not know about Ezra's good spells or the labor of the bees. Least of all did they know how Lady Alicia had forgiven Emma from the bottom of her heart.

It was a wonderful summer with one happy thing after another falling into place like pearls threaded on a string. The children worked hard at their lessons, spurred on with the promise of a month's holiday in September if they deserved it, but they had fun, too. They spent a lot of time with Lady Alicia and her son. Nan and Betsy helped Lady Alicia sweep away cobwebs and make new cushions and curtains for the Manor, and Robert and Timothy helped Francis weed the garden, and day by day, as house and garden came slowly back to their old order and beauty, Lady Alicia and her son grew younger and younger and happier and happier.

But Francis still kept his home in the Lion rock. He had it as his workshop and did carpentry there and painted beautiful pictures on canvas with oil paints. He had always wanted to do this but had never had enough money to buy the paints. Of course he was not really daft, and he never had been, he had only been called daft by the country people because in his efforts to speak he had made queer noises. He was really a very clever man as well as a very good and charming one. All the children loved him but especially Nan. She often went with him to his workshop and read aloud to him while he painted. Neither of them had ever been so happy as they were when they read and painted together. At these times Nan felt she would have nothing left to wish for if only her father were here. And Francis felt very much the same. If only, he thought, the father whom he remembered so vividly had not been so foolish as to lose himself. If only he were here too how perfect life would be.

Robert also was happy and content because he had at last saved up enough money to buy a real bridle for Rob-Roy and gallops on the moor became more wonderful than ever. Sometimes Moses came too, riding a dappled-grey horse, Abednego perched proudly up front.

It was on a day in August, when the moor was purple with heather and the fern was just beginning to turn gold, that a cab with two men inside and luggage on the roof came bowling across the moor and came in sight of the three riders. One of the two men inside called out to the driver and the cab stopped. The two men jumped out of the cab and came striding toward Moses and Robert. They were tall men, much of a height, their faces tanned golden brown, and one of them had a fine lionlike head and gray hair and a gray beard.

"Moses!" he cried out in a ringing voice. "And Abednego!"

And the other man, who was fair with a fair moustache, called out, "Robert!"

Then followed one of those times that are afterward remembered as though they had happened in a dream, or in heaven, or on another star, because they seem too wonderful to belong to earth. Moses, Abednego and Robert fell off their mounts and ran to meet the two men, who seemed as they strode over the heather to be gods, not men, so strong and tall were they, so golden, gay, laughing and splendid in the sun. But Moses, Abednego and Robert, though their hearts were nearly bursting with joy, could not laugh. Moses, as he ran across the heather to the lion-man, was sobbing, and Robert, springing into his father's arms, was crying too. Abednego, having leapt to the lion-man's shoulder, wiped his eyes on Gertrude. It was as though for the first time in their lives they saw the sun burst out from behind a cloud. The two horses and Rob-Roy watched for a few minutes and then, coming slowly nearer, whinnied and gently thrust their soft muzzles against the necks and chests of the men and boy and monkey. They did not altogether understand what was happening but they knew it was an occasion that called for the unobtrusive steadying influence of their marvelous equine sympathy. The horse who was drawing the cab whinnied too and the driver thrust his bowler hat to the back of his head and stared.

A little later the sound of wheels once more brought the village to its doors to watch another carriage procession, as the three riders triumphantly led the cab over the bridge and up the hill to the Vicarage. The villagers were puzzled but they laughed and waved because the faces of the men and the boy told them that this was a matter for joy. At the Vicarage door Robert, Rob-Roy and some of the luggage and one of the two godlike men were separated from the main cavalcade. As the cab went up the hill to the green, with the remaining godlike man leaning forward and waving, the emotion in his face and his likeness to his son told them who he was. When they saw the cab drive in through the manor-house gates they began to cheer wildly. The lost squire was not dead after all. The squire was home.

He was the man who had lost his memory, whom the children's father, Colonel Linnet, had met in Egypt, and his memory had returned to him when Ezra had taken the pins out of the head and feet of the figure of the tall man. He was delighted to be home and Lady Alicia and Francis were delighted to have him home. It was of course a great shock to Lady Alicia to have her lost husband restored to her so suddenly, and so soon after the restoration of her son, but she had longed for him and she was a strong elderly lady, and the air of the high moors is invigorating and so she not only survived but became younger and happier than ever.

They did the same thing at the Vicarage, for Colonel Linnet had applied for special leave to bring

Hugo Valerian back to his home, and in the very peculiar and special circumstances it had been granted him and he could stay for three weeks. The first fortnight of the three weeks was wonderful, but during the last week a certain gloom made itself felt, for even though they had Uncle Ambrose and Ezra the children felt they could not bear the dreaded parting. And their father felt the same. And so did Uncle Ambrose and Ezra and all the animals. The gloom grew steadily worse until suddenly one day at lunch Colonel Linnet said to Uncle Ambrose, "I wish to heaven I could leave the army, live here with you and the children and take up farming."

"Why not?" asked Uncle Ambrose.

"These same children," said Colonel Linnet, indicating his offspring. "The boys must eventually go to boarding school. Possibly Oxford or Cambridge later."

"Certainly," said Uncle Ambrose sternly. "Why do you suppose I am wasting valuable time and strength hammering knowledge into their wooden heads?"

"I doubt if I could afford it on what I'd make farming," said Colonel Linnet gloomily.

"I share your doubt," said Uncle Ambrose. "But farm by all means if you wish. Any one of the local farmers will be delighted to instruct you and your total lack of talent will give great pleasure. In time you may develop some slight efficiency in the art and be able to contribute toward the education of these young blockheads. But even if you do not I am happy to inform you that my own financial means will be equal to the strain. In my youth I had the good fortune to escape matrimony. Having never been under any obligation to waste good money on feather bonnets, woolly boots, rattles and so forth, I have put by a considerable sum. Before making the acquaintance of these children I had thought to leave it to my old college but have lately changed my mind. These children are the most troublesome I have ever encountered and you yourself as stubborn, unintelligent and reactionary as any soldier I have ever had the misfortune to meet, but I am nevertheless attached to the lot of you. I should welcome a joint home and a joint bank balance. And so I know would Ezra."

Ezra, clearing away the beef and kidney pudding and bringing in the apple dumplings, was grinning, Hector was flapping his wings and hooting, Absolom was barking and the children yelling with joy. Their father tried to put before his brother the disadvantages of the scheme from Uncle Ambrose's point of view, before it was too late, but he was shouted down. By the time the apple dumplings had imposed their own silence it *was* too late. The thing was as solidly real as the dumplings themselves.

"A very excellent dinner, Ezra," said Uncle Ambrose, laying down his spoon. "Only requiring for its ultimate perfection that we partake of some soothing digestive mixture in order that future memory, as well as past participation, may be equally happy. A thimbleful of ginger wine all around, Ezra. You will join with us, I beg, while we drink the toast of happy ever after!"

Epilogue

It merely remains to say that they all worked hard to make that toast come true and it did come true. High Barton became the happiest village in the whole of Devonshire with no more ill-wishing, poaching, pin-sticking, quarreling, or anything at all that anyone could take exception to. Emma Colbey and Frederick remained at the village shop and appeared so trustworthy that even Ezra took to buying soap there, but not anything to eat because he was never quite sure about the inwardness of Emma's and Frederick's virtue. He thought it might be merely skin-deep, all right for soap but not to be relied upon for bacon. But skin-deep or not it lasted and when Frederick died at the age of twenty, and eventually Emma herself at the age of a hundred and two, they were much mourned. And so was Tom Biddle, who only lasted till ninety-eight, but then he, it was thought, had been somewhat bewitched by Emma and so when she behaved well, so did he. A local man took over the inn, the Falcon Arms, and it became a gay and happy place. Ezra, coming to the conclusion that he could set a good example to the children just as well by moderation as by total abstinence, took to going there instead of to the Wheatsheaf, and every Saturday night he banged his beer mug on the counter and sang his drinking song. Everyone else joined in and a loud and cheerful noise rolled out through the open window of the inn and across the green, under the crescent of spring or the harvest moon, or the frosty stars of Christmas, and everyone abed in the village would wake up and smile. Sometimes the two Valerians, father and son, joined the merrymaking at the inn and when the singing was over they would all listen spellbound to the wonderful tales of his adventures that the squire had to tell.

Hugo Valerian still went abroad sometimes, because he loved traveling, but he did not go alone. He took his wife and son with him because the love between the three of them was now so great that they could not bear to be parted. Moses went too because he could not bear to be left behind. And of course they couldn't go without Abednego. As the years went on and she grew older they would take Nan with them to be a companion to Lady Alicia when the men and the monkey wanted to go adventuring on their own. And sometimes, because they were the two youngest, Francis Valerian and Nan would go adventuring alone and he taught her to paint nearly as well as he did himself. He loved her very much, so much that on her eighteenth birthday, midsummer day, he married her in High Barton church. Uncle Ambrose married them, blowing his nose a good deal while he did it, and the bells pealed and all the animals were allowed to come into church. Hector and the bees came too. It was a remarkable wedding and made quite a stir in the countryside. Thereafter Nan lived at the Manor, but as a day never passed without all the people at the Vicarage visiting the Manor, or all the people at the Manor visiting the Vicarage, there was no real parting. Nor was there when Betsy grew up and married the Vicar of Pizzleton, because Robert gave her Rob-Roy, who never grew old, as a wedding present, and Uncle Ambrose gave her the governess cart and she was always driving over with the little cart stuffed full of her round fat babies. She had six, three boys and three girls, and she was a very bustling mother. Nan had only two children, beautiful lion-hearted Valerian boys, but as she was less busy by nature than Betsy she required less outlet for her bustle.

Colonel Linnet was a very bad farmer but a very happy man and everyone loved having him farming badly at High Barton. Uncle Ambrose was able to finish his book once Robert and Timothy had been sent off to boarding school. He was pleased to finish it, heaved sighs of relief and immediately started another. Robert did quite well at school because though he wasn't clever, Uncle Ambrose had taught him to work hard, and then, to his father's delight and Uncle Ambrose's great annoyance, he went into the army. He was a good soldier and managed to win both medals and honor and to stay alive at the same time, and once he had got over his annoyance Uncle Ambrose was very proud of him, and of the beautiful wife, four children and six polo ponies which he collected in due course.

But it was Timothy who was his uncle's chief delight, for both at school and at Oxford he won scholarships and prizes, and was such a brilliant scholar that as the years went on his name was spoken with bated breath wherever learned men were gathered together. He did not get married but became a Fellow of his college and lived in luxurious rooms looking out on green lawns, and wrote books and poems and was very happy. He was also very nice. His head did not swell at all and he was devoted to his relatives, but especially perhaps to Uncle Ambrose, and he visited High Barton every vacation without fail. Uncle Ambrose also visited him and the greatest pride and joy of his old age was to walk down the Oxford High Street arm in arm with his brilliant nephew, with Hector, who appeared to be gifted with eternal life, sitting proud and erect upon his shoulder.